902911284 0

Please return/renew this item by the last date shown.
Items may also be renewed by the internet*

https://library.eastriding.gov.uk

* Please note a PIN will be required to access this service
- this can be obtained from your library

D1345441

DEATH IN PRINT

DEATH IN PRINT

G.M. Malliet

**SEVERN
HOUSE**

First world edition published in Great Britain and the USA in 2023
by Severn House, an imprint of Canongate Books Ltd,
14 High Street, Edinburgh EH1 1TE.

severnhouse.com

British Library Cataloguing-in-Publication Data
A CIP catalogue record for this title is available from the British Library.

ISBN-13: 978-1-4483-1120-0 (cased)
ISBN-13: 978-1-4483-1121-7 (e-book)

All Severn House titles are printed on acid-free paper.

MIX
Paper from
responsible sources
FSC   FSC® C013056
www.fsc.org

Typeset by Palimpsest Book Production Ltd.,
Falkirk, Stirlingshire, Scotland.
Printed and bound in Great Britain by
TJ Books, Padstow, Cornwall.

Praise for G.M. Malliet

"Gripping . . . Malliet draws the reader in with elegant prose and distinctive characters"
Publishers Weekly on *Death in Cornwall*

"For fans of old-fashioned cozies"
Booklist on *Death in Cornwall*

"Low-key, highly professional work right up to the unmasking of the surprisingly well-hidden killer"
Kirkus Reviews on *Death in Cornwall*

"The reader has a real treat in store . . . Malliet's writing is both smooth and elegant and her humor delicious"
Booklist Starred Review of *Death at the Alma Mater*

"Fans of Dorothy Sayers's novels and other Golden Age British mysteries will enjoy this contemporary salute"
Library Journal on *Death at the Alma Mater*

"Lots of humor and a bit of 'guess who this writer is' make this one a good choice for readers who enjoy intelligent cozies and traditional mysteries"
Library Journal on *Death and the Lit Chick*

"Top notch . . . readers will find a tasty tale that doesn't disappoint. Perfect for fans of the wickedly funny cozy writers M. C. Beaton and Catriona McPherson"
Booklist on *In Prior's Wood*

About the author

Agatha Award-winning **G.M. Malliet** is the acclaimed author of three traditional mystery series and a standalone novel set in England. The first entry in the DCI St. Just series, *Death of a Cozy Writer*, won the Agatha Award for Best First Novel and was nominated for Macavity and Anthony Awards. The Rev. Max Tudor series has been nominated for many awards as have several of her short stories appearing in *Ellery Queen Mystery Magazine* and *The Strand*. She was a graduate student at the universities of Cambridge and Oxford and now lives in the US with her husband.

www.gmmalliet.com

In memory of Donna Lefeve

ACKNOWLEDGMENTS

Once again, many thanks to my agent, Mark Gottlieb of Trident Media Group, and the team at Severn House, in particular Joanne Grant, Sara Porter, Mary Karayel, Martin Brown, and Piers Tilbury. Because books are not created in a vacuum. It takes a talented group of villagers (agents, publishers, editors, copyeditors, marketeers, publicists, jacket designers and soothsayers) to help stories reach their audience.

Thanks also to Dr Brittany Wellner James, Director of Development and Fellow, Jesus College; Bruno Mollier, Head of Catering, Jesus College; and Professor Philip Burrows, also of Jesus College, Oxford, for making themselves available to answer my questions about college black-tie affairs and ancient wine cellars. All mistakes, wrong-headed suppositions and embellishments are my own.

And as always, thanks to Bob.

'It is easier to forgive an enemy than to forgive a friend.'

~ William Blake

Cast of Characters

- Sir Boniface Castle, founder of Castle Publishing, Oxford, UK
- Lady Ursula Castle née Blackenthorpe, his wife, whose family money funded her husband's dreams
- David Castle, their son and editor-in-chief at Castle Publishing
- Imogen Castle, their daughter and head of marketing
- Gita Patel, assistant at Castle Publishing
- Jason Verdoodt, St Rumwold's College tutor and bestselling author on whom all hopes for Castle Publishing are pinned
- Minette Miniver, Jason Verdoodt's long-suffering girlfriend
- Professor Titus Ambrose, lecturer in theology, whose rooms are across the staircase from Jason's
- Professor Mortford 'Morty' de Witt, college doctor and professor of medicine, often called in by Thames Valley Police to advise on a case of murder
- Lord and Lady Yale-Lequatte, deep-pocketed supporters of literary causes and guests at the celebration of the sale of one million copies of Jason Verdoodt's *The White Owl*
- Tricia Magnum, aka Dame Patricia, bestselling but frequently remaindered author of children's books. She had a fling with Jason she claims is all in the past.
- Professor Alice Davies, expert in artificial intelligence, former MI5 agent, and master of St Rumwold's College
- Sir Bartholomew Tremaine, St Rumwold's College librarian, who resents those who would turn his sacred library into a 'nightclub' for celebrating a bestselling novel

- Dimitri Smirnoff, St Rumwold's College butler in charge of catering the private party for Jason
- Professor Charles Monet, the college's wine steward
- Tess Babbage, a college scout who sees too much
- Gregory and Amber Verdoodt, parents of the deceased author
- Detective Chief Inspector Arthur St. Just of the Cambridgeshire Constabulary
- Portia De'Ath, crime writer, University of Cambridge criminologist, and Arthur's fiancée
- Detective Chief Inspector Ampleforth of Thames Valley Police
- Detective Constable Daisy Lambert of Thames Valley Police. No one at the police station ever listens to the young constable, and they probably should.

PROLOGUE

The Turf was crowded despite the weather. If you waited for good weather in Oxford you might never leave the house.

And she had had enough of never leaving the house. Kevin was gone and as much as she wished things were different, that was a fact.

It was time to get back out there in the world. All her girlfriends said so. But the fact was there was only one Kevin and she'd been lucky to have him. Besides, at fifty, she was getting too old for this sort of carry-on. She was more likely to make a fool of herself after more than twenty years out of the dating market than find tolerable male companionship, let alone true love.

Her friends told her there were dating apps for older people, an idea that turned her rigid with horror. She'd likely end up with one of those blokes who emptied her bank account and scarpered off back to Russia. Maisie, her sister, a religious type, thought she could meet someone if only she would join her church, showing a complete lack of understanding that any hypocrisy like that was beyond her. God had abandoned her, so she had returned the favour. The last church she had set foot in had been for the funeral service for Kevin (who had also not been religious. A man in black from the funeral home who had never met Kevin stood up before the small crowd of Kevin's friends and pub buddies and done what he called a 'celebration' of his life. It might have been a celebration of any man, good or bad, with prizes just for breathing, and it carried not a trace, not a hint, of Kevin within the words, the empty words).

Still, on a Wednesday evening, it made a nice change to put on a colourful frock, the one with poppies and the belted sash that Kevin used to love. He told her she looked like a movie star in that dress, and she told him she looked more like a character actress, but ta very much. She wore a red sweater over the dress to keep out the weather.

Readying herself for these expeditions, she'd combed up her hair and even put on a little red lipstick. Not because she was trying to attract anyone but because, after a bare existence of work-eat-sleep for so long, it made her feel human. As close to human as she might ever feel again. She didn't invite any of her friends to join her, or Maisie, who was teetotal anyway. They'd all start in with their dating nonsense, talking about how their cousin Sally met a bloke on the *It's Your Turn* app, when what she really wanted was to be alone. Alone in the company of a crowd, if that made any sense at all. It made sense to her.

In the days and months after Kevin's accident, people said wasn't it lucky she and Kevin had never had children. Her *own sister* had said it – her with her twins who were 'the light of my life'. People talked no ruddy end of rot, and as soon as she'd shut the door on them she'd say out loud – there was no one to hear, after all – all the many things she might have said but had kept inside. Only one of those many things was that she would *kill* to have a small version of Kevin running around the house, or a small version of herself that was part Kevin. It would be, either version, girl or boy, a child who was good with its hands, good at making things, good at getting fiddly things *just right*. Kevin had been a carpenter for Brice Builders, and he was so good they put him on doing the finishing work, inside and out. Mr Brice had even turned up for the 'celebration', which he didn't have to do – that's how much Kevin had meant to him. He was an artist, was Kevin, and Mr Brice had said so. Not just good at his job, but an artist. It meant everything to Kevin to reach the end of the day knowing he'd done better than his best.

All the rich folk with their fitted cabinets could thank Kevin every time they opened a perfectly balanced door that didn't creak or come off in their hands and beheld all the expensive things they owned. Every time their roof didn't leak, or their windows shut tight without sticking, they could thank Kevin.

But of course, they never did thank Kevin. They never knew Kevin Bottle existed. For folk like that, things they wanted to make their lives better just magically appeared. If they paid enough for the best, things would magically appear. And if some bloke fell off the scaffolding at his job building their house in a gated estate, what was it to them? They couldn't know and they wouldn't want to know. They would come to think of their new luxury home as a place of bad luck, haunted by a tall man with a red beard, dressed in workman's clothes and carrying a hammer and a measuring tape. No, they wouldn't want to know and certainly Brice Builders wasn't going to tell them. Kevin's accident had rated a brief notice in the Oxford newspaper, a 'worker injured' notice, with no follow-up when he died in hospital three days later. The world had moved on by then. The Kardashians and that lot were busy getting married again.

Yes, the world had moved on, leaving her to wish she'd never met Kevin, or that she'd never been born, or that she'd been born somewhere else than England. Anything to ease the gnawing pain that was life without Kevin.

The pub wasn't hard to find if you were in the know, but it had become a student prank to send tourists in the other direction – to pretend they'd misunderstood and send them down Turl Street instead to the vanished pub of that name. The Turf Tavern, a completely different animal, was reached by way of St Helen's Passage, a winding, narrow, dark alley running between a college wall to one side and a brick house on the other. Halfway along the alley was a sharp turn, but eventually the alley ran into the little ancient pub, crooked and teetering with age. It looked as if it would collapse in on itself, but according to the sign over the door it had stood since the twelfth century. Looming over it was the top of a college bell tower.

The pub was crowded but she found her favourite seat in a far corner, away from the bar, where she could be alone and observe people. She enjoyed blending into the background, keeping her eyes and ears open. Her Yorkshire granny used to say there's nowt so queer as folk, and she was right about that. The Turf was perfect for people watching, and it had soon become a habit on her one day off a week to dress up a bit and come here for a pint on her own.

She had lived in Oxford all her life, and she had worked in an Oxford college for three years, ever since Kevin passed, for a little extra money (Kevin *did* like to spend) and for something to do. So she knew all the types.

The students, of course, were rowdy on a weekend night, but this was a weekday, and maybe some of them had tutorials the next day or were mindful they needed their rest. She wanted to tell them *you can rest when you're dead*. You're only eighteen, only twenty, only twenty-one, and you're full of life and energy and you don't have arthritis (yet) and the world's all at your feet. You leave this place with an education the rest of the world can only envy and some of you will go on to great things. This is no time to rest up. Rest up for what – for being old and alone?

Others were tourists, and those were the fun ones to watch, easy to pick out of any crowd. Germans, Japanese, Arabs, Swedes – you name it. They were different but all the same. The Americans were the easiest to spot, however hard they tried to blend in. God bless them they tried, but everything they did gave them away, from over-tipping the barmaid on down. Their expensive travel clothes, and their accents too, of course. Their tendency to talk just that bit too loud.

Of course, in a pub they needed to shout to be heard, but not quite so much and not so often as they did shout. Their sense of belonging was what surprised her, of fitting in wherever they were, and because they had a great-great-great-uncle from Wales or Cornwall or whatever, the entire country must be their home, too. But at the same time they had this sense of wonder, like a child's, at being surrounded by all the history – the history she herself took for granted. They were amazed at all the beautiful buildings which had been created before the United States was ever thought of. Places built by men like her Kevin, in fact.

Their shopping bags and clean new backpacks and tourist maps and tickets sprouting from their pockets – all these were clues that gave them away, but the shoes most of all. While things had changed over the years in Oxford, with people getting more casual (sloppy, she thought) all the time, the one thing that still surprised her was how easy it was to spot Americans by their shoes. All ages and sorts, the Americans wore some variation of the same brand of trainers beneath their travel pants. Maybe it was because they were on holiday and they were dressed for comfort, but she suspected they dressed like this at home, too, in what they called 'leisurewear'.

The usual waitress came over to her to take her order, which was kind – the ritual was the customer should order a drink at the bar, however teeming it was with people, but she'd never get a drink by herself, she wasn't the pushy type, and being here alone was enough of a personal challenge for her. It was getting easier, but still, she felt this was what Kevin would have wanted. She was easing herself back into the world, not sitting at home going slightly mad, pretending to watch some rubbish on the telly and thinking of him.

The Turf had not been her local with Kevin. That was in Cowley near where they lived. The Turf was their special occasion place when they'd been dating, and where he'd proposed, and where they'd celebrated every anniversary. Today would have been their twenty-third anniversary, and she would drink a toast – maybe two – to his memory.

The place was starting to fill up, but she'd nearly finished her pint anyway. Her second pint. She was drinking Kevin's favourite, her own being a glass of white wine. She wondered sometimes if this was a problem, the pints. When Kevin had been around she'd never drunk much at all, really, not to speak of. But two little drinks? That was supposed to be good for the heart and the bones wasn't it – beer especially was good for bones? Anyway, the waitress had learned her ways by now and brought the second pint without her having to ask.

She put a ten-pound note on the table as she was getting ready to leave. The £4.57 pint was highway robbery, it was, but she'd leave the change – it wasn't the girl's fault. She'd just been to the cashpoint and taken out a hundred pounds; carrying round that amount of cash made her feel rich. They always said the queen never carried money, even though it had her face all over it. In the queen's place, she'd carry a very large purse stuffed with money and she'd buy everything in cash.

But £4.57? The world had gone mad. Supply chain issues, they said. She pictured barrels of beer sitting on a big barge out in the middle of the ocean. The second beer was starting to work its magic on her arthritis. She'd worry about becoming an alcoholic another day. Maybe she was a little woozy standing up. She sat back down until it passed.

The crowd had overflowed into the beer garden at the entrance to the pub. Smoking was no longer allowed, hadn't been for some time, and that was a blessing. She'd given up years ago at the same time as Kevin and they'd both survived it. She wondered now why either of them had bothered, but she was glad not to be tied to the habit. With the low-beamed ceilings of the tavern, it must have been like a smelly London fog in here in the past.

'Have another, luv?' the waitress asked, collecting her ten-pound note. 'On the house.'

She shook her head, making its insides seem to slosh about. She was definitely feeling woozy – probably shouldn't have had the second pint.

'No, no. Work tomorrow,' she said, and rose to leave. She sensed more than saw the man sitting not far from her stand up also. A tourist, well-dressed, shoes polished to a high gloss. Not American, then. Former military. Kevin had done his time and got out. He always said there were two types of people who made a career of the army: those who needed to be told what to do and those who wanted to be told. Kevin was neither type, and look how well he'd done for himself.

This time the room didn't sway quite so much. She walked past the bar and out the door and wove her way past the throngs of students, shouting and laughing. They didn't even see her. She was invisible. At her age she was used to being invisible among the students at the college and she didn't hold it against them. She loved every one of them, the ones from the posh backgrounds and the ones on scholarships who were frightened so they put on airs, afraid they couldn't keep up. Oxford had the occasional suicide at the beginning of term; that was unbelievably sad. There had only been one from her college in the years she'd been there, a boy from India who felt he was letting down his family when he couldn't keep up with his studies, when he couldn't fit in. She always wondered if she should have known, if she could have prevented it. She'd often seen him wandering around the quad and he looked no more lost than the rest of them. No more happy or sad than the rest of them, but it had struck her after his death that she'd never seen him in a group.

It meant so much to them to succeed, to make someone proud of them. They were all so young they made her heart ache.

She reached the lane leading from the beer garden. It would dog-leg around and take her to New College Lane and the Bridge of Sighs, her favourite spot in Oxford. It was where Kevin had first kissed her. She'd take the bus from Queen's Lane in Oxford City Centre and she'd be home well within the hour.

She heard steps coming up behind her, heavy steps, pounding harder as whoever it was began to run. She edged to the left side of the narrow alleyway to make room. She was used to undergraduates thundering about, or zipping past her on their bicycles, never watching where they were going, nearly knocking her over a couple of times, barely stopping to apologize. The last time it had happened, a well-brought-up young man had helped her collect all the things he'd made her drop, making himself even later getting to wherever he'd been going.

But whoever this was stopped when she stopped and when she turned, looking to see who it was, what was the matter, the knife bit into the base of her throat before she could fully turn her head – it was over that quick. She never really knew who killed her, only that they were strong and they smelled of beer and cigarettes. And she knew that however much she missed Kevin, she also knew she didn't want to die.

Not this way.

ONE
Boniface

Six months later

Sir Boniface Castle's lifelong dream had been to own a publishing house. To be a publisher in the tradition of the giants of the past who had discovered and nourished writers like Dickens and Thackeray and the Brontës and Matthew Arnold and all the greats.

Well, Arnold maybe not so much, but the others. The bestsellers of their day who, along with Shakespeare, had made the UK the beating heart of the English-speaking world.

Sir Boniface's advantageous marriage to the like-minded Lady Ursula Blackenthorpe of the Mayfair Blackenthorpes had given him the wherewithal to follow his dream. While his background was in manufacturing (wallpaper), he believed his skills would transfer easily, since despite his ambitious harking back to famous writers, books to him were merely widgets made of paper and ink, and his favourite bedtime reading was the profit-and-loss spreadsheet, and his knowledge of current authors was based solely on their book sales and rankings, numbers he could recite by heart. If pressed to make small talk at book fairs and literary soirées, he did have perfect recall of reviews appearing in publications like the *Daily Telegraph* and the *London Review of Books*.

On his fiftieth birthday, Sir Boniface bought a crenellated wedding cake of a Victorian house in North Oxford's Jericho neighbourhood, and from there began luring talented staff from London. Jericho's bohemian vibe was a draw, and he snared many of the best editors and book marketers with enormous salaries and promises of profit-sharing and bonuses. His plan was to offset this outlay by offering prospective authors the lowest possible advances and royalties that the market would bear. He got away with this by refusing to deal with literary agents and accepting only unsolicited manuscripts from authors, who were subsequently offered the most extortionate terms imaginable. But desperate as they were, not only to be published but to work with the world's most renowned editors and a powerhouse publicity machine, they signed.

Other publishing houses scoffed but many, after losing some of their best staff to Sir Boniface, followed his lead, increasing salaries across the board.

Meanwhile, Sir Boniface sat back to await the submission of the one author who would bring him fame and fortune. The wait took longer than he'd thought, but as with every maker of books since Gutenberg, the hope for another J.K. Rowling or James Patterson to brighten the doorway sprang eternal.

Sir Boniface named his new enterprise Castle Publishing, installing himself at the top of the management pyramid as publisher, his son David as editorial director, and his daughter Imogen as head of marketing and publicity. The company logo was a rampant unicorn, borrowed from the arms of a noble ancestor to whom Sir Boniface was (very) distantly related, most likely on the distaff side. After three years of running in the red, the house was beginning to turn a profit with its science fiction imprint (David's particular interest), but it was having trouble discovering new mainstream, romance or crime fiction authors of good or even good-enough quality. One after another, books acquired by Castle Publishing failed to sell enough copies to earn out even the tiny advances paid to its small stable of desperate authors. Some editors, bored despite their large salaries and bonuses and trendy surroundings, began yearning for a return to the brighter lights of London, where they might once again work with a powerhouse writer. Many of them openly discussed with their fellow inmates over drinks at the Duke of Cambridge how they were salting away their monthly salaries, anticipating the day they would leave Castle Publishing behind and resume their former careers.

Sir Boniface caught wind of these conversations, for he was not above a bit of corporate espionage (editors and others would have been wise to inspect the potted plants in their offices for bugs of the electronic kind). Panic at the thought of a general exodus began to set in for the first time with the otherwise wildly optimistic publisher. His house of cards had been built on having the best team of editors, marketers and publicists in the world, his long-term plan being to get the company up and running and then revert to a more traditional publishing model, paying low-level editors barely enough to buy their own red pencils. If they left before he was ready to push them out, he might face ruin.

But in true fairy-tale fashion, one day an obscure Oxford tutor named Jason Verdoodt arrived, changing everything at Castle Publishing. His over-the-transom submission titled *The White Owl* created quite a furore within the walls of the publishing house – eventually. Every editor wanted to claim *The White Owl* as their own, there being no clear path to ownership at Castle Publishing. Every publicist wanted to be the one to publicize it. Every marketeer wanted to negotiate the merchandising and production rights, which were the real money-makers, more so than the book itself.

The irony was Jason's book came very close to never making it on to bookshop shelves. According to company by-laws, all acquisitions had to be approved by the publisher or, in his absence, his son David. When it finally thudded on to David's desk (a literal thud, for one of the eccentricities of the submission requirements at Castle was that the manuscript be submitted in hard copy), Boniface was on holiday and David, drunk with unleashed power, rejected it out of hand. He was too steeped in science fiction to begin to understand the experimental mystery genre Verdoodt was exploring: *The Da Vinci Code* meets *Death on the Nile* by way of *David Copperfield*, as the cover sheet explained. But fortunately for everyone involved, the manuscript was rescued from the rubbish bin and eventually found its way to the desk of a tanned-and-rested Sir Boniface.

The rest is publishing history. As a PR story it had all the magical elements that can hoist an author to bestsellerdom: handsome young tutor from working-class background submits manuscript to struggling publisher, who instantly recognizes the genius behind the work. (As with all PR stories, some truths were edited out.) The humble genius is summoned to the publisher's office, where instantly a bond of mutual respect is forged and an industry is launched. The genius agrees to a laughably small advance on sales, perhaps not knowing his book's true value.

Still, no one could explain to anyone's satisfaction the quality of *The White Owl* which made it climb to the top of every bestseller list, let alone why the author had chosen Castle Publishing over the more traditional London publishers requiring agented submissions. His story, which seemed incredible even for a starry-eyed author, was that he had submitted *only* to Castle Publishing because a) they were an Oxford company and b) he had heard they were the best publishers with the most talented staff. Besides, c) he couldn't be troubled to look for an agent. If Castle did not accept the manuscript, he was going to quit writing fiction and resume full-time his profession as a tutor in arch and anth (archaeology and anthropology) at St Rumwold's College. The reading world gasped at the thought of this near-miss, and he himself might have fainted to hear how close his book came to rejection, even though he was among the happy few humans who seldom suffered a moment's self-doubt.

He never came to hear of the near-miss because assistant Gita Patel engaged in a bit of coverup, claiming her boss David had recognized the enormous sales potential in the manuscript immediately and had sat on it to await his father's return. David did not contradict her version of events.

To this day, few can justify the rapture of those reaching for words to describe the quality of the writing and storytelling in *The White Owl*. Reviewers ran out of superlatives to describe the book, and many compared its author to Evelyn Waugh, for the book's opening chapters had been set among the upper classes at Oxford in the 1920s, a theme reminiscent of *Brideshead Revisited*.

It helped of course that the author was young, but many a young author had been left by the wayside as older, more established writers chugged past with their generous advertising, marketing and promotional budgets. Verdoodt was handsome in a Byronic way, with shiny locks of dark hair and flashing eyes, but many a young and handsome author had been stranded likewise once it was discovered he had no talent.

No one could quite put their finger on it, but of course the clamour for more instantly arose and the author was reported to be at work on a follow-up novel, writing late into the night when his tutorial duties allowed. It was said he wrote by candlelight and by the moonlight seeping through the leaded glass panes of his college rooms, which only gilded the myth growing around him.

Those who thought he might abandon his college post were wrong; he told interviewers he grew up in poverty, the child of immigrants, instilled with a belief that a steady pay cheque was preferable to a pot of gold that might vanish in wartime. It was the sort of modest comment that sent sales rocketing ever higher.

Boniface had acquired Jason Verdoodt's second book for an eye-popping advance which earned huge amounts of media attention (and stoked the envy of other Castle authors) before the author had written a single paragraph. Thanks to a stroke of marketing genius by the daughter of the house, Imogen Castle, much of this attention was generated by false claims of first copies of *The White Owl* being pirated during break-ins at the book manufacturing plant in Cornwall, and of later attempts to hack into the computers of Castle Publishing itself.

Soon the Verdoodt name was invoked as a matter of course when contenders for the year's literary awards were discussed. He was considered a shoo-in for the Booker prize, but *The White Owl* was a cross-over phenomenon, 'devoured and discussed in hair salons and literary salons around the world', according to eminent book reviewers.

It was heady stuff for a tutor used to living in spartan college rooms to now be able to afford a suite at the Ritz whenever he chose and a limousine to take him there. College accommodation, however picturesque tourists might have thought it, was often cold and lacking hot water, but again he diffidently emphasized he was used to this ascetic poverty, it was how he had been raised.

Imogen did, however, leak news of his 'secret' week-long stay at the Ritz to work on the new novel to ensure media coverage of the author waving to photographers from his hotel window. She spun this as the author's desperate need to get away from fans.

In sum, the success of his book showed that the world was literally at Jason's feet – the world of willing young women with literary ambitions in particular.

It was enough to turn the head of a humbler young man. In the case of the already insufferable Verdoodt, it went a long way towards turning him into a monster.

TWO
The Wunderkind

It was late September, close to the start of the full Michaelmas term, and Jason Verdoodt was organizing his wardrobe for the evening. There was to be a black-tie dinner in his honour on the premises of St Rumwold's College, starting with drinks in the Fellows' Library and continuing into the college's stately dining hall with its massive fireplace, ornate plaster ceiling, and centuries-old paintings of college luminaries.

The library venue with its elegant stonework, arched windows and vaulted ceiling had been chosen over the strident protests of the college librarian, Sir Bartholomew Tremaine, who predicted the ruin by wine and canapé stains of furniture already darkened by centuries of spilt ink and the tears of failed scholars. His concerns had been overruled, although the master had instructed the tables be covered with white table-cloths for the occasion, and the more precious leather-bound volumes be stored safely away.

But having a celebrity like a Verdoodt on the premises, drawing attention and honours to the college as J.R.R. Tolkien had brought renown to Merton and the Reverend Charles Dodgson to Christ Church, the master felt a few rules needed to be broken. Wealthy donors loved this sort of thing and wealthy donors were what allowed the college to thrive even in the lean years. In particular, the master was hoping to impress alumni Lord and Lady Yale-Lequatte into endowing a college scholarship in creative writing or donating to repairs of the leaking roof of the junior common room.

At the moment, St Rumwold's College was closed for learning, except for some left-behind graduate students who had told their faraway families they were too busy working on their theses to travel home. In some cases, this was true. In others, a new love beckoned, further weakening family ties.

But in October the term would begin, and the Oxford quads would again overflow with scholars.

As mentioned, Jason Verdoodt had remained at his humble teaching post despite his success, but his reasons had nothing to do with his modest origins. For one thing, apart from bookshop signings, where else could he find the kind of adoration he received daily from his students?

For another, he was wise enough to know fame was fleeting and authors were only as good as their last book. He therefore intended to milk *The White Owl* for all the attention it could get. Meanwhile he needed something to do with his time, and he happened to like teaching.

He was a born teacher, a charismatic in the tradition of a megachurch pastor, and he thrived on being around his disciples, as he thought of his students. He looked forward to leading tutorials, to the power of testing and training not just good minds but the best minds in the country, if not the world. His combined fields of archaeology and anthropology let him explore the best of both worlds, and the department's director of studies had given him free rein from the start. He was obliged to give six sessions a week, coaxing something besides nonsense out of the students who sat before him in cushy chairs with varying expressions of comprehension on their faces. They handed in their essays once a week, and he was diligent about reading these and offering insightful comments which they ignored at their peril when it came to exam time.

He taught from three locations: the Institute of Archaeology in Beaumont Street, the laboratory (radiocarbon dating and crop isotope analysis), and the Pitt Rivers Museum in Parks Road. He had a paramour in each location, deftly juggling the three women so none of them suspected the others existed. It was for this reason he tended to avoid local book signings: *quelle catastrophe* if they should all turn up at once. But he was a risk-taker by nature and thrived on creating this sort of chaos: living on the edge of exposure and figuring out ways to avoid consequences for his actions.

Of course, there were others besides these three. Tonight's 'date' was his publisher's daughter Imogen Castle. If she'd taken more after her father, she'd have been a beauty. Part of

Jason's gift was finding the attraction in a woman that others might overlook. Imogen, who had beautiful eyes, was forty years to his thirty-two, but his oldest conquest had been nearly sixty, and he seldom saw age as a drawback. His dalliance with Imogen was clearly an advantageous pairing; it was nice having the head of marketing at Castle Publishing in his pocket.

At least, for now. He'd extricate himself from Imogen's clutches when the time came in his usual fashion, introducing her to someone more suitable, feigning mild jealousy as the sparks ignited, then standing back to admire his handiwork before disappearing from her life entirely. He was good at this, this pairing up of people, in the process disposing of those no longer of use to him, and he thought of himself as a sort of gifted matchmaker. He supposed it had something to do with his training in anthropology, which is in essence the study of human biology and behaviour across time.

That and the inborn instinct of the predator in finding and disposing of vulnerable prey.

Of course, it was important to remember Imogen came from a wealthy and well-connected family. Marriage might not be completely off the table in her case. After all, there was nothing to say he'd have to permanently curtail his dalliances after marriage, was there? Something to keep in mind for the future.

Jason Verdoodt did not see anything immoral or dangerous in his behaviour, since the women were all adults. The one thing he had taken to heart from his readings in anthropology was the concept that morality was relative to time and place. The undergraduates were another story, in his and most other cultures. But one civilization's taboo was another's orthodoxy.

As he was choosing a tie for the evening, cursing his scout who shuffled things about to demonstrate his rooms had been cleaned – he'd have to have another word with the head housekeeper – his mobile buzzed with a message from Minette Miniver, another long-time girlfriend. The longest, in fact, as they'd been undergraduates together. He ignored the message, as he'd ignored several others from her in recent days.

He would soon have to bring Minette into the picture and update her on her approaching change in status, but the moment hadn't quite yet presented itself, and even Jason felt it would be churlish to drop her by text message. It might even be dangerous. Minette could be rather . . . excitable.

Besides, he hadn't thought of anyone yet to introduce her to.

Fortunately, she lived in London. He had been counting on distance making the heart grow indifferent since that had always worked well for him, but she had been more tenacious than he'd anticipated. He supposed her damaged childhood with her skinny horror of a mother had something to do with her clinginess and general instability. Once Minette got wind of his new house, however, he'd have to dampen any expectations she might have that the house was being prepared for her occupation. That they might – God forbid – actually live together.

Or worse, get married.

He had an awful feeling that was in her mind. But he'd never said anything like that to her, or even implied it. Had he? Well, no matter if he had. It wasn't happening.

Things had changed since the two of them had been together at Cambridge, she reading English and helping him write both his master's and PhD theses. Well, she'd helped him polish his grammar, which he had to admit wasn't his strong suit – imagination was. But *polish*, that was it. No need for her to practically claim authorship as she tended to do when frustrated by the long wait to get him to the altar.

He had never promised Minette a rose garden. She should acknowledge that and move on. What was wrong with women?

Which wife of Henry VIII's was it who had gone away quietly, literally keeping her head on her shoulders? Anne of Cleves? Yes, Anne of Cleves. Why couldn't Minette be like that? Sensible. The case had altered, and she needed to accept the fact.

He laid out his sartorial choices on the bed, admiring the skill of his Savile Row tailor. Jason's taste in clothing had always been impeccable and now he could afford to indulge it. One of his shoulders was slightly lower than the other – an accident of birth – and Mr Farnsworth had cleverly disguised this slight defect with discreet layers of padding.

Verdoodt's room on the third floor of Staircase B in Second Quad was ensuite, a sink and a toilet and a coffin-like shower having been wedged into the far northeast corner of the medieval chamber. He would soon be moving to posher digs in North Oxford once renovations were complete on the small house he'd paid for in cash. The estate agent couldn't quite believe her luck, for he had made his choice without demands for alterations or hesitations or haggling over the price. In fact, he had had his eyes on this house for some time, had researched it thoroughly, and had known it was coming on the market. From the moment he had written 'The End' on the last page of his manuscript, he had dreamed of it becoming a bestseller, and had planned accordingly.

He'd come a long way and there was no question in his mind that he'd earned his success. They hailed him as an overnight success, but no one knew better than he, overnight success took a long time. The years of swotting in Belgium and the Netherlands, toiling away at Leiden and Cambridge before coming to Oxford. He'd kept moving up the ladder. And now look at him.

All the more reason to make sure Minette got the message. The sooner the better.

Simply put, he didn't need her any more.

It was as well to be prepared for the next move up in the world. He liked to say, with Hannibal, 'I will either find a way or make one'.

THREE
Minette

Minette Miniver was dithering over her own wardrobe for the evening. She stood in front of a sort of funhouse mirror in a short-term bedsit in Cowley, just up the road from Oxford proper but worlds away from the preserved splendour of its Cotswold stone architecture. The stairs and hallways of the two-storey building, crouched lopsidedly along Marston Street, always seemed to smell of cooking, although none of the rooms came equipped with kitchens and there were hand-printed signs everywhere to remind tenants of the penalties for using unauthorized appliances. This didn't seem to stop the man in Room B-1, who had a fondness for curry dishes. Nearly as bad, the full-length mirror added twenty pounds to her hips and an extra chin to her face.

Cowley was a land of fish-and-chips shops, local pubs and Indian food takeaways, and bedsits stocked to the attics with impoverished graduate students. Minette could have afforded better accommodation but better was not what she wanted. She wanted anonymity. She was afraid she might run into Jason if she had stayed at the Randolph or any of the high-end hotels in Oxford.

And she didn't want to run into him or anyone, for she was on a secret mission.

She had overpacked. She always did when she was anxious. She didn't need three dresses for that evening's occasion, like a celebrity bride with elaborate changes of costume for each wedding day event. Minette needed only *one* dress. But her insecurity was overwhelming because, insofar as her relationship with Jason was concerned, she had reached a do-or-die moment – a moment that required the proverbial dress to die for. It was fair to say she was consumed with self-doubt, and a few baser emotions besides.

Jealousy being the root emotion from which sprouted all the rest.

She and Jason had been together for *years* and *years*. And that had to count for something. They had met in college and stayed in touch, if sporadically. When she was honest with herself, she admitted she had done all the keeping in touch. Jason had just sort of gone along and made himself available when he felt like it.

They had what she thought of as a long-distance but exclusive relationship, ideal for her because of her hectic, erratic schedule as an intern and then a doctor. She had never questioned that idealness. At least, she had never allowed herself to question it. Her job kept her in London and his kept him in Oxford. Their lives intersected *perfectly*. Almost. But as far as she was concerned, it worked well – distance making the heart grow fonder – and would continue to work until the day he and she could live together forever and truly cement their relationship.

That day had surely arrived now. With his success, Jason could no longer cry poor over buying a house for them in Oxford.

She did wish she had never brought up the subject, however. Men, especially men like Jason, didn't like being pressured.

This party tonight had brought things to a head. This big celebration of Jason's book, a celebration he had failed to mention to her, and which she'd only learned about by chance when a friend happened to mention it, having assumed Minette was invited. The friend had heard about it through some publishing newsfeed on Twitter.

It was a book he had hinted at in passing over the years but which Minette had, if she were honest, paid zero attention to. Every doctor she knew was writing a book on the side about their experiences in A&E, although some of them were branching out into fiction, hoping to become the next bestselling medical thriller writer. She had put Jason's ambitions in the same category of wishful thinking, and that was on her for doubting him. He had had such a successful career at such a young age as an Oxford tutor and was clearly on the path to a fellowship at his college. She assumed any writing he did would be an academic treatise on ancient dyes or whatever, a book destined to be read by perhaps a hundred people. She never understood that he was trying to reach a wider audience with a popular novel. She never foresaw how wildly he would succeed in this ambition.

No matter how she looked at it, the fact he hadn't invited her to tonight's do was her own fault. She should have known, or at least have asked what he was up to. She should have been more supportive.

It wasn't as if she had no belief or faith in him. Far from it. She had adored Jason from the first moment she'd set eyes on him. Simply adored him. But now with his newfound celebrity, with the articles in book sections of major magazines and newspapers, and television interviews on morning programmes, she could feel him slipping away. She couldn't quite put her finger on it but there was a difference in him now. A coldness. He was always perfectly polite and correct but there was an increase in the number of unreturned texts and phone calls, and a lack of apology for these slights.

She couldn't kid herself anymore. He was trying to free himself from her. He wanted someone more suitable for a superstar author.

Not someone with hips as wide as the Thames and more than one chin.

All those years of being young together were slipping away.

She didn't think she could stand it.

She couldn't *stand* it.

She stood before the distorted mirror in the cramped bedsit tugging at the low-cut white silk dress she had packed as one of her three options for the night. The dress said 'sexy'. It said, 'small-ish waist'.

It also said 'wedding'.

It said, 'Miss Havisham'.

Too obvious?

Yes, she decided, tugging the dress roughly over her head, leaving a bright red lipstick stain on the neckline. So much for that, she thought, throwing the ruined garment back on the bed. It could be dry-cleaned but there wasn't time. At least her choices were narrowed to two now.

Then there were the shoes. Four pairs, none of which seemed to go with anything. Too casual, or too trying-too-hard. *Arghh.*

Her patients would be amazed to see her now. In an emergency, her brain became robotic, admitting no room for error. *Give me that, hand me that, get the IV ready stat.*

She knew common sense had fled the moment she heard about the book party and decided to come to Oxford. It hadn't been robotic thinking – it hadn't even been a decision, just an impulse.

What she thought of as her Jason brain was now in the driver's seat.

Probably the black dress with its modest neckline was more appropriate for an elegant dinner at a world-famous college, and while it flattered her shape it did have about it the look of widow's weeds. It only needed a veil to complete the look. It was, in a word, boring, and she was sure half the wives and girlfriends at this affair would be dressed similarly, afraid of putting a foot wrong, of attracting negative attention at such an august gathering. It needed a pearl choker or something glamorous like that to set it off, and she didn't happen to own a pearl choker or any other proper jewellery. Her daily costume consisted of blue scrubs and a hairnet, mask and safety goggles. Over the years she'd got rather out of practice with dressing to make a statement.

The one outfit in her arsenal that *would* make a statement was the red satin number her mother had given her one Christmas as part of her ongoing campaign to push her into the marriage market. Marla thought Jason was a player and would never marry her daughter, a topic on which she and Minette had quarrelled more than once. The dress wasn't inexpensive, but it was eye-catching and flash, cheap looking. Minette hated it. She looked like a gangster's moll wearing it. It sent all the wrong messages for a dignified dinner at a stately college.

But now . . . Now Minette wondered if it weren't just what the occasion called for. Bold. Yes, bold, that was the ticket. She was, after all, crashing a party, and surely the best way to do that was to make sure she stood out from the crowd.

Which she would. Surely Jason wouldn't have her thrown out.

It was as if she were possessed by a sort of derring-do, like a woman preparing to be dropped behind enemy lines in World War II. She had to be like that. Brave like that.

Do or die.

Because everything else she'd tried with Jason had failed. And if tonight pushed him over the edge somehow, well. At least she'd know.

She'd know what she already knew. He was leaving her. He wanted her gone. This was her last chance to reel him back to her side. To remind him what they'd been to each other.

And if that didn't work . . .

If the red dress didn't work, there was always Plan B.

And while the specifics of Plan B were vague in her mind, the plan overall was to make Jason pay. Make him sorry.

She would either have Jason for her own, or no one would have him.

FOUR

Ursula

'I thought you said the company was solvent.'

'Did I? Did I say *sol*vent? I think I said something more along the lines of it was "turning a corner". Yes, that was it. I said we were "turning a corner".'

Lady Ursula knew the technique well by now. Rather than reply to what she had said, rather than 'stay on topic', as her children would have it, her husband would attempt to divert and derail the conversation by debating the precise wording used. Like a politician trying to wriggle out of the trap he'd set for himself: was it a forbidden party during lockdown or was it a business gathering that happened to include drinks and canapés?

She had learned over the years – sometimes – to avoid the pitfall of being too specific, as in, 'You said you would call at four'. To which Boniface would reply, 'No, I said I would call around four. Or was it five? It was definitely closer to five'. This technique drove her right round the twist, but only because she fell for it so often, entering the debate as to what exactly he'd said and never getting him round to the topic of *why* he'd been late calling.

She had on occasion been able to cut through her husband's nonsense (her children had another word for it), but it required constant vigilance and it was exhausting. All that back-and-forth, attempting to wrest the truth from him. Downright and forthright herself, she preferred honest and open communication, however painful – and however often she was shot as the messenger.

She would have done well not to have married Boniface. In fact, she'd been engaged to another man when they met. A suitable man from her own class, as her mother never tired of reminding her. But to be honest – and Lady Ursula was nothing but honest with herself these days – there had been something irresistible about Boniface. Something that promised a lifetime of adventure, of risk, of taking chances. Of *life*. He'd been good looking, but more than that he'd possessed the sort of Stanley Kowalski allure that had been the undoing of many women before her and would be the undoing of many to come. Everything in his nature ran counter to everything in hers. She never realized how exhausting that imbalance would prove to be over time; how wearing, how soul-destroying.

Still, she stayed in the marriage. Having made this match against her parents' wishes, she simply *had* to make it work. She could not admit failure and defeat, in their eyes or her own. Besides, the family were descended from Catholic nobility and none of her ancestors had ever been divorced. Although the rules had loosened considerably in recent decades, and annulments could always be bought given the right price, her family lived in the sort of Brideshead world where divorce was never discussed, let alone considered. It wasn't clear to Ursula if any of them believed in hell and damnation for the unfaithful; it was more as if they were carrying on the way they always had done out of ingrained habit.

It wasn't until her former beau Sir Roger had come back into her life that she started to revisit all the choices she'd made. Most women would look at their children and think, 'Well, maybe the *marriage* wasn't a success but at least we managed to produce these two wonderful human beings'. But Lady Ursula couldn't even cling to this fiction. With David, the apple had not, in many regards, fallen far from the tree. He was as cagey and mendacious and as hard to pin down as his father, if for different reasons: His head was always in the clouds of the science fiction and fantasy worlds where he had dwelt from the age of thirteen, living out his days on Planet X, starring in some video game playing in the windmills of his mind.

His sister Imogen had a practical nature, which should have warmed her mother's heart and drawn her closer, but her affinity for marketing had nourished a manipulative streak. A cold, calculating and ruthless little girl bargaining for cakes and later bedtimes had been transformed into a stone-cold woman who put a price on everything. Everyone was a mark, a target, a figure on a chessboard to be moved into place or eliminated by trickery and guile. No wonder Imogen was unmarried. No man in his right senses would take that on, despite Imogen's wealthy background.

Lady Ursula had only recently become aware how far Jason Verdoodt had wormed his way into Imogen's life. He was intelligent and charming, and certainly he was good looking, but Lady Ursula, being a realist, knew her doughy daughter with her blackcurrant eyes had limited appeal to the opposite – or any – sex. At least Jason was an even match for Imogen in the manipulation sweepstakes. It was going to be interesting to see who bested whom. For even viewing Imogen through the prism of her small reserve of motherly love, Lady Ursula knew he would hang about her daughter only for so long as he found the relationship advantageous. She wondered not for the first time how far he might go to attach himself to her noble family. Was he thinking marriage? She couldn't countenance the thought of history repeating itself.

'Turning a corner, then,' she said now to her husband. 'Have it your way. You led me to *believe* the company was in good shape. You led me to *believe* this Jason person was the saviour of Castle Publishing. What has changed?'

'It's Jason Verdoodt. You could at least remember his name. He helped pay for that designer frock you're wearing.'

'No one says "frock" anymore. What century are you living in? And I paid for the dress.' This was a mistake. Boniface hated being reminded how much he owed her and her family. 'Besides, you know I only read non-fiction and biographies.' Realizing she had fallen again for her husband's diversionary tactics, she repeated, 'What precisely has changed?'

Boniface's face began to crumble, like a medieval castle wall under attack by a trebuchet.

She had him. She only had to maintain silence.

'There's been a development.'

Silence.

'With his next book.'

Silence.

'He's threatening to move to a different publisher.'

Ah. At last, we near the truth.

'How much?' she asked. For this could only be about money. Castle Publishing had deep pockets thanks to her family money but, like most of England's old families, they were land poor. They couldn't go up against the big guns – the 'Big Five' or the 'Big Four', depending on the current state of flux in the industry – in New York. Jason Verdoodt (she knew his name perfectly well, and only pretended indifference to get her husband's goat) was threatening to leave for greener pastures, taking his new book with him, despite having already accepted their very generous offer. It was a shame that, after the initial fanfare, Jason had been stalling on signing the contract.

But who could blame him, the ungrateful wretch? Still, it was potentially a disaster.

It wouldn't destroy Castle Publishing, since legally they could continue to reprint Jason's first book until the end of time, or until it stopped selling a certain low number of copies, whichever came first (Jason's book contract had been reviewed by a rather careless entertainment lawyer). But all the new money would chase after Jason's newest book. She knew enough about the industry to know this was not great news for Castle Publishing. Jason needed to be persuaded to stay.

'How much?' she asked again. 'The truth. I can't help here unless you give me solid figures. I could go to Father and see . . .'

'Already tried,' said Boniface.

'Already tried?' Ursula was stunned. Boniface had never done this before; she knew he was secretly terrified of her father. 'You went behind my back to my own father? To ask my own father for money? No wonder he was so strange on the phone. I suppose you told him to keep it man to man. How *dare* you?' How dare both of them? While her father had no great admiration for Boniface (the wool had long been pulled from his eyes regarding the integrity of his son-in-law), he'd rather talk to a man, any man, about a collapsing business venture than trust his own daughter. Even at sixty-plus years of age, it still stung, this undermining of her confidence. It had gone on since she had made her first tentative baby steps.

'It's business,' said her husband. 'You have made a point of not wanting to know the fine details.'

This was demonstrably not true. She had simply given up over the years. And now here they were.

'I'll tell you what is going to happen next,' she said. 'I will speak to him myself. To Jason Verdoodt. I will find a quiet corner during drinks in the Fellows' Library tonight and I will speak to him this very evening. I will find a moment.'

'Ursula, that's a bad idea. I—'

'Boniface, I am not going to let you drive this company into the ground. If it takes my last breath, I will talk him out of leaving.'

A tiny gleam of hope sparkled in Boniface's eyes. Ursula could often be relied upon to do the impossible.

'Maybe these New York publishers have money but what we have – what *I* have – is a family name known throughout Britain for centuries. A name bestowed by a king and glorified by kings and queens through the ages. A name always on the winning side of history.'

That last was a bit of an exaggeration. Many a Blackenthorpe had taken the wrong side in some skirmish or other in a failed attempt to seize the throne and had had his head handed to him on a chopping block, so to speak. But the thrust of what she said was true. The Blackenthorpe name today had the sort of clout that got one invited to the royal enclosure at Ascot and to royal weddings and to tea at Buckingham Palace. Things that mattered.

She knew the main motivation for most writers was respect. Money, yes, but respect above all was inextricably bound into the needs of these anxious, desperate creatures – a weakness that smart publishers had learned to exploit to ensure their own survival. She had things to offer Jason no other publishing company, particularly no *American* publishing company, could offer. Tea at the palace? As easy as picking up the phone and speaking with one of the palace secretaries. It helped that the royals, particularly the younger ones, saw themselves as patrons of the arts.

'What I have, and what I lend to Castle Publishing, is *class* and *breeding*,' she continued, in the same ringing tones no doubt used by Queen Elizabeth I to rally troops to fight the Spanish Armada. 'And those things can never be bought.'

'But—'

'But me no buts. I shall speak with him tonight and make him see sense. See if I don't. I'll find a private moment.'

Now Boniface was growing alarmed. Ursula in such a state had to be carefully managed. 'What is it you have in mind?'

'Never you mind. I'll handle it.'

'But I—'

'But first,' she swept on, 'I'll have a word with Imogen and David. This is time for the family to unite and move forward as one. Everything is riding on it.'

Boniface, who knew his children as well as his wife (that is to say, hardly at all), could predict as accurately as the next man that a vessel would sink when it was riddled with holes.

He had led his manufacturing company to success. Was it his fault producing books had turned out to be a bit more complicated than manufacturing wallpaper? All these tedious, needy authors with their constant clamouring for attention and their ever-escalating demands for more everything – money, marketing, publicity. It never ended.

But Jason Verdoodt held all the cards in this instance and Boniface was smart enough to know it. His wife might get the family marching in lockstep, but the likelihood was great they would march straight off a cliff together.

Wisely, he kept his own counsel. Once Ursula got up a head of steam like this, it was best to let her run.

He was worried, though. If she didn't get her way with Jason, she might prove dangerous.

FIVE
David and Imogen

As Boniface and Ursula were having this discussion, their children David and Imogen were downstairs in the living room of the family home in North Oxford. The plan was for them all to drive together into the city centre around six thirty, allowing plenty of time for traffic and parking.

Castle Mansion (as their father always called it) was technically their home now – the spacious grounds held two separate guest houses where the siblings had taken up permanent residence. They'd been at boarding school most of the time they were growing up, but they considered the family residence in Notting Hill to be their home, not this absurd, new-built Tuscan villa.

'*So* bourgeois' had been Imogen's verdict on first seeing the interior, all stuccoed walls, plaster ceilings and wooden beams. Recesses held pottery and reproduction busts of Roman emperors, including no one's favourite, Caligula. The floors throughout were of terracotta or marble, the staircase was of black wrought-iron, the artwork reproduction Michelangelo and da Vinci. 'I can't imagine what Mother was thinking to allow it. It's her home, too.'

'She tried to talk him out of it for months while the place was being built, remember? This is his idea of high class. I don't know where he gets half the rubbish he believes.'

'From all those visits to Italy? Those "In the Footsteps of Lord Byron" tours? Maybe he thinks the emperors and popes lived like this, but it's more like something out of a holiday issue of a women's magazine.'

'It's embarrassing really,' David was saying now. '*So* pretentious. I can never invite any of my friends here.'

'He's very common, is Father. We've had so much to overcome.'

They looked at each other in perfect understanding, lamenting the hardships of being born to wealth and privilege, cosseted as far as was possible by two bewildered parents with few nurturing instincts, who in turn wondered where these two could possibly have come from. Their father thought of them privately as the evil twins, although they were two years apart in age.

They were opposites in appearance, David tall and lean to Imogen's short and round – what she thought of as comfortable, womanly proportions. She was not a beauty but no one had ever dared tell her so, because of her social status and her vile temper, and she viewed every flaw through the prism of total self-love: her large, high-arched nose was noble; her sunken black eyes deep wells of intelligence (Jason Verdoodt often commented on her eyes); her rough, untended complexion evidence of the expensive outdoor pursuits in which she excelled, particularly drag hunting, however much she missed the days of riding to hounds.

For the most part she had got through life free of the self-doubt that tormented lesser mortals. Her vanity showed up particularly in her style of dress. Tonight she wore something that might have been based on a peasant costume from South America but was handstitched with semi-precious stones, making it a designer effort costing several thousand pounds. Since most of her costumes were similarly unforgettable, she would wear them once and donate them later to charity. It was anyone's guess what Oxfam did with them.

David, while aware of his shortcomings in the looks department, shared his sister's blind spot when it came to clothing. His textured burgundy tuxedo clashed with the red brocade sofa against which he lounged, cocktail in hand.

His gangly skeleton stretched to six feet, but with his short torso all his height seemed to be in his legs. He marched rather than walked, throwing each foot out in front of him before stomping it to the ground.

David said, 'Weren't you going to this do as Jason's date?'

'I am,' Imogen replied, standing to untangle the ruffles of

her skirt from the underlying petticoat. She turned, looking down over her shoulder to make sure the petal effect was complete.

'So why isn't he picking you up?'

She doubled her fussing about with her dress, her eyes not meeting his, which told David the question was both dreaded and unwelcome.

'He had an urgent piece of business at the college and couldn't break away in time,' she said at last. 'So I'm meeting him there.'

'Urgent, hmm. I never knew an archaeologist have anything much to do with urgent business. After all, most of what they uncover has already waited for centuries.'

'Anthropology *and* archaeology are his subjects,' she explained with exaggerated patience. 'Anthropology being the study of humankind, which is full of nothing but last-minute crises, wouldn't you say? However, I gather this had to do with a student needing his help at the last minute. He is devoted to his students, and they in turn adore him. Rather than inconvenience me he gave me plenty of notice he might be late and urged me to drive in with the family.'

If rumours were true, thought David, the student in crisis would undoubtedly be young and female, for Jason's reputation was that of the swashbuckler mothers warned their daughters against dating. This young female was most often blonde and svelte, although Jason didn't really seem to have a preference. If anything, variety was his watchword.

David had little doubt that his sister – middle-aged before her time, hirsute, plump and ungainly – was not merely Jason's latest attempt at variety. Meaning, he had a purpose in dancing attendance on her, the purpose having everything to do with getting maximum attention for his book. Watching her peck at the ruffles adorning her décolletage, it occurred to David that if Jason decided to move on to another, bigger publisher, there was nothing to make him cling to Imogen a single moment longer than was necessary. He, David, did not want to be around to pick up the pieces when that happened. It was clear that his sister was as besotted as a teenager in the first throes of love.

He wondered if – as a loving brother – he should warn her, but of course that would be futile lunacy. Anyone who came between her and her newest true love (oh yes, they'd been down this road before) was putting their lives on the line. Imogen and her infatuations were countless and, without exception, doomed. She did however have a remarkable ability to move on to her next target with very little looking back, her invincible confidence a sort of bulletproof shield against ridicule or humiliation.

So far, anyway. Jason was in anyone's estimation a catch, though, and she might not be able to wash him from her mind quite as easily as she had done all the others. Furthermore, a great deal of his success could be attributed to Imogen's constant work on his behalf: air-brushing his image, artfully doling out intriguing if imaginary titbits about his past, arranging his interviews and appearances, making sure he connected with the right media people. Whatever her faults, his sister was a master manipulator and saleswoman who could take a ho-hum book and send it soaring up the bestseller charts. She had been accused of bribing reviewers – probably not true, although David wouldn't put it past her to try.

To give Jason his due, he had come up with a real page-turner, making her job easy for once. If she was going to have trouble letting him go, certainly Castle Publishing in the form of his parents was going to have the same problem, possibly even more so.

Again, David thought overall it would be best if he stayed out of the line of fire as much as possible this time.

He did dare venture a question about the possibility of Jason's leaving the firm. After all, romance aside, it was vital to the firm's finances that Jason should stay on board and sign his new contract. This was no time for niceties and Imogen might know something he didn't.

'Has Jason said anything to you about any new offers from any other publishers?' he asked tentatively. 'Not that he'd think of leaving after all you've done for him, but—'

'He's hinted at it,' she said darkly. Her small eyes narrowed into dangerous slits. 'I'm going to do everything in my power to stop that kind of thinking.' This was said with a toss of her hair over her shoulder, a sultry move that suggested she believed seduction was the answer here. David's heart sank, but he forged ahead.

'And how do you propose to do that?'

'Well, Mother has this theory that what writers want is respect. We simply must up the respect quota.' Did a shadow cross her eyes? It was hard to tell with Imogen. Clearly she was thinking, planning. This was Imogen in a dangerous state.

At times she reminded him of their mother.

'If writers wanted respect, they'd have become doctors,' said David.

'"No man but a blockhead ever wrote except for money",' she quoted.

'I don't see how we can pay him a penny more than we have.'

'I think he's after a higher royalty rate. Something around thirty per cent – for the hardbacks. More for the eBooks. He keeps wanting to tweak the terms and this latest demand . . . He seems to think contracts are made to be altered.'

David, his drink half raised to his lips, settled his glass against his thigh, his hand trembling. 'He's mad,' said David. Fearing she might take that as a criticism of the object of her affections, he amended hastily, 'That's madness. There's no way we can afford anything like that and stay in business. He must realize that.'

'I'll talk with him,' she said, that same dangerous confidence ringing in her voice. This was not a woman used to hearing the word 'no' and, when she did hear it, she always misheard it as 'yes'.

Sometimes David wondered if his sister was quite sane.

SIX
DCI St. Just

D etective Chief Inspector St. Just of the Cambridgeshire Constabulary was also an invited guest at Jason Verdoodt's party, pressed into service as a plus-one for his fiancée Portia De'Ath, crime fiction writer and Cambridge don, for the weekend.

As the pair entered the elegant lobby of the Randolph Hotel, Portia was saying, 'Many of the actors and crew from the *Inspector Morse* films and spinoffs stay here. Once I was in Oxford for a conference and after dinner in the hotel, my colleagues and I saw two of the show's leading stars having a drink in the hotel bar. We were thrilled to bits but no one had the nerve to approach them.'

Portia never seemed to grasp that an interruption by a stunningly attractive woman was always welcome, thought St. Just. Perhaps particularly so among actors.

They joined the queue to sign in at the front desk.

She added, 'Colin Dexter was a regular and worked on some of his books at the bar. That's why it's now called the Morse Bar.'

'How nice,' said St. Just. 'And how apt. He brought the world hours of entertainment. You know, one day they'll brag that you stayed here and worked on one of your novels. They'll probably put a plaque outside the room to commemorate your stay.'

'Don't be silly,' she said, but he could tell she was pleased by the idea. 'I may, however, just have time to scribble a few lines this weekend. To make true any claims of "working on a novel" while I was here. Just in case.'

'Just don't disappear.'

'What?'

'I was thinking of Agatha Christie. They have a plaque

outside the room of the Harrogate hotel where she stayed during her famous disappearance.'

'Oh. No, I won't go anywhere, promise. I also need to go over my notes for the influx of new postgraduates at the Institute.'

'Speaking of time . . .' he began, glancing at his watch. 'What's the schedule for this evening?'

'Drinks at seven, dinner at eight. The drinks party will be in St Rumwold's College library and dinner will be in the college hall.'

'And all in honour of Jason Verdoodt.'

'That's right. He teaches at St Rumwold's. He was an undergraduate at Cambridge, though.' She added with a smile, 'Which university now claims to have taught him all he knows.'

The queue inched forward and at last they were given a key to their room. They and their luggage were whisked upstairs by a hotel porter. As they were unpacking in the opulent room, sorting out their clothes for the evening, St. Just asked, 'Have you ever met him? Jason?'

'Strangely enough, I have not. The mystery-slash-crime-slash-thriller arena is small and one does tend to run into the same people over the years. But Jason Verdoodt is quite a new author and frankly, given his fame, he's free to ignore the conference circuit if he chooses. He's barely had time to pause for breath with the success of his first novel. He's received the kind of critical attention debut authors can only dream of.'

'And tell me again why we're here?' St. Just knew the party was to be hosted by Castle Publishing, and that Castle was a rival to Portia's own publisher. During his time with Portia, he'd learned a great deal about the publishing business at second hand. And he had come to feel that as an industry it rivalled the Borgia franchise for bloody coups and hostile takeovers.

So while he wasn't surprised the owner of Castle Publishing might be trying to poach Portia from her current publisher, to the extent he was picking up the tab for their weekend stay at the famous Randolph Hotel, St. Just was a bit surprised she would entertain the thought of leaving her current publisher, where she was happy with her editor and well-compensated for her work.

'It's a bribe, I'm well aware,' she said. 'Sir Boniface has been reaching out to me and my agent for some time, wanting me to write a new crime series for his house.'

'What made you decide to consider accepting the bribe? Are things with your publishers suddenly going downhill?'

'No! Not at all. It's just that the event is also a fundraiser in aid of my favourite literacy foundation, which made it difficult to say no. But to soothe my conscience, I will hand Sir Boniface a large cheque for the foundation at the end of the evening. He persuaded me that by lending my name to the cause, he could attract potential donors with deep pockets to the event. Lord and Lady Yale-Lequatte will be there, as well as Tricia Magnum. Of course, Tricia shows up for every barn-raising so that's not much of a coup.'

St. Just had caught on the more familiar name. 'Lord and Lady Yale-Lequatte? There was some scandal or other, wasn't there?'

Portia placed a slender hand against her chin in thought. 'Yes. Financial, I think. Or was it that she ran off with the chauffeur and he with the nanny? It's always one or the other thing. Love or money. I don't suppose there's a polite way to ask them.'

'I have always found people most eager to share their side of the story in any scandal.'

'You would, wouldn't you, in your line of work? The trouble is knowing whether they're telling you the truth.'

'Precisely. And what do we know about Tricia Magnum? Help me tie this thing, will you?'

Portia expertly knotted the tie at his neck as she said, 'You must know her. The children's author?'

'Yes, even I have heard of Tricia Magnum,' said St. Just. 'Beyond that, I mean. Family? Foes? Any gossip there? She's a Dame now, I believe. Her name appeared on the last honours list?'

'Yes, and it was long overdue, in my opinion and probably hers as well. I wonder what we're meant to call her now.'

'Dame Tricia, presumably, although Dame Patricia might be her formal title.'

'I don't even know if she's married, but my sense of her is that she's single. She may have a child; I'll try to ask.'

'It seems fitting that the woman who for so many years soothed a nation of children to sleep should be made a Dame. Perhaps they gave her a medal for courage in the face of adversity. She wrote fifteen books before she struck gold with the one book.'

'I remember every word of *Moon Over Wiltshire*. My mother would read it to me, or my father sometimes.' She paused at the memory. 'I learned to read by memorizing what the words looked like on the page.'

Portia smiled as she turned away from the mirror where she had been tucking a stray hair into place. If only she knew how that smile stopped his heart every time. That such a woman as Portia had consented to marry him both amazed and frightened him, knowing he had somehow to live up to the honour.

'Let's go or we'll be late,' she said. 'I don't mind admitting I'm anxious to meet the rising star author whose name has dominated book news for months.'

'Surely he's not that good?'

'Surely he is. As an author. Perhaps not so much in his personal life – rumours are rife he gets up everyone's nose. Anyway, you must read *The White Owl*. I'll lend you my copy. It's a remarkable story. Not just the book, but how he and his book got "discovered".'

'A real Cinderfella story, was it? Rags to riches?'

'Yes. More or less. But we need to be moving along. I'll tell you all about it later.'

SEVEN

Tess

B ehind the three-storey front of St Rumwold's College with its golden stone entrance tower, a scout was racing to finish her chores even more quickly than usual.

She really would have to hurry now to have time to change for the evening. She was doing double duty for the book celebration party at seven and it was already six. She had two sets of rooms yet to clean and Jason Verdoodt occupied one, no doubt getting ready for his party.

She could just barge in and ignore him but why tempt fate? He was unpleasant to deal with at the best of times, clearly aiming to get rid of her.

Let him try. What difference would it make? She'd be on her way under her own steam soon enough.

A nap between shifts would have been nice, she thought, but a jolt of coffee would have to do. She'd treat herself to something sugary, too. And why not?

She thought she was starting to look like a fire hydrant from too much pastry and too many packets of crisps, was why not. Her diet, combined with the physical nature of her work, had made her muscular beneath a layer of fat, like an aging dock worker. If being a waitress was hard, looking after the cream of the nation's brightest was harder. She seldom did more with her thick hair than tie it back with a scrunchie hidden beneath a flower-patterned kerchief. Over her daytime clothes, usually jeans and a T-shirt, she wore a bib apron with deep pockets to hold the brushes and dusting cloths the college issued to cleaning staff.

But her smooth complexion, her best asset, remained unblemished despite layers of makeup. One day soon she'd set to work on getting her figure back; it was a matter of a gym membership and a high-protein diet but right now she couldn't set aside time or money for either. She was still in her six-month probationary period and was a hard worker, despite what Jason Verdoodt might claim. Being such an exemplary employee was why she was allowed to do for some of the professors – plum jobs beyond the very menial work, like cleaning the common rooms. The undergraduates must have been raised in barns, she thought, and she was lucky to have escaped having to clean up after them.

She thought now she'd just throw a quick mop around the rooms of Professor Ambrose, who lived across the hall from Jason in Staircase B. She wouldn't have time today for hoovering. Ambrose had his faults but underneath it all he was a poppet and always seemed to recognize her lot was not an easy one. But he also refrained from any Professor Higgins-like tendencies and had left off having a go at trying to improve her cockney accent. He merely said, one day when he was clearly in his cups, that even though a college education wasn't for everyone he felt she could do better and offered to write her a letter of recommendation if she should choose to apply to the Open University.

His 'in his cups' moments were increasing in number, to judge by the number of empty bottles in his rubbish bin.

'Who does he think he's kidding?' she thought, as she removed the bottles and replaced the bin liner. The college would probably step in soon if he couldn't get his drinking under control, but she would never turn him in.

Ambrose was a wine snob, which in her experience meant an alcoholic attempting to hide his habit behind business lunches and afternoon tutorials that lasted into the night – tutes which she imagined amounted to arguments over how many angels could dance on the head of a pin (Professor Ambrose taught religion – for his sins, he liked to joke). She knew his corkage fees at local restaurants were lofty, also, as he left restaurant bills out on his desk for anyone to see. She'd learned about corkage fees during her brief employment at one of Oxford's fine-dining establishments, which she'd left when a place for a scout opened up at St Rumwold's. There was prestige in being attached to one of the colleges, even though the pay was rubbish, and nothing like as good as she'd made as a waitress.

She generally did Jason's rooms after Ambrose's, and she was always anxious to get into the lair of the famous author on the occasions she knew he was gone. This meant sometimes the rest of Jason's colleagues got short shrift (she was responsible for cleaning the rooms of five other tutors and thank God they were mostly neat and tidy).

Professor Ambrose returned to his rooms as she was dusting the bookshelves, thinking what an awful lot of rot was published about 'the nature of God'. To her mind, theology was very simple. God helped those who helped themselves. End of.

Also, she was more than willing to believe God might more properly be called Goddess.

'Oh,' said Ambrose, surprised to see her. 'I thought you'd be gone by now.'

'Just finishing up,' she said.

'You have His Majesty's rooms still to do, do you not?'

She thought one of Professor Ambrose's more endearing traits was a wicked sense of humour despite his theological grounding. Or perhaps because of it. He had made it clear on more than one occasion that he did not care for Jason Verdoodt.

'I have read some of his work and I have found it to be rather unsound,' he would say. 'Like the man himself. Never trust an academic getting by on his looks alone. Also, he's from the Other Place.'

She always looked at him, hoping for further enlightenment on this score, which did not come. Professor Ambrose also had veered very close on occasion to accusing Jason of fudging the data from his lab results, but he had never crossed that line. To someone like Ambrose, that sort of carry-on should be punishable by life in prison, or worse. She did know that the Other Place was Cambridge and that every academic in Oxford avoided saying the word aloud.

Ambrose was apparently feeling rather talkative today, and she could guess the reason: the big do for Jason was a thorn in the man's side, especially since he had not been invited.

'I suppose he'll return late from this party of his,' he said. 'And not alone, if history is any guide.'

'Oh?' she said. It was enough to open the floodgates.

'It has not been easy having someone like that on the same staircase. Music at all hours – if you can call it music. Noisy friendships with persons of the female persuasion even though that sort of thing is *strictly* prohibited in the rules of conduct for instructors at St Rumwold's College. If he wants to carry on like that he needs to move out of the college and spend some of his ill-gotten gains on buying a new house, preferably one in the woods miles away from quiet, law-abiding people.'

Stashing her duster inside an apron pocket, she said, taking pity, 'I believe you may get your wish very soon. He's been looking at property to buy for some time now.'

'Oh, but how wonderful,' Professor Ambrose exclaimed. 'I suppose you've seen brochures and suchlike in his rooms.'

She was torn about admitting the truth of this. She wasn't meant to snoop and she didn't like Ambrose thinking she did.

'I don't mean to snoop,' she said. 'In fact, it is like a badge of honour with me. I never snoop.'

'Of course, you don't, my dear,' he said. 'What else have you seen? I mean, can you tell me. *Where* is he looking for a house? What sort of house?'

This struck her as more than idle curiosity. The poor man was clearly eaten up with jealousy of his more successful colleague. She imagined attracting students to a dying art like theology might put the professor's job on the line, sooner rather than later. Even though he looked to be older than God, he was probably only in his seventies. There was nowhere for him to go but downhill if they kicked him out. He'd have some sort of pension, yes, but nothing to do with his time but drink even more. She'd watched her own father go to pieces that way.

'It's small, and it looks like it needs a lot of work. *Loads* of work. These old houses, you know. And it's not a good neighbourhood either. I think he'll have problems. Robbers and suchlike.'

Professor Ambrose did not trouble to conceal his smile at the thought.

Within half an hour, she was bustling over to the Fellows' Library in Second Quad, where this knees-up was being held.

She had to duck at the low entrance to the library, sparing a moment as she did to glance at the carving over the door of a tiny stag reading a book. You could never say those medieval stonemasons didn't have a sense of humour. She'd seen a documentary on the telly about how a stonemason got his revenge when the people who had hired him didn't pay him for his work – something about a mooning gargoyle.

The stairs behind the library door were steep and would have been hell on her arches, but the butler had had the good idea of using the book lift as a dumb waiter, sparing everyone the heavy lifting. This was particularly important when it came to the boxes of wine, of course.

She knew the librarian had petitioned with all his might against the party being held in 'his' library, citing the inconvenient stairs as one excuse, along with a sudden concern for staff safety, but the use of the book lift to solve that problem had left him with no more arrows in his quiver. He had retired from the field bloody, but unbowed. If she knew the librarian, he'd find a way to spoil the event, if only by hanging about with a sour look on his face, chasing after everyone with napkins and wiping away imaginary stains on the furniture, and generally getting in everyone's way. At least, it would keep him busy while the real work got done.

She was excited to have wangled her way into helping out this evening. She had no literary pretensions – she knew her strengths as well as her weaknesses – but if people-watching was a sport, she was an expert, and this gathering of the great and good was more than she could've hoped for. The ladies in their finest, the men – most of them not cut out for such occasions – trying to disappear into the stacks. The fireworks promised should Jason Verdoodt's girlfriends collide like comets in the sky. For yes, she had got wind of that. If these people would leave private letters and such about, how was it her fault she perhaps knew too much of their private lives? There was a woman in London who seemed positively unhinged. If she turned up – boom!

Overall, she thought, it would be a night to remember.

EIGHT
Where Is Jason?

'Where is he?' Sir Boniface had buttonholed the St Rumwold's College butler, practically dragging him by his lapels into a corner of the Fellows' Library for a private word. That server was all ears.

'I was asked to organize the food and wine, sir,' replied Dimitri Smirnoff, taking a step back as he delicately shook off the man's hands. Smirnoff was a tall man, as tall as Sir Boniface, and the fact they could literally see eye-to-eye was unfortunate – it leant an aggressive note to an already fraught situation. In all other ways they were worlds apart, in temperament and background.

Smirnoff was not enjoying this evening with its added frisson of fear and anxiety. If a single drop of madeira got spilt on any of the college's library holdings, there would be hell to pay. Sir Bartholomew Tremaine seemed to regard the library as his own private property and resented the use of the facilities 'by illiterate barbarians', as he put it.

Smirnoff continued, 'I was not asked to be responsible for the whereabouts of the guest of honour. Sir.'

'Well, you're responsible for him now. Go and have a look in his rooms, will you? Ask the porter if he's been in or out this evening. Don't just stand there, man – do something.'

A resentful Smirnoff was glad to comply if it got him out of the line of fire but, in fact, he would be held to task by many people if this were not resolved. Silently he cursed Jason Verdoodt as the pain in the arse he'd been since taking up his position at the college. Smirnoff could always tell the upstarts from the true nobs; Verdoodt had the tendency to overcompensate, which was common to people who simply didn't belong in the rarefied atmosphere of an Oxford college. He was not an Eton man, for one thing (Smirnoff had looked him up).

One way Verdoodt tried to overcompensate was by being churlish to the college staff, bossing them about and complaining all the time. Big mistake, that. Verdoodt positively loathed his scout Tess and had demanded she be moved elsewhere or fired, a demand Smirnoff and the head housekeeper had thus far managed to ignore. Tess was a hard worker. Smirnoff had instead taken every opportunity to set the man straight.

But it was a work in progress. Showing up late for a celebration in his honour was not upper-class behaviour as he may have thought, but a dead giveaway to his common roots. Verdoodt was not Lord Sebastian Ruddy Flyte, no matter his pretentions.

Smirnoff could feel the eyes of Professor Davies, the master of the college, on him from across the room, a rather pleading look in her eyes: *where is Jason Verdoodt?* It was Smirnoff's job to make sure these affairs ran smoothly, although why he was supposed to oversee the whereabouts of that Don Juan of a jumped-up tutor, he didn't know. If rumours were anything to go by, Verdoodt could be anywhere, in any bed in Oxford, and the head butler would much rather not have that conversation, particularly with a female master of the college.

'Yes, sir,' he said to Boniface. 'I'll see what I can do. Sir.'

The 'sir' was once again tacked on a moment too late. Sir Boniface gave Smirnoff the stony glare of a housewife who had paid good money at the fishmonger's for fresh trout and been given yesterday's mackerel instead. Guests had been gathering for some time – it was close to eight p.m. now – and the string quartet of music students on loan for the night was screeching away in one corner, getting on his last nerve. It wasn't like Verdoodt to be late. Or was it? How well, after all, did he know his famous author? He wrote like a dream, yes, but that didn't mean he was punctual. Most authors were a bit unreliable, in Sir Boniface's experience, their heads in the clouds. Why had he thought Verdoodt would be an exception?

Oh, God. This was a nightmare. All Boniface's snobbery, latent and active, was stirred. For all these literary dignitaries to be stood up . . . after talking the master into this spectacle . . . unthinkable.

'See to it, man. We'll have to start moving them along to the dining hall soon, with or without him.'

Having sent the butler on what he suspected was a fruitless errand, Boniface turned his attention to his guests, realizing his role as gracious host might have to be expanded. He felt like a stage actor who'd suddenly forgotten his lines, and he took a rather long sip of his madeira, desperately wishing for a whisky instead. He supposed that so long as they all had lots to drink, the missing guest of honour might not be missed for a while, but he knew it would be noticed immediately by at least one attendee.

He surveyed the small, crowded room, quickly finding his daughter in that ridiculous get-up of hers. Imogen was dressing too young for her age – short skirts, sequins, little hats perched at crazy angles on her head – and the reason wasn't difficult to guess. The arrival of Jason Verdoodt in her life had caused a stunning transformation in a daughter he had long since relegated to the sidelines as of little use in his plans to found a dynasty. She was useful in her marketing position, of course – useful to the company. But that was different. He had reached a time in his life where he thought more of grandchildren, of establishing a vast empire that would command the respect of historians, of someone to pass the torch to. It bothered him greatly that a lifetime of work and planning and sacrifice might end with his own demise. He had little faith in his son David's business acumen and even less belief that grandchildren would come from that source.

David happened to be talking with his sister now, although from the way her eyes turned constantly to the room's entrance, she was barely paying attention. Boniface sighed.

It was not that he lacked understanding. He had known hopeless love in his day, back before he was Sir Boniface, back before anyone thought he'd amount to anything – before Gracie Spratt from his grammar school had thought he'd amount to anything.

If there was anything sadder than unrequited love, he didn't know what it was, but his experience from those days as an awkward, knobbly-kneed boy had taught him a valuable lesson

– or rather, Gracie's laughter at his back had taught him a valuable lesson.

He'd begun holding something of himself in reserve, realizing that for someone from his blue-collar background, making an advantageous match was the best way out of obscurity. This he had gone on to do. His wife was no beauty, but she *was* pedigreed. So what if so many of the Blackenthorpes carried more than a drop of madness in their veins, living out their lives in genteel asylums for the nobility? All that inbreeding.

But Imogen and David were mostly all right in that department, thanks to his infusion of Castle blood. Weren't they?

He had seen photos of his schoolyard nemesis, Gracie Spratt, not long ago. When he was knighted, he had hired a private investigator to learn the basic facts of her life. He'd been gratified to learn she had married a local factory lad who drank too much, that they lived in a terraced house in a dodgy part of town and had produced four unremarkable children. It had been utterly pleasing to learn this. The PI had provided photos, which were the icing on the cake. Gracie had very much let herself go. He'd never noticed before how thick her ankles were.

With that, the last of the romantic notions he had acquired from novels had left him. But he knew infatuation when he saw it, and in middle age his daughter was on a collision course with folly, or worse. He didn't see a way to stop her.

He supposed a word in her ear months ago might not have gone amiss – but no. When did any fool falling in love listen to reason?

He looked around, eyes still scanning the crowd, as if Jason might magically appear. Imogen wasn't the only woman dressed inappropriately for the occasion. The children's book author over there in the corner, Tricia Magnum, pretending an interest in the book titles – it was as if she frequented the same dress shop as his daughter. For someone writing in her genre, one might forgive a certain lack of coordination when it came to colour and design, but she seemed to feel that children expected her to dress like a clown. Even now that she was Dame Patricia, little had changed, although he supposed her dresses were more Gucci than Marks and Spencer. He hoped rumours of her involvement with Jason were just gossip. Imogen wouldn't like her being here if she knew. He caught his breath as Imogen moved away from her brother, heading in Tricia's direction. *Please*, he prayed to the literary gods, who as usual would not respond. *Please* let her not make a scene.

And who is that woman over by the drinks table, the one in the red dress? He didn't recognize her as one of his authors or in any way connected with the Castle Publishing boiler room. His wife had drawn up the guest list – Ursula knew instinctively who should be invited. Maybe red satin had become the style but it made the woman look cheap. That and all the makeup. And those *shoes* that made her tower over everyone.

The writer Portia De'Ath he recognized, of course, and wondered again what it would take to get her to jump ship from her current publisher to join Castle Publishing. The woman could write crime, yes – and, given her position at Cambridge, knew its details better than most. But more than that, she had a presence that would translate well to television online interviews, and that was where the traction was to be gained these days in getting books into readers' hands. That must be her fiancé – what was his name, now? St. Justinian? Something like that. According to her bio and various online interviews (of course, he'd looked her up), he was a policeman. Big fellow, dark-haired and lantern-jawed. The sort who'd look good on a police recruitment poster. What a handsome couple they made. He must speak with her later, while he had the chance. But for now, finding Jason was the priority. Where had the butler got to?

A distinguished-looking man stood talking with the college master. He supposed calling Alice Davies 'mistress' would have been out of the question, but the whole 'master' business certainly was confusing. It was enough that centuries of misogyny had been overcome in welcoming the influx of female heads of colleges to Oxford. She was Professor Alice Davies, expert in artificial intelligence, former MI5 agent, and urbane head of St Rumwold's College, speaking with a man he recognized as Professor Mortford de Witt, college doctor and professor of medicine. He was often called in by Thames Valley Police to advise on local cases of murder, and Boniface had approached him not long ago about writing a book on his more famous cases. The man had demurred, but Boniface was never put off by initial refusals. That was not how races were won.

He watched these two illustrious guests, studying their relaxed body language, momentarily diverted from the vexing question of Jason's absence. The doctor was debonair in his bespoke dinner jacket, and the master above reproach in her unremarkable but expensively cut dress that fell in an A-line to midcalf. They both looked tanned and healthy, as if – despite being academics – they also enjoyed outdoor pursuits. Boniface knew he should go and make small talk with them but hesitated, recalling that the master was an expert on a topic on which he himself drew a blank. What, when it was at home, was AI anyway?

With relief his eye fell on Lord and Lady Yale-Lequatte, with whom he had more in common. It was important to keep in their good graces. They'd been thrilled to be invited, realizing close-in access to the famous Jason Verdoodt was getting rarer by the moment. Authors were receiving death threats every day, after all, not that that had slowed Jason so far.

He'd go and have a word with them now.

Just then there was an unholy commotion. The sound filled the room all at once, almost like an explosion, seeming to emerge from the staircase leading to the ground floor of the library. It was an unholy, keening sound, as if some ghost from the college's past had been resuscitated, returning to claim his diploma or avenge being sent down for gambling.

The keening stopped suddenly, to be taken over by the sound of glass breaking as several guests dropped their madeira to the stone floor. This was followed by the thunder of someone running up the steps.

The muffled thud of someone stumbling could also be heard, along with a loud curse – those winding steps had been worn smooth by a million footfalls over the centuries and were never designed for running. The butler appeared finally in the doorway at the top of the steps and announced, after a dramatic pause to catch his breath, 'He's dead.'

There was an audible gasp from his audience. Heads turned almost in unison, people looking, as people in a panic will do, for someone else to take charge of a confused situation. Out of the corner of his eye, Boniface saw Portia De'Ath's large policeman stride across the room, pushing past anyone in his way.

'Who is dead?' he demanded of the butler.

The butler, noticing all eyes were on him, seemed to collect himself, his training in discretion at last coming to the fore.

'Verdoodt,' came the whispered reply. 'It's Jason Verdoodt.'

NINE
Dumb Waiter

S t. Just turned away from the lifeless form sprawled head-first at the bottom of the stairs. Looking up those stairs, DCI St. Just could see a crowd gathering like a herd of sheep.

'Stay back,' he commanded. 'Get the doctor down here. Get de Witt.'

They stayed frozen in place for a long moment, but slowly they began to move as de Witt pushed through them, parting their bodies like the Dead Sea. He trotted quickly down the staircase, careful to touch nothing on his way. His usual remit was dealing with students and their educators with viruses and stomach aches, but he was not a stranger to dealing with sudden death.

'He's dead,' St. Just told him. 'For some time, I'd say. But you tell me.'

He rose and stood back to allow the doctor to kneel in his place. A quick check of the pulse, which St. Just had already performed. A look into the clearly dead eyes, staring out from beneath well-groomed eyebrows. De Witt shook his head and rose, massaging his hands in what St. Just took to be a nervous habit.

'About an hour, I'd say. Of course, we won't know until—'

'Until you get him on the table,' St. Just finished for him. It was a code of honour among doctors at a crime scene never to hazard guesses on the spot. It was the sort of wire trip that prosecutors looked for in court if examiners later had to contradict their first impressions.

'Any guesses as to cause of death?'

'Stairs,' he said briefly.

'I gathered as much. Anything else?'

'I think you should look at the staircase for scuff marks on the stone matching the polished leather shoes of the victim. See here – and here.' He pointed at abrasions on the otherwise immaculate shoes. 'I think you'll find scrapes made on the stone as he tumbled down the stairs.'

'A likely accident?'

'If he were older and less fit, an argument could be made for that,' said the doctor.

'From your tone of voice, it sounds doubtful,' said St. Just.

'I never said so.'

'I won't try to claim you did, don't worry.'

'But if he were drunk, perhaps,' said the doctor thoughtfully. 'The tox scan will reveal that if so, but I don't detect the overwhelming odour of alcohol.'

'Nor do I.' St. Just leaned in towards the face of the corpse and sniffed. 'A slight trace, merely. Of course, he never made it to the drinks party. Any alcohol in his system would've been consumed ahead of time, probably in his rooms as he was dressing. I suppose it's possible he wanted to get the party started early – it must have been a big night for him – but, overall, I'm thinking, no . . . He'd want his wits about him.'

'If you'll forgive me for saying so, St. Just, I don't believe you have any jurisdiction here. While your reputation generally heralds your arrival – oh, yes, I know who you are – we need to get the locals in on this or there will be wounded feelings. The politics of the thing, especially if we're dealing with a crime committed in one of the colleges . . . well. It doesn't bear thinking about. And the media! My God, the media will lose its collective mind.'

'I agree. I'm sure the Thames Valley Police will be more comfortable dealing with you than me, jurisdiction or no. Do you want to make the call? They'll probably send Ampleforth.'

The doctor looked surprised. 'You know him?'

'Yes. Sound man. Loads of experience.' *If given to jumping to conclusions.*

De Witt called it in to Thames Valley Police, giving a clipped summary of the circumstances and location. While they waited for the response team, the two men looked around them at what was already to St. Just's mind a crime scene. For one thing, it looked to him as if the body had been moved.

He echoed this thought aloud.

'Where is the blood? Not on the stairs or along the wall of the stairs, not that I can see. You're the expert, but wouldn't you say if this was an accidental tumble down the stairs, or if someone pushed him and he suffered a fatal head injury, he'd have left traces as he fell? There is some blood around his head but not as much as one would expect, especially since he's basically upside down on the stairs and the blood should've drained.' He turned and looked round him. 'Let's have a look inside that dumb waiter.'

'The book lift?'

'Yes. I want to see if it's large enough to have held a body. And there will be blood in there if I'm right.'

He was right. On opening the thick wooden door to the book lift, so dark with age it must have been original to the building, they could see the space inside was large enough to contain a man of Verdoodt's stature if his body were folded over.

'There's the blood,' said St. Just, pointing to one side of the interior. 'He'd been hidden there for a while, by the look of it. By the time he was removed from the hiding space, the blood flow had essentially stopped. It's funny there are no traces of it on the floor here. Someone must have wrapped his head in a cloth to make sure he didn't leave a trail as he was dragged.'

'Either that, or they carried him.'

'It's possible. It's just possible if they took care not to get blood on themselves in the process.'

'Why would they care about that?'

'They would care if they were re-joining the party and wouldn't have time to change into clean clothing or to wash up.'

The doctor looked again at the staring eyes of the victim. 'The corneas aren't cloudy,' he said. 'He's been dead less than two hours. Don't quote me. But there's something odd about his eyes . . .'

'I see it, too. You think perhaps he was drugged? Poisoned?'

'Funny you should mention it. Of course, everything is poison taken to excess, especially if mixed with alcohol. Again, the tox scan will confirm, but the pupils of his eyes shouldn't look like that, even or especially on a dead man.'

In fact, Verdoodt's eyes looked as bright and shiny as they must have done in life. His expression almost carried the hint of a smile, too, adding to the unsettling sense that he might at any moment jump up, laughing at the practical joke he'd played on everyone.

He'd been a handsome man, thought St. Just. It was sad to see him all dressed up for death in his well-tailored finery – however did a humble tutor afford that? The book profits, of course, came the answer. Here he'd been looking forward to an evening of fine speeches and toasts and praise for his work. In the midst of life—

St. Just's own eyes were caught by an object in one corner of the small stone area. A book, by the look of it. Only to be expected in a library.

A hardcover book, still in its glossy cover, its pages splayed out as if it had been carelessly flung there. St. Just went over and, using his mobile phone's torch, took a closer look. He was careful not to touch, especially once he saw the blood.

'I think we've found the murder weapon,' he said over his shoulder to de Witt.

'What is it?'

'It's Jason Verdoodt's bestselling book. The hardback version.' St. Just rose and turning to the doctor said, 'One corner of it is soaked in blood.'

TEN
DCI Ampleforth

Detective Chief Inspector Ampleforth looked the sort of man who might one day require a Boswell to document his exploits. In his mid-fifties, with a rounded belly and thick stalks of greying hair sprouting back from a large forehead, he managed to look irascible and ill-tempered even when he was smiling, which he seldom was. But at the sight of St. Just, whom he evidently regarded as a long-lost friend, Ampleforth made an exception, pulling his lips back into a fearsome grimace that would intimidate anyone not familiar with his displays of joy.

The men knew each other from attending police conferences and conducting training courses over the years. Most recently they had spent many hours in a pub outside the police academy in Warwickshire, preparing a joint presentation on interviewing witnesses and victims for trainees at the College of Policing.

'What's all this then?' he asked St. Just. 'I was just sitting down to dinner, telling the wife what a quiet week we've been having at the office.'

'That's an invitation to disaster,' said St. Just, shaking Ampleforth's hand.

'Is this what it looks like?' Ampleforth demanded, taking in the body's position as well as the long staircase leading up from it. 'An accident? I suppose not or de Witt wouldn't have called me in. Would you, sir?' He turned his massive head to take in the college doctor and expert on the art of death, who just then was teetering on his haunches four feet away from the body, taking in the angle and distance from the hardback book. Spying the offending object in the corner, Ampleforth said, 'Please, for the sake of all that is holy, do not tell me that is the murder weapon.'

'It would appear that it is,' said de Witt. 'Of course, I can't say with any certainty until—'

'Until you get him on the table,' finished Ampleforth. 'I assume everyone's been told not to leave until the police take down their names and vitals?'

De Witt nodded. 'I sort of deputized the butler to keep them upstairs,' he said. 'He's used to being in charge.'

Just then a woman constable appeared at the open door.

'Upstairs,' Ampleforth commanded her curtly. 'Keep them quiet and keep them together.'

Spinning around – Ampleforth was surprisingly light on his feet, rather like a spinning top, thought St. Just – he said, 'And what do you know about all this, St. Just? I heard your intended was in town, but I didn't know you were with her.'

'How did you hear about Portia?'

'It was in the local paper, of course. This shindig or whatever we must call it. It was in the society news, or what passes for society news in Oxford. It's mostly frightfully boring stuff about Oxford dons getting awards for doing things no one understands. But your good lady is a celebrity in her own right, if you didn't know it. Boldface names and all that – she's one of them now. Everyone loves a good mystery, including my wife, who was all over this news story. I try to tell her crime novels have nothing to do with real-life investigations, which are a long slog in the best of cases, but she doesn't want to hear it. She thinks everyone in a stately home is ripe for slaughter and there's nothing I can say to change her mind.'

St. Just, thinking he was lucky Portia had so few illusions, said in answer to Ampleforth's earlier question, 'As to what I know, very little I'm afraid. I didn't know the victim.'

'Who is . . .'

'Oh, of course, I'm sorry. You don't know even that much yet. The victim is Jason Verdoodt, tonight's guest of honour.'

'I knew him, as it happens,' said de Witt, standing to join them. 'He was a lecturer here, and as he had rooms in the college he was one of my patients. For the common everyday stuff, you know. Like a cold or the flu. Otherwise, he saw his own doctor for routine maintenance. He was generally in perfect health so he didn't need me.'

'Right. I'll let the doctor fill you in on time and manner of death when he knows more, but it's looking as if Jason was killed shortly before the party started and was deposited, if I may use the term, in this sort of dumb waiter that you see here.' St. Just gestured to the book lift, the door of which was now standing open. 'We found blood in there telling us the space was used as temporary storage until he could be displayed at the foot of the stairs in a manner indicating a fatal tumble down.'

'Suspects?' Ampleforth asked.

'Potentially as many as stars in the sky,' replied St. Just. 'At least as many as were invited to this celebratory party by Sir Boniface Castle, owner of Castle Publishing. And I estimate that number to be about fifty to sixty persons. Though how many of them had a reason to want the guest they had supposedly come to honour dead is anyone's guess. The party was being held in a small room upstairs which got quite crowded, given that large library tables take up much of the space. And of course, the walls are lined with stacks of books. You can get a more accurate head count from the butler – the college butler, that is. He was the master caterer for the evening and he was the one who found the body.'

'Always a bad position to find oneself in,' said Ampleforth darkly. 'Being the one to find the body.'

Remembering Ampleforth's penchant for jumping to conclusions, St. Just said, 'In most cases yes but again, there are many suspects. By the time the butler raised the alarm, the man had been dead for an hour or thereabouts. I have come up with that number,' said St. Just quickly, with a glance at the doctor who looked ready to protest, 'because that's how late Jason Verdoodt was to his own party. It was to have been drinks at seven and dinner at eight in hall. Guests would have been arriving for drinks close to the time he died. Now, I only know the man by reputation, but I don't think any writer worthy of the name would be late to a celebration of his talent. Listening to Portia, one gets the definite impression that burnishing their reputations is at least a part-time occupation for most full-time writers. In other words, he would have been here on time or before, given any chance. Let's say perhaps five to ten minutes fashionably late to build anticipation, but even so. Common sense dictates that he absolutely would have been here and not kept everyone waiting too long.'

'If he hadn't been murdered on the way,' said Ampleforth.

'Precisely so. And whoever killed him would have wanted to avoid detection, of course, so they may have arrived early to lie in wait.'

'That suggests to me Jason may have been early, too,' said Ampleforth. 'Otherwise, someone might have witnessed the murder. So, the suspects are many. Given Sir Boniface's position in society and Verdoodt's notoriety, the situation requires careful handling and quick solving.'

'Quick and accurate, yes,' agreed St. Just. He was beginning to feel relieved that he was on the scene. It wasn't as though Ampleforth was in anyway corrupt or unintelligent – being shown the error of his ways he would generally climb down from any hastily adopted positions. But his opinions tended to be quickly formed in a headlong rush to solve a case. It was not a good trait for a police officer to have. Besides, this would no doubt develop into an unsavoury business and St. Just was glad to be here to protect Portia as much as possible.

'Did Verdoodt have any enemies that you know of?' asked Ampleforth.

St. Just had a clear memory of Portia's saying to him only that morning that Verdoodt got up everyone's nose.

'I gather there was some jealousy,' he said mildly. 'You only need look at the man to imagine the nature of some of that jealousy.'

Just then the flash of a camera repeatedly illuminated the area as one of the crime scene technicians documented the setting in photos. This process with both still photo and videos had to be followed before the body could be removed to the morgue at the hospital for examination.

Ampleforth stared at the body of the handsome author and shook his head. 'Wife?' he asked. 'Girlfriend? Friends of any kind?'

'I'm sure we'll learn more about that,' said St. Just. 'I gathered from overheard conversations at the party that more than one woman considered herself to be in the running for the position of wife or girlfriend.'

'More than one?'

'I'm afraid so, yes. That will complicate things, also. I—'

Just then the uniformed constable who had arrived just after Ampleforth appeared at the top of the stairs.

'They're getting restless,' she announced. 'What do I tell them?'

'Tell them we'll be up in a minute,' Ampleforth replied. 'We're only getting in the way down here, anyway.'

'And in danger of being photographed,' agreed St. Just. 'Come along and I'll introduce you to our potential suspects. I mean, witnesses.'

ELEVEN
First Steps

'There are so many potential witnesses we'll have to take them in some kind of order,' St. Just added as the men slowly ascended the wide stairs together, DCI Ampleforth not being given to taking the stairs two at a time. ('Arthritis in the knees,' he explained. 'It's a scourge. Before long I'll need everything replaced.') St. Just slowed his pace to match the older man's. They stopped halfway up, where they could continue their conversation without being overheard – and where Ampleforth could catch his breath.

'The doctor's first impression was that Jason might have something unusual in his system. Of course, a drug or poison could have come from anything he consumed earlier but there was an odour of wine about him. We'll have to wait for de Witt for news of stomach contents, but meanwhile we need to start somewhere. We should have a look in his room, see if he left any open bottles lying about.'

'We'll go through his belongings. He lived in the college, didn't the doc say? At least we won't have to travel far.'

'Yes. And the college must have a head of catering, someone who knows the set-up,' said St. Just. 'There may still be a bottle somewhere in the library that's been tampered with, although I doubt the killer – or killers – would be so reckless if they were trying to target a single person.'

'Unless they simply didn't care how many people were harmed.'

'Yes,' agreed St. Just. 'Or perhaps . . . perhaps this tragedy falls more into the category of a prank gone wrong – you never know. What was meant to inconvenience led to something far worse.'

'Good point. But would one of the students be so reckless? Don't bother answering that,' said Ampleforth. 'Now, some of these places put a fellow in charge of doling out the bottles of wine. Well, you know that. Aren't you a Cambridge man?'

St. Just nodded absently. 'We'll need to have a word with whoever oversees the wine cellar for the college.'

'I went to one of the red-brick unis myself,' said Ampleforth. 'Leeds. But a college like this would assign an expert, if only to guard the bottles, some of which can be quite expensive. We investigated a case of burglary at one of the other colleges not long ago. St Edmund Hall. The colleges often appoint someone whose real expertise is splitting atoms or debunking Viking mythology or whatever, but who also knows a bit about vintages and so on and can be relied on not to drink the profits.'

'So we need to find out who had access, how many people had access, when they had access – all of that,' said St. Just. 'The wine didn't get altered by itself – that is, if it was the wine that was tampered with. But if that's the case, something happened between the time the bottle was uncorked and the time some of the contents ended up in the glass that Jason drank from. I'm assuming it was a glass, of course – that he wouldn't chug from the bottle, or be forced to. There'd be signs of that on his clothing. What I wonder is why . . .'

'Wonder why what?'

'Why they bothered. If the idea was to give him a mighty shove down the stairs, was it necessary that he be drugged?'

'It probably helped – a pliant, disoriented victim is easier to manipulate. The popularity of date-rape drugs like GHB is one example. But those drugs are designed to make the victim forget what happened. Whoever killed Jason didn't care if he remembered. They knew he wouldn't be around to remember a thing – if we are eliminating the possibility he simply lost his balance and fell, which I'm gathering does not fit with what little we know so far. Otherwise, the doctor wouldn't have felt the need to disturb me at my meal.'

'You may be right – subduing Jason, who was young and fit, would be necessary if his opponent were neither of those things. The last thing the killer would want was a victim putting up a fight or being able to run away.'

'Right. If it was a crime, there's a good chance it was premeditated.'

'In a way, we're only suspicious because there seems to be some feeling surrounding the man and his unfettered success as an author. Most authors stumble along the way, but Jason seems to have bypassed the usual challenges to publication and bolted straight out of the gate to the front of the pack. And he did all this without an agent, I'm told.'

Portia had told him it was possible Jason had been turned down by agents, who would be gnashing their teeth at the loss. But as a motive for murder, St. Just thought that a stretch. How many agents were there in the world anyway? The task for the police would be nearly impossible and the motive – an anguished agent – rather feeble.

St. Just continued, 'We won't know, until the toxicology results come in and the body has been thoroughly examined, if we really are dealing with a deliberate, planned assault that ended in death. I would imagine the mortuary department will handle the post-mortem?'

'That's right.'

'They'll need to be told to step it up, since what we're dealing with here is liable to land us all on the front page of the newspapers. We'll need answers to reporters' questions at our fingertips.'

'The butler should know something about the wine catering situation – where it came from, how many bottles, how distributed, if it was left unattended.'

'Distribution may be the key,' mused St. Just. 'It's unfortunate this was a black-tie affair.'

'Beg pardon?'

'Men in black-tie dress look alike.' St. Just glanced down at his own costume for the evening. 'Different heights and weights and complexions, of course, but they look alike, in much the way all penguins look alike – even if not all penguins are the same size. So if anyone in black tie was seen acting oddly, or messing about with wine bottles with his head lowered and his back turned . . . you do see. It could have been a waiter, or it could have been a guest. At least with the ladies, we have colours and brocades and silhouettes to make them memorable. To tell them apart.'

'You're right about that. Serving staff for a formal do have much the same look as the men they're waiting on. The women caterers, too, who've all started wearing trousers instead of skirts.'

'Still, one of the waiters, male or female, would have more chance to duck out of the party undetected, talk with Jason, quarrel with him, and dispatch him. All without arousing suspicion. And if he cried out as he fell – as the party was getting in full swing, I doubt anyone could hear him over the string quartet, which was too loud for the room.'

'I see . . .'

'We'll need background on Jason, of course,' said St. Just. 'Anyone who knew him well may hold the key to his death – even if they weren't actually moved to kill him. From what I understand, his author enemies may be many but well hidden. Most people don't want to own up to a rivalry. It seems too petty. What difference does it make who sold more books than you did? But according to Portia, the rivalry can be intense.'

'Even she could be called a rival. It's the sort of profession where the big prizes are few and many are scrambling after them. Even I know that.'

'Portia is free of that sort of pettiness,' said St. Just firmly.

'I am sure she is,' Ampleforth said quickly. 'She doesn't need to play the game. Now, let's see what my constable may have overheard while holding the party at bay.'

Detective Constable Daisy Lambert of Thames Valley Police had bad news for them once they reached the room where the party had been held. It seemed she had allowed several of her captives to slip the net.

'There's a back staircase, sir,' she explained to her senior apologetically. 'Before I knew what was happening, or noticed the crowd was thinning out, they had scarpered. I told them to stay put once they gave us their names and numbers but some of them left.'

'You did manage to get *all* the names, didn't you?'

'Yes, sir. I'm ninety per cent sure I did yes. Yes, sir.' Off

Ampleforth's look of outrage, she straightened the jacket of her uniform and said, 'Ninety-five. But it was while I was going about taking names that some of them slipped away.'

'We will talk about this later, Constable,' said Ampleforth. 'Who do you know for certain has left?'

'Lady Ursula, sir. She left. She said she'd taken a sedative and that she didn't feel well. Said she wanted to go home and we had no right to detain her. It was only me here, sir,' she added defensively. 'I told her we'd need to speak with everyone but when I looked for her later, she had gone.'

'What about Sir Boniface?'

She pointed to the tall man with greying hair standing near the drinks table, pouring himself a refill.

'For God's sake, woman. What is it about the words "crime scene" that you don't understand?' Ampleforth stepped quickly over to the table, telling the man to put down the glass and bottle. An argument ensued which Ampleforth appeared to win.

St. Just turned to Constable Lambert. 'Who else has left?' he asked.

'I don't know, do I?' she said.

'*Think*. It could be very important.'

'I don't know who was here to begin with, or what they look like . . . Oh, hang on. The two grown children of Lady Ursula. I forget their names. I've got them written down, but they said they were going to drive their mother home together. The daughter's name was Imogen. Imogen Castle. She said we should play close attention to Minette somebody, that we should question her.'

'I do so appreciate receiving interrogation advice from the public,' said St. Just. 'Did she happen to mention why, this Imogen person? Why we should do that?'

'She told me she was distraught – her words – and someone named Minette was the reason. This Minette had introduced herself to Imogen as the fiancée of Jason.'

St. Just, realizing this could be important, asked impatiently, 'So where is this Minette? Not here either, I gather?'

'Imogen said she'd left. Before . . . before the body and all that, sir.'

'Before the body was found. I see. Interesting.'

'I thought so,' she said, clearly welcoming the chance to redeem herself by having thought-provoking information to offer. 'Imogen got so upset she threatened to have the butler remove her if she didn't leave.'

'So it came to that, did it?'

Constable Lambert beamed. 'Yes.'

St. Just was intrigued. Had this Minette woman crashed the party? It would be easy enough to find an unusual name like that on the guest list.

Ampleforth re-joined them. 'What a cock-up,' he said. 'The college master is nowhere to be found, and presumably left earlier, too. The place is like a sieve.'

'I really am sorry, sir.'

Ampleforth ignored her. 'Why don't you have a word with the master, St. Just? I'd be grateful for your insights in this investigation. It's as well to start at the top and work down in a case like this. In the meantime, we'll try to speak to as many as we can.'

In St. Just's experience, starting at the bottom often exposed better clues for a police investigation. The top was too adept at covering its tracks. But this was an Oxford college and protocol should be followed. After all, the police would need permission to search and round up any suspects who might be attached to the college and it was far better to get willing permission than to show up looking threatening and waving a warrant about.

'I'll see what I can learn,' said St. Just.

TWELVE
The Master

Speaking with the Master of St Rumwold's College, Professor Alice Davies, was a bit like interviewing a female David Niven – all suave urbanity with a hint of steel behind a debonair smile. It would not surprise St. Just to learn that steel had been used as a stiletto – figuratively speaking – on her way to the top of her profession. He was saddened but realistic about what it took to storm the bastions of formerly all-male enclaves like St Rumwold's. It had only been a matter of decades since women were properly admitted as undergraduates so, taking the long view, the recent influx of female dons, principals and masters was heady progress.

For Dr Alice Davies, the top would be the vice-chancellorship, a position currently held by a woman, as well. Possibly she was aiming for the chancellorship itself. St. Just knew from the brief he'd been emailed last night from DCI Ampleforth's team that the master was a renowned expert in the field of artificial intelligence and was former MI5, to boot. St. Just wondered about the word 'former'. In wartime, for example, there was no such thing, simply agents who never spoke of what they later got up to 'on holiday'. And the world was always at war, whichever way one chose to look at it. And a spy was always a spy.

The only exception might be an Anglican priest of his acquaintance, who vehemently denied continuing a clandestine existence, posing as a vicar of a tiny village in southwest England. St. Just supposed it wasn't the man's fault that murder seemed to follow him wherever he went. No more than it was St. Just's fault that every attempt to escape the bonds of Cambridge landed him in a murder investigation.

Asked how everything was going at the college, generally speaking (apart from the odd murder, St. Just did not add), the master swung into full PR mode. She might have been being interviewed for the student newspaper, so relentlessly upbeat was her response.

'Things *were* going swimmingly,' she said, leaning back in her leather desk chair. 'Thank you for asking.'

'Except?'

'Except,' she acknowledged unwillingly, probably realizing that it generally paid to be as transparent as possible when dealing with the police, 'every college has its problems. Mostly of a financial sort these days.'

'Oh?' St. Just adopted an attitude just short of indifference, brushing away a non-existent speck on his sleeve.

'Yes, well, it can have nothing to do with what you're . . . investigating. It's just that, well. This just came to my attention, the extent of the situation.' She tapped one finger against a sheaf of papers on her desk. 'It transpires that some recent investments made by the college were not as sound as they might have been. The war in Ukraine upset everything, as you know. I'm not complaining, fighting the Russian invasion had to be done, but stocks and futures that looked stable suddenly were not. Oil, for one example.' She shook her head. 'We should have pivoted to silver to offset the losses but did not do so in time, it seems.'

'I understand,' said St. Just. 'I think we are all feeling that pain but, as you say, we are willing to shoulder part of the burden in a broader cause.'

'When liberty is at stake—'

'Quite,' he said, pre-empting her before she swung fully into patriotic mode. This was where her MI5 training would come to the fore. 'I assume the bursar is in charge of making those investments.'

She didn't seem to notice they were veering off the topic of murder, but St. Just had decided to follow the conversation wherever it might lead.

She was quick to reply. 'Not he alone! The final decision rests not only with me but an advisory board. I didn't mean to mislead you. At St Rumwold's College there is no consolidation of power into one person's hands. History has shown what a mistake that can be.'

'I quite understand. So, I would imagine, given the somewhat changed financial situation of the college, fundraising
has come to assume a larger role in your day-to-day
existence.'

'That is well put,' she said. 'Larger than I'd like, to be
honest. I'm here to educate young minds, above all else. But
we rely on alumni donations, especially in perilous times like
this.'

'And many of them are strapped for cash as well, I would
also imagine.'

'Yes,' she said. Her voice carried a note of hesitation.
Where was he going with this?

St. Just wished he could enlighten her, but the fact was, he
was still just fishing.

'So,' he said, 'I would imagine the value of the cachet of
having Jason Verdoodt on the teaching staff could not be
overstated.'

The statement seemed to come as a relief to her. Her shoulders visibly dropped, and as she shifted in her chair to swing
one knee over the other, she assumed a more relaxed posture.
It was this that made St. Just realize she had been metaphoric-
ally holding her breath throughout their conversation. And he
wondered why that was.

'Were you worried he might eventually leave his position
in the college?' he prodded. 'Take up writing full time?'

Her internal debate before answering was obvious, but
wisely she chose not to stonewall on this topic. 'I was
concerned, to be honest with you.'

St. Just nodded. How much easier his life was when
suspects and witnesses were honest.

'He often said – to me, to journalists, to whomever would
listen – he had no such plans.'

'But you didn't believe him?'

'It's not that, exactly. I thought that after a certain amount
of time had passed, he would change his mind, is all. Perfectly
natural. The college life has many attractions even for a – erm
– well, a lively young man, but for Jason, the world suddenly
was at his feet. I thought that in due course, he'd move on.
He'd already bought a house in Oxford, so literally, he was

moving out of his rooms soon enough. He may have been thinking of applying for a position at another college.'

'Something along the lines of an honorary position with fewer duties but with full privileges at a, well, a better-known college.'

'Quite. St Rumwold's has a fine reputation but places like Christ Church and New College, well. We have the *Harry Potter* franchise to thank for their popularity. Jason would have been snapped up immediately. With a worldwide platform such as he had . . . He'd also been published to some acclaim in his field – not just his fiction was well-received, you know. He was fluent in several languages, the recipient of several awards. No, he'd be gone in a trice. I can't say I'd blame him, but I did hope we could entice him to stay.'

Jason's leaving would be in her eyes the ultimate betrayal, thought St. Just. The least the man could do would be to join the brain drain from Britain to the US and remove himself completely from her sight.

Well, someone had removed him, all right.

'Help me understand what happened last night.'

'At the party, yes. I can only say I wish I understood it myself.'

'Some of the attendees seemed to vanish before the police could reach them. How did that happen?'

'Obviously, something was amiss. So, to alleviate panic, the attendees were told only that there was a disturbance at the front entrance and that they could leave via the back entrance of the library through a door that led into the master's garden – my garden. They probably assumed some sort of protest among the students over something or other. It does happen on occasion. We educate them and this is how they repay us.'

'When you knew the police were arriving, you allowed this to happen?'

'But I didn't know there was a murder, did I? Just some sort of ruckus brewing. Some sort of accident, perhaps. I guess my training kicked in and my first thought was crowd control. I didn't even know the ruckus had to do with our guest of honour. I just knew our dinner was waiting. The chef kept texting the butler, who kept asking me what I wanted to do.

So I made a decision. From the master's garden there's a narrow door in a brick wall that gives access to the quad and would allow them to enter the hall.'

So while the investigation was going on, some of them sat having a good time at dinner. *Unbelievable.*

St. Just sighed, deciding nothing would be gained by registering his outrage. He said, 'The police will be speaking with Jason Verdoodt's colleagues here at the college and within his department, as well as his students, but I wonder what your general impressions were of the man?'

Definitely, this put her guard back up. She began to fan the edges of the offending sheaf of pages, avoiding his eyes, probably seeking the diplomatic response. He decided to press his advantage.

'And I would especially like to know,' he continued, 'if you were aware of any problems surrounding his tenure here at the college. Fame such as his, sudden as it was . . .' St. Just allowed the question to hang between them in the air, open-ended, heavy as a cloud, for the thrust of his meaning was not lost on her. Her bearing resumed its wary stance, and her posture was now rigid. He was surprised a woman with her background wasn't better at hiding her reactions, but either lack of practice or stress had her on edge.

She seemed to him to teeter between placing full confidence in him as a professional investigator who could clear up the current mess, given her full cooperation, and fear of being misunderstood and making matters worse. Or of repeating gossip, which generally did have a way of blowing back on the gossiper.

'I don't think his neighbour across the hall was fond of him. Professor Ambrose. But he wasn't at the party. He told me a few days ago that he had dinner plans with his brother, and I saw them leaving together on my way to the library. Jason and Ambrose weren't, erm, friendly.'

'Anyone else you can think of who wasn't friendly?'

At this, she decided to punt. 'You should speak with his scout who, after all, knows everything. They may all try to say nothing, discretion has been drilled into them, but . . .'

But, thought St. Just, she preferred to leave the gossiping to those lower down the social scale.

She continued, 'If she gives you any resistance, say I've given permission and full cooperation is needed. I'll have the head housekeeper look up the name for you.'

'Thank you. I had thought of speaking to his scout. We will also have a word with the wine steward or whoever would have overseen those bottles being placed ready for the party.'

'Of course. I've already had a word and he has expressed his willingness to provide the police with whatever information might be of help. This time of day you'll likely find him in the Senior Common Room. First Quad.'

'Thank you,' he said, noticing how she'd leapt ahead to see the police's need to speak with the wine steward. She couldn't have known that foul play in Jason's death had been confirmed. No doubt she'd had a word with the college doctor by now, though.

On his way over to the college that morning, St. Just had received a call on his mobile from Ampleforth. The preliminary blood tests had indicated the presence of a strong sedative in the victim's blood. 'Enough to knock him for a loop,' Ampleforth had said. 'If someone caused him to fall down those stairs, they could have done so with the mere push of a finger. The cosh on his head with the book may have been for show.'

'Or the *coup de grâce*.'

'Perhaps. They can't say with certainty.'

Ampleforth had also mentioned that the police had pulled CCTV footage from the college, both inside and out, and his team were reviewing it to see if anyone unauthorized had breached the grounds via the side gate into the college. St. Just expected to hear this would turn out to be Minette, who likely had waited until a student or don had entered via that route and had simply followed them in.

Ampleforth informed him that the college porter was willing to swear no outsiders entered the college through the main gate, at least none without a right to be there or without an invitation to the party. The porter had kept track, checking invitations as people entered and keeping a list. A comparison with the list of names police had taken at the party would show any discrepancies – if anyone had left early and not made their way to the dining hall with the others.

So, probably an inside job – unless the CCTV review revealed otherwise.

'The matter must be resolved,' the master was saying, adjusting her glasses. 'And quickly. You do understand why, don't you? You're clearly an intelligent man.'

'It had occurred to me this kind of lingering stain on the college would not be to anyone's advantage. Of course. We're doing all we can and will continue to do so. You have my word on that.'

'You're from . . . the Other Place, are you not?'

'I am a detective chief inspector with the Cambridgeshire Constabulary. Yes, ma'am.'

'I meant you are a graduate of one of their colleges.'

He didn't know why he was unnerved by this comment. But of course, anyone with an MI5 background would have uncovered this basic information. It was the speed of that research that perturbed him.

'That is correct. I matriculated at Peterhouse.'

This information seemed to mollify her, as Peterhouse was the oldest Cambridge college. She nodded her head slightly: At least the case wasn't in the hands of a complete idiot.

'Thank you in advance,' she said, with all apparent sincerity. 'This was the last thing the college needed right now. I'll be spending a great deal of time, I'm afraid, on my least favourite chore.'

'Spin control,' said St. Just.

She nodded, adding, 'Don't forget about the scout.'

'I won't,' he said.

THIRTEEN
The Wine Steward

Given the news about the blood test results on Jason's body, St. Just felt the talk with the wine steward had gone to the top of his list of priorities for the morning.

As the master had suggested, he found him in the college's Senior Common Room in First Quad, just finishing his morning biscuits and coffee. St. Just declined the invitation to join him.

'I wonder if I might have a word.'

'About the party last night? Yes, the master briefed me first thing this morning and told me I should expect to hear from you. Rather awkward situation, isn't it?'

The wine steward was Professor Charles Monet. St. Just recognized the famous name, but he knew him not as a relative of the famous painter but as an expert in chemistry, frequently quoted in the popular science news in the papers. He proved to be very proud of the college's wine collection.

He led St. Just from the SCR to Third Quad and on to a door on the ground floor of Staircase C. He produced a large iron key from his jacket pocket and proceeded to pull back the massive wooden door. This revealed a narrow staircase to the cellar where the wine was kept, a sort of catacomb running beneath the grounds of the college.

All very *Cask of Amontillado*, thought St. Just.

He was no great wine connoisseur but, having pulled out the small torch on his keyring for a closer look in the inadequate overhead light, he recognized what looked like a half-dozen bottles of Château Latour 1988 that had to be worth a few quid. St. Just said something to this effect and Professor Monet beamed.

'We also have over fifty bottles of Château Mouton

Rothschild 1970 and over seventy bottles of Château St-Pierre St-Julien 2005.'

'Those alone must be worth a great deal of money.'

'Indeed. It's a matter of public record so I am free to tell you. The contents of our cellar are worth in total around six hundred thousand pounds. Our wines are second to none in quality if not quantity, if I do say so.'

'You're not serious,' said St. Just.

'Quite serious. The only colleges that surpass us are those with a drinking problem in the population. They tend to order wine in excess out of a fear of running out. Our cellars are not drawn down so carelessly and the bottles are allowed to age in place, accumulating wealth for the college's future.'

'I confess I'm torn,' said St. Just. 'Although I see the wisdom in letting them earn interest, so to speak, I'd be very tempted to open a few bottles, myself. In a celebratory sort of way.'

Monet cracked a smile, displaying rather pointed white teeth. It was like watching the opening of a seldom-used portcullis.

'Quite,' he said. 'Was there anything in particular you wanted to see? The area down here is divided into eight separate rooms or compartments, all under lock and key. They are of course temperature controlled, and – before you ask – there is an accounting system for any bottles brought in or taken out.'

St. Just was still turning over in his mind the sheer value of all these bottles. Like works of art, the prices were no doubt inflated beyond the real value of the contents, but putting a price tag on rarity was impossible. There was no slide rule for this, apart from whatever the market would bear.

Still, he didn't imagine he was there to investigate a potential robbery of the tidy fortune accruing below the ancient walls of St Rumwold's College. He supposed he could stretch his mind to make some connection, perhaps a burglary gone wrong or aborted when things got out of hand – a quarrel among thieves thwarted of their prize, perhaps – but try as he might, he failed to see any immediate link to the death of star author Jason Verdoodt.

Just in case, he said, 'I assume the accounting system is computerized?'

'Yes, it is,' Monet replied, if reluctantly. His face fell in disappointed lines at this intrusion of the twenty-first century into what St. Just was sure he thought of as his private vault. 'But of course, I also keep a handwritten ledger as has been done for centuries. Computers and cloud storage may fail but our written archives never do. Apart from that unfortunate fire in the fifteenth century, of course; it left a gap in the records. The cellar master at the time died trying to save all the records but failed. Otherwise, we are quite up to date.'

'Quite so,' said St. Just. 'Highly commendable of you to have a backup system. Might I ask you to confirm all the bottles are present and accounted for? The bottles used yesterday evening, I mean. Please confirm nothing has gone missing. It might be important.'

'Certainly, sir.'

With that he pulled out an old ledger that looked like it might contain an original text set by Gutenberg, all leather binding and iron clasps. Donning a pair of white gloves, Monet eased it open to the relevant page.

'We had fifty guests, and for an aperitif I generally allow a quarter of a bottle for each guest. There was to have been more wine at the dinner in hall, of course, red and white, but . . . you know what happened. Anyway, thirteen bottles were sent up to the library to be served for the seven o'clock drinks party. Then the guests were to walk over to the college dining hall for dinner at eight.'

'Thirteen bottles,' St. Just repeated. 'Can you show me where those bottles would have come from?'

Monet walked over to a door labelled with a large number seven and, selecting a key from a key ring, opened the door.

'How many sets of keys are there?' St. Just asked.

'Two,' he replied. 'I have a set and the master has a set.'

'No one else?'

He shook his head decisively. 'It's been done this way from time immemorial. Or course, back in the day we had a cellar master. Now, *I'm* the jack of all trades.'

'An honorary volunteer position, is it?' asked St. Just. At the man's nod, he said, 'I see.'

'What do you see, Inspector?' The tone conveyed that umbrage had been taken.

Restating Ampleforth's words of the night before, St. Just said, 'It's not a job that can be left to just anyone. It requires knowledge and dedication. I would imagine not that many members of the Senior Common Room have the expertise. Nor do they want the responsibility.'

This seemed to mollify him.

'Quite,' he said. 'The last fellow left in charge, well . . .'

St. Just waited hopefully for a tale of drunken orgies among the wine racks but none was forthcoming.

'When was it you took over?' he asked.

'About five years ago,' Monet replied.

Unless he'd developed sudden criminal tendencies, that seemed to leave Monet outside the framework of this investigation.

'The bottles came from right over there,' Monet pointed, standing back to allow him to enter the area labelled #7. Something seemed to catch his eye as he followed St. Just inside. 'But that's odd.'

'What's odd?'

'It's just that it's usually dusty in here. A bit cobwebby, in fact. The scouts are not allowed in except under supervision, so generally no one comes in here unless they are retrieving bottles of wine under my gaze. Even the butler rarely comes in here – there's really no need. His part is keeping the keys under lock and, well, key.'

Which was saying that *three* people had access to the keys, not just Monet and the master. St. Just let it go for the moment, but the super-secret keys suddenly did not seem so secret.

'But the butler could come in here at any time?'

'Theoretically, yes. He's supposed to ask permission, but perhaps no one was around to ask. The man can be trusted implicitly, I do assure you.'

Inwardly, St. Just sighed.

'I'll have to ask him if he got someone to clean up in here. This entire wall of shelves looks dusted, or at least as if the dust has recently been disturbed. And the floor looks as if it has been recently swept.'

'But nothing's missing, as far as you can tell?'

Monet scanned the shelves carefully before answering. 'No.

It all looks as it should. Everything accounted for. And if you're suggesting the butler may be up to something, you must think again. Dimitri Smirnoff is a sound man.'

'I'm sure he is,' said St. Just. Then contradicted this sentiment by asking, 'Is there accounting? I mean, do you take a yearly inventory?'

'Of course we do,' Professor Monet replied sharply. 'The last inventory was taken during the summer. Dimitri and I did it together. It took hours; it's a two-person job. Every bottle was present and accounted for.'

At a nod from St. Just moments later, he ushered him out of the room and made a show of carefully locking the door behind them.

'Was it unusual to serve drinks in the library?' St. Just asked halfway through this security demonstration.

The professor's mask slipped for a moment, revealing intense annoyance. He said stiffly, 'It would be more usual to serve drinks in the master's garden or drawing room.'

'So why the change of venue?'

'I'm sure I wouldn't know, sir.' From the look of disapproval settling on his face, St. Just was certain he did know but was not going to comment. There was little question his loyalty was to the college and its inmates.

'I would imagine it was more inconvenient for you to serve drinks in the library.'

'It was a question of the stairs,' Monet replied neutrally.

Presumably the very stairs where Jason Verdoodt had met his fate. 'Of course there is more than one staircase.' Down which several witnesses had escaped, he could have added, but decided not to bring Monet in on that most frustrating aspect of the investigation.

'Indeed, there is. The staircase used by regular visitors is wider and more accessible. But we were forced to use the book lift as a silent butler, in a manner of speaking, because the back stairs to the library are too narrow and rickety for people carrying heavy trays up and down, not to mention cases of wine.'

'A sort of dumb waiter, is it? The book lift?'

The man nodded.

'And the main stairs had to remain open for guests to use. I see. So altogether the master's garden or lodgings would have been more suitable from the point of view of the staff.'

'Ours not to reason why, sir. Now, if there's nothing else?'

St. Just imagined he'd get little more out of Professor Monet than what he'd already wrung from him. It was clear the change of venue had not been his decision. It sounded more as if Verdoodt, the golden-haired boy, had determined that the library was the glamorous setting he wanted and the college, probably in the form of the master, had acceded to his desires.

Besides, Castle Publishing likely had been paying for this event and could call the tune. Or perhaps the college had shared the bill to give the college the extra sheen needed to draw future alumni donations – almost certainly they had. He made a mental note to ask.

He thanked Monet, who hustled him out of the gloomy domain and into the fresh air.

St. Just thought it was time to hunt up Jason's scout.

FOURTEEN
The Scout

Following directions from the head housekeeper, a sturdy woman with a tight cap of curls framing her broad face, he went to speak with Tess Babbage, who was responsible 'among many other things' for the care of Jason Verdoodt's rooms in college.

'We none of us have time to stand about killing people, if that's what you're thinking,' the housekeeper assured him, news of a murder investigation clearly having travelled fast.

She was steadfastly unhelpful, apart from directions on where to look for Tess. In a thick Eastern European accent, she did drop one useful titbit. 'Dr Verdoodt tried to get Tess fired. We never got to the bottom of that before . . . you know. Before all this happened.'

'Fired over what?'

'Better you ask Tess. It was the only complaint we received about her in all her time here. She's about to end her probationary period and then this. I almost wondered . . .'

'Hmm?' St. Just waited patiently.

At last, she said, 'I will not speak ill of the dead. Except to say, Jason had a bit of a reputation with the ladies. Maybe he was turned down? Some men don't take rejection well. But in Tess's case, it's unlikely that is the case.'

'Why do you say that?'

Again, she hesitated. 'You'll see for yourself. You'll find her in the Senior Common Room this time of day, cleaning up after. Or the Junior Common Room. Tell her I gave you permission to see Jason's rooms. She has the key and needs to get them ready for the next occupant.'

'I'm afraid that's impossible. It's a crime scene. We'll have to have it roped off.' St. Just was surprised this hadn't been done already and pulled out his phone to warn Ampleforth.

'Crime scene? I was told he fell down the stairs.'

But you thought differently.

'Thank you for your time,' said St. Just, dialling up Ampleforth.

He found Tess not in the SCR or the JCR, but tidying up in Jason's rooms, vaguely waving a feather duster about. He swore softly under his breath.

'Put down that duster,' he commanded, as if she were armed.

Tess looked mystified, as well she might. She retreated to a dark corner of the room near the sagging bookshelves, holding out the duster as a defensive weapon.

'And who might you be?' she asked.

'I am DCI Arthur St. Just of the Cambridgeshire Constabulary and this is a potential crime scene. I must ask you to stop what you're doing.'

'What? He fell down the stairs, I was told. And what has Cambridge to do with it, anyway?'

That was a long story and he rather wished he hadn't given his full title.

'It's still possible it was an accidental fall, but we have an obligation to the deceased to investigate every angle.'

No need to stir panic unnecessarily, thought St. Just.

'So I guess that's why you're here talking to me,' she said, her voice shaking. 'You heard Jason tried to get me fired. Am I a suspect because of that? Because believe me, I didn't really care. You have the wrong idea here.'

'But it must have been unpleasant to be accused.' He left that open-ended in case she wanted to mention what she'd been accused of doing. But she was not so obliging. Perhaps, after all, it was the predictable story. Jason had been grabby and when she resisted, he'd reported her for some imaginary offence. In which case, he was liking Jason Verdoodt less and less.

'I was planning to quit anyway,' she said stoutly. 'Who needs this kind of grief, cleaning up after a bunch of grubby toffs who think they're better than me? Who wouldn't give the time of day to my sort? I've already applied up the road at the Turf. Better pay, less hassle, good tips – very highbrow for a pub. Very.'

He knew of the Turf Tavern, which featured in every tourist guide as one of Oxford's most historic venues. It could be reached only on foot down a dark and narrow medieval alleyway.

Still, he found her comment interesting. Perhaps the woman was a bit of a snob when it came to her places of employment, going after prestige and history wherever she could find it. Still, being employed by one of the most exalted places of learning in the world must carry a certain cachet. Would a job at an old historic tavern really make her want to leave?

He decided to face the grabby-Jason question head on. 'Did Dr Verdoodt ever accost you in any way? Harass you?'

This elicited a hollow laugh. 'He managed to resist,' she said.

'So what was his problem with you? Why would he file a complaint?'

'He said I moved his things about. Which I did. You wouldn't have any idea, the mare's nest some of these dons leave in their wake. I'm always careful not to disturb their rubbish too much in case they're using some filing system invisible to the naked eye, like, but none of them get in a tizz about it. Only his lordship, the "Great Author".'

St. Just wondered. Was Jason working on something he didn't want anyone else to see? He supposed it would be natural for him to be secretive about a work in progress that had already garnered so much attention.

'To be sure, there was nothing more . . . untoward in his interactions with you?'

'Like I told you, he managed to resist.'

She emerged timidly from the shadows where she'd hidden on his entrance, a mature figure dressed in loose-fitting work clothes. She wore a colourful kerchief round her hair, and as she neared him, she pulled it back from the right side of her face.

It was difficult for him not to flinch at the unexpected sight.

A healed burn scar that ran from eyebrow to temple disfigured her face, pulling the skin up around her eye into a permanent squint that must nearly have been blinding.

'To be fair on the man, Jason had prettier targets than the likes of me.'

FIFTEEN
At the Randolph

As St. Just left the college, his mobile buzzed with a call. It was Ampleforth.

'More detailed results are in,' he said. St. Just could hear in the background the sort of shouting, laughing, and printer racket that suggested Ampleforth was calling from police headquarters. St. Just felt a momentary pang of longing for his own noisy headquarters office. 'It's definite his bloodstream was carrying a potent cocktail of prescription drugs and alcohol – not a lot of alcohol but enough to disguise the taste of ground-up medication. It's doubtful he would grind up his own medication, so it seems clear someone else did it for him. I didn't know they could tell the pills were ground up, did you?'

St. Just shrugged, then realized Ampleforth couldn't see him.

'No, I didn't know that. I suppose it means he'd just recently been drugged. In other words, the medication would have had a more immediate impact on his system.'

'That's what de Witt said.'

'It's just possible, is it, that Jason chewed up the tablets? Some people do, to get a hit of the drug faster.'

'Possible, I suppose, but the doc is taking the view that the pills were meant to be disguised by a glass of wine. I do have one bit of news that is irrefutable.'

'Oh, what's that?'

'That book we found of his. The one in the corner. We can't say with any certainty it was the murder weapon – that it was the direct cause of his death – but there's a slight gash on his forehead that matches the corner of the book.'

'I thought I saw something like that,' said St. Just.

'Here's the kicker. It was a signed first edition copy of his famous book.'

'Signed? Please tell me you mean he signed it with a dedication. Something along the lines of, "To the person I know wants to kill me with this book", followed by a clearly legible name.'

'Unfortunately, only his signature is scrawled on the title page – there is no date or dedication.'

'That's too bad. It would have made our job much more straightforward. I suppose it's too much to hope for fingerprints.'

'Fingerprints there are none. Whoever handled the book must have worn gloves. I've had my people over at Castle headquarters today. Rumour around the water cooler has it that Jason Verdoodt was threatening to leave for greener pastures. They can't have been happy about it, but they are protesting it's all in the game.'

'I wonder. But a dead author is even less use to them than a defecting one, I should think. At least with a live author, there's hope they'll come crawling back.'

'I suppose.'

'You said drugs, plural,' prompted St. Just.

'He was drugged with anti-anxiety medication and two antidepressants. Mixed with alcohol – in this case, a dry madeira *apéritif*, matching the wine being served that night – they'd disorient him to the point he'd easily lose his balance. That's handy if you're planning to hit him and push him down a staircase and finish him off with a book, in case the stairs don't do the trick.'

'Did he take prescription drugs?'

'I asked de Witt, who of course as the college doctor could have prescribed for him and would have access to records showing his prescriptions. De Witt says he prescribed nothing to Jason that couldn't be purchased directly at the chemist's, over the counter. He says Jason was a health nut, jogging and running and so forth, and very careful what he put in his system.'

'All very interesting. Not proof – Jason could have come by the drugs in any number of ways: "borrowed" from a friend, or prescribed by another doctor, of course.'

'We're looking into it. But the health nut angle seems to be universally acknowledged. He had been heard to say he didn't need drugs and alcohol to have fun.'

'I'll just bet,' said St. Just. 'Interesting they could narrow the alcohol down to a dry madeira *apéritif.*'

'Not one hundred per cent, of course, but what are the chances? Did you get anything from the wine steward?'

'Not a lot. He prides himself that the vault where the wine is kept is burglar-proof, but in fact the keys could have got into the wrong hands in any number of ways. It's not a question of slack security, it's a question of trust. These positions at the college, from master on down, are positions of honour. No one wants to jeopardize their coveted position.'

'No one but the killer, and the killer wouldn't necessarily need access to the wine cellar. He or she could have been any of the guests at the party. Still, it's most likely a college wine that came from the cellars of the college. The empty bottles have not been tampered with − no drug residue − but one glass, undoubtedly the one used by Jason, showed traces.'

'Oh? And where was the glass found?'

'Sitting on the table with the rest of the glasses and the rest of the unopened bottles.'

'Interesting. No prints there either, I'll wager. The killer could have slipped the glass inside a pouch or handbag, but why bother?'

'Indeed.' Ampleforth could be heard to heave a sigh down the line.

'Anything else?'

'Not really. There's one report says a man in black-tie dress was reported to have been seen leaving the scene in a hurry.'

'Only one? There must have been dozens fleeing out the back way. The gardens would have been black with men in formal dress.'

'Humph. We need to look at motives, and the problem is, we may have too many.'

'I'd like to start with the publishing angle,' said St. Just. 'Perhaps devote part of the day to the love affairs angle. You wonder where Jason found the time. There's a lot of jealousy to go round.'

'We're gathering even Imogen Castle, the daughter of the publishing house, felt she had a special claim on Jason's heart. Jason had created quite a mess for himself in the romance department.'

'I suppose we must also investigate the professional jealousy as it relates to his colleagues in academia. Did he scoop one of them by finding an Egyptian mummy or a Viking hoard or something?'

'But,' said Ampleforth, 'we have to start with the obvious. I don't have the manpower to spread out all over Oxford in some sort of dragnet of the intellectuals.'

'Agreed. So, while Sir Boniface might have been unhappy when his author threatened to leave for another publisher, taking his guaranteed next bestseller with him, would he be jealous enough of Verdoodt's success to kill him? And how about the other Castle Publishing authors?'

'The tabloids indicate we should pay attention in particular to the children's book author.'

'Not Tricia Magnum?'

'She's been seen out and about with Jason. If the tabloids can be believed.'

'That is disappointing. A large part of me wants her to be as nice as her books would indicate.'

'If she was having an affair with Jason, and he was busy earning his bad reputation, he may have exhausted her supply of niceness. She's staying at the Randolph and I gather is eager to speak with the police.'

'That will make a nice change from people bolting at our approach,' said St. Just. 'Have you reached Jason's next of kin yet?'

'Yes, and they live very nearby. I wonder, could you go and talk with them? The locals already gave them formal notification.'

'Weren't they at the party?'

'No. I've got hold of the guest list and their names aren't on it. And therein lies a tale, I'm sure. I'll send a driver to pick you up whenever you say and let the parents know when you're on the way.'

'That's fine. I'll fit in a visit to the publishing house

sometime today, if you're all right with that, and I'll arrange to speak with Tricia Magnum – Dame Patricia – at the Randolph, but first I'll stop in and check on my fiancée. I left her working on her next book in our room at the hotel. I'm afraid most of our plans for touring around Oxford have fallen by the wayside, but Portia is always glad of a quiet moment to write.'

Portia's face as she peered into her laptop carried an expression with which St. Just was familiar: unshakeable focus and concentration tinged with a soupçon of concern and frustration. She looked up dazedly from her work as he entered.

'*Why*,' she cried, 'will Reginald not do as I say? *Why* does he ask his nitwit sidekick to investigate the family when Lady Anne is standing right there? And surely someone needs to walk the dog by now.'

It always took Portia a moment to emerge from her pool of creativity into the real world. By now St. Just knew better than to ask, 'Who is Lady Anne?' or to make some fatuous comment about pets in stories. He never read Portia's 'pages', as she called them, for a work in progress. She explained it was because she was superstitious about letting her raw material out into the world ahead of time. He suspected also she didn't want to hear criticism from him or anyone on an unfinished project, so he viewed his waiting role with some relief.

Still, it made him wonder if Jason had been the same. Because in taking a cursory survey of Jason's rooms, he'd not seen a stack of manuscript pages or piles of research that would indicate a new novel in progress.

He said as much aloud to Portia.

'Oh, my, Arthur,' she said. 'You are living in a different century when it comes to how books get written – and read – aren't you?'

St. Just found this comment unfair and said so.

'I not long ago downloaded *Baudolino* to my laptop so I wouldn't have to carry it about with me on holiday,' he said, hoping she'd notice his use of the, for him, high-tech word 'downloaded'.

'Commendable,' she murmured, smiling. 'How far along are you with it now?'

'Oh, you know. Halfway through.' This was perhaps a slight exaggeration. The truth was he'd been reading the same book on holiday for about a decade. It was a massive book that rewarded close reading, but the real problem was every time he settled in to read it murder erupted around him, and he had to drop the story in favour of investigating the case to its conclusion.

'I'm sure Jason, like most of us these days, wrote at a computer, some type of laptop for preference,' said Portia. 'It would be a rare writer who resorted to pen and ink, and most editors have moved on to using the online editing function. It saves hours of time and frees the author from trying to interpret any chicken-scratch handwriting.'

St. Just had noticed a computer screen in Jason's rooms but no laptop. That was certain to be seized by forensics and, in due time, they'd reveal what was on it.

This led him to wonder briefly about Jason's estate. Who inherited? He made a mental note to ask Ampleforth what he knew about Jason's will – if he had one – at the first opportunity.

'You really must read it,' Portia was saying. 'Jason's book, I mean. Although I doubt it has anything to do with the case. It's simply a wonderful job of storytelling. Elements of fantasy mixed in with the mystery but nothing too silly, if you know what I mean. He is – was – a master of world-building. You buy into the fantasy even if, like me, you tend to run from stories with dragons and wizards and magic amulets.'

'Good to know. I'll *download* it on to my *mobile app* when I get back. For now, I'm off to see another sort of wizard. Tricia Magnum. The children's book author.'

'Oh, do tell her I said hello. I wonder how she's taking it – Jason's death. Never mind, I can guess. I don't suppose you can tell me more about what's going on?'

'Not just yet. Maybe never. You know how it is.'

'I do. And for a crime writer, it's absolutely maddening.'

Portia resumed her writing struggles as he walked out,

closing the door behind him, reminded again of how writers all seemed to know each other. He had heard the term close-knit used to describe the writing world more than once.

'A star has been extinguished, and the skies will remain forever dark,' said Tricia Magnum.

He had arranged via one of Ampleforth's people to meet her for coffee in the Randolph bar, thinking showing up at her room might be misinterpreted. What might have seemed normal procedure for a police officer only a few years ago was now more likely to generate a formal complaint of harassment. Not that St. Just questioned the wisdom of playing it safe with every suspect, male or female.

He stopped to correct himself – she was simply a witness, not a suspect, until events proved otherwise.

She had floated into the room five minutes late, a cape billowing behind her. As St. Just watched, a small boy in her wake was nearly enveloped in the folds and was only extricated by the quick thinking of his mother.

Bestselling children's book author Tricia Magnum extended her hand in greeting as she offered her views on the skies darkened by Jason's passing. She sat down on one of the hotel's leather chairs, smoothing the skirt of her mid-length dress. Beneath the cape she wore a cardigan over a starched white blouse with a Peter Pan collar. St. Just did not think he had seen an outfit like it on a woman of her age, which he knew to be late thirties, outside of World War II documentaries about the war effort on the home front. He wondered if her choice of staid headmistress wear was deliberate.

Her complexion, bare of makeup, was as soft as a child's, her eyes a twinkling blue. He had seen her on the telly, reading from one of her books to a group of entranced youngsters.

'Tragic!' She cried now. 'Jason Verdoodt was so full of . . . so full of . . . well, *life*.'

St. Just thought an award-winning author such as Tricia Magnum might have come up with something better than this old full-of-life chestnut, but he was willing to make allowances for grief. Especially if rumours were true and bright-star Jason had held a special place in her personal firmament. At least she seemed genuinely to mourn him. Considering Jason's reputation, St. Just knew her sentiments might not be universal.

She pulled an embroidered handkerchief out from somewhere and began dabbing at what looked like authentic tears.

St. Just, not to be outdone in the cliché department, said, 'I am sorry for your loss.'

He took advantage of the lull to snag a nearby waiter and ask for coffee and biscuits, ordering for them both.

He faltered at knowing how best to address her, his knowledge of *Debrett's* failing him. He tried, 'Dame Patricia, a few questions if you don't mind,' and she did not correct him.

'Thank you, Detective,' she said, getting his own title wrong.

'Inspector St. Just of the Cambridgeshire Constabulary. At your service.'

She acknowledged this with a regal nod, one potentate to another.

'Now, I would like to ask you how you knew Jason, where you met him, how long you knew him. Whatever you can tell me.'

'Oh!' she cried, and St. Just's heart sank, fearing she would launch into some romance-for-the-ages speech that would be short on fact and tall on imagination. She did not disappoint.

'Jason and I met, fittingly, at the London Book Fair. In April. I was being interviewed by the BBC. But of course, Jason was really the man of the hour, it was him they wanted, and his interview followed right after mine. His book had taken off into the stratosphere where it remained. I – to be honest, but a poor scribe in comparison – I could not believe it when Jason went out of his way to speak to me. I was tremendously flattered.'

St. Just thought she protested too much. 'But surely,' he said, 'you are someone he would seek out. As a famous, award-winning author, and, well . . .'

'As a woman?'

'Yes,' St. Just said simply. Tricia was an attractive woman despite the costume, so prim it might be her version of mourning-wear. He thought it might be out of character for her – though he had too little knowledge of her to say for certain. She was older than Jason by a few years, but St. Just had not gained any impression a few years' difference would stop the man. If he wanted to be 'adopted' by women well-established in the field of writing, it might almost be inevitable they would be older than he.

'I assumed his interest in me was – how shall we say? – professional. We were both at the same publishing house, after all, and had the same editor.'

'That would be David Castle,' said St. Just. 'I hadn't realized that David edited children's books.'

'Do you know, that surprised me too – that they handed me off to David, whose head is entirely absorbed by space aliens and so on. He is a science fiction aficionado and makes no apologies for it. But an editor's job is not what anyone imagines. Emerging writers think editors will spend hours holding their hands and discussing troubling paragraphs and quoting Sartre over cocktails – I think all that sort of thinking was engendered by the New York, Algonquin-table people of literary lore. In fact, an editor is more akin to a train conductor, keeping the thing on the tracks, keeping it on schedule, keeping it safe until it can be handed off to marketing. No publisher in his right mind acquires a book that needs too much polishing. And correcting grammar? Forget about it. They don't have the time or the inclination. My own books are as print-ready as I can make them by the time they reach the first stage of publishing. Not perfect – there will always be typos and leaps in logic and forgetful author lapses – but by no means are my manuscripts haphazard piles of words to be whipped into shape by the publisher.'

'I see,' he said, somewhat taken aback by her fervour on the topic. 'So you and Jason chatted about David, did you?'

She shook her head vehemently. 'We spoke of . . . other things.'

'Ah.' Here it came. Time standing still, hearts beating as one, and so on.

'We were soulmates from the first. He felt it, too, and often said as much to me.'

'Wonderful. And how often were you able to get together?'

'It was difficult. His life was in Oxford. Mine is miles away in Cumbria. Not far from Beatrix Potter's house, in fact. I find the nearness of her memory invigorating when it comes to writing my own little stories.'

St. Just judged this was the moment to praise her 'little stories', which he could do honestly and without hesitation. 'Your stories are a national treasure,' he said. 'Congratulations on being on the honours list, by the way.'

She blushed a becoming pink and began fussing with her skirts to hide her sudden embarrassment. 'I never in a million years expected it,' she said. 'We writers are alone so much, you see. Most days it's just me and the geese and the ducks. The occasional lamb wanders by from the farm next door. So I'm basically writing for an audience of one.'

'Yourself,' he supplied.

'Myself as I was at the age of six. I have perfect recall for those days. I can't tell you what I had for lunch yesterday, but I can tell you every detail of my childhood. I didn't use to be able to call up these things so easily, but I was a shy child, an only child, easily bullied – children can be cruel, make no mistake! – and instead of hiding all those feelings away, I can easily dig them up and bring them to the fore now. I've been told by parents that my books help them with their children who have trouble joining in a group, and for that I'm glad.'

'That explains a lot about how children's books come to be written,' said St. Just. 'I really had no idea what the process was. But anyway, I would imagine it's a lonely life?'

'Yes and no. You don't realize you are lonely until that one person comes along and you realize how much you've longed for a companion – for a like soul, in this case.'

'Jason Verdoodt.'

'Correct. Meeting him changed everything.'

'But where you live, it has to be four hours away.'

'It didn't matter. We spoke daily. Well, nearly every day. Love cannot be measured in moments, but we did make every moment we had together count.' She paused to dab again at her eyes. 'I truly do not know what I will do without him.'

As much as St. Just was loath to throw a grenade into the middle of her grief parade, he knew he would get nothing but platitudes from her unless he provoked her into some sort of indiscretion. What were the chances Jason was staying faithful to her, given his reputation, with such a distance between them? Not to mention Tricia Magnum did not strike him as being Jason's type – even though, it was hard to know at this point what type Jason was honestly drawn to.

'The relationship was exclusive, was it?'

She began without hesitation, 'When true love strikes—'

'Yes, quite. But I understand that at the party there was another woman who considered herself to be exclusive to Jason.'

He let that hang in the air while she processed it. From her expression she was torn between pretending she didn't know and letting her glee at what she did know shine through. She chose a modified glee.

'You mean Minette. At least I think that's her name. I don't know her last name. But someone named Minette showed up to the party, dressed to the nines in a truly frightful red dress, completely inappropriate, and she was ousted from the party by the daughter of the publishing house – Imogen, I mean. Told to *leave* or be thrown out.'

'The dress was that bad?'

She laughed. She had the tinkly, high laugh of a child. 'No, of course not. Well, it *was* bad, but Imogen told me she was there without an invitation. Crashing the party – can you believe the nerve? She claimed to be some girlfriend of Jason's from way back. Well, the threat of being thrown out soon put an end to that. The room was crowded as it was, and anyway, especially since the height of the pandemic, crowded parties with people standing shoulder-to-shoulder are simply not allowed. Conferences, book fairs, book launch parties – they've all been scaled back. It's done no end of damage to the industry and we're all still crawling out from underneath. However, showing up without an invitation! That is simply not done.' Tricia didn't bother at this point to hide her glee at her rival's disgrace.

And St. Just had no doubt she saw this other woman as a

rival. Which prompted him, having forded this stream partway, to continue until he reached the other side.

'Perhaps the daughter, Imogen, also felt she had a special relationship with Jason Verdoodt.'

'Well, I can't control thoughts, you know,' she answered hotly. 'I can only tell you that Imogen is mistaken. She's not a *writer*, she's in marketing. She and Jason have nothing in common.' Hearing her words, she corrected, '*Had* nothing in common. Oh my God – whatever am I going to do without him?'

Her voice carried far enough into the room that several people turned to see what the matter was and whether the man was somehow to blame for the woman's distress. One woman in a group of four having tea recognized the author, loudly whispering to her companions that it was the famous Tricia Magnum.

Overhearing this, she seemed to struggle to collect herself. She could never grieve anonymously like most people – not ever again, not now that she was recognized probably everywhere she went, like Margaret Atwood. St. Just was familiar with the problem from his time with Portia. She hadn't reached superstar status like Dame Patricia, but occasionally he noticed people adjusting their behaviour in her presence, hanging on her every word. It was as if they were waiting for her to perform a magic trick.

St. Just shifted his position so his back was more to the room. He said, 'But there was some, shall we say, competition for Jason's attention? Something that may have caused someone to feel, let's say, slighted? Not you, necessarily, perhaps, but *someone*?'

Her expression changed from grief to wariness. A small woodland creature in one of her books might have adopted exactly that look on hearing the approach of Mr Wily Fox.

Tricia may have been realizing for the first time she might be a suspect in Jason Verdoodt's murder. There had been a sense of chaos surrounding the scene of his demise, with no one clearly accounted for, so she was as much a suspect as anyone else. And in her case, if she had come to doubt Jason's commitment to her, all the ingredients for a strong motive for doing away with the source of her unhappiness were there. She only had to stir them to create turmoil within herself.

St. Just was unwilling to press her without more to go on, and certainly not in such a public setting. Could this seemingly gentle writer of tender children's tales really get riled up enough to kill her lover? Had Jason perhaps provoked her deliberately – just for fun? Tried to dump her as being of no further use to him?

If that proved to be the case, it made St. Just's job harder. Bringing someone to justice was a difficult task at the best of times, requiring him to set aside any personal feelings. When the victim was unlikable, as Jason appeared to be, it was doubly hard to remain neutral.

'You must find whoever did this,' she said, and if he had ever doubted Tricia's ability to be other than a gentle teller of tales, the look in her eyes just then told him she was more than capable of vengeance. Her books might have been sugar-coated with optimistic endings, but they still described the dog-eat-dog nature of the animal world of which humans were a part.

St. Just would now lay odds that Tricia Magnum was more than capable of taking revenge as it suited her.

SIXTEEN
Meet the Parents

The driver sent to transport St. Just to the home of Jason Verdoodt's parents turned out to be Detective Constable Daisy Lambert, the young woman who had responded with DCI Ampleforth to the discovery of Jason's body. It was difficult to say if being relegated to this minor task was meant as some form of punishment for botching up the crime scene, or if Ampleforth had felt a woman's touch might be needed on what was essentially a bereavement call.

She didn't say much as she drove, possibly afraid of putting another foot wrong, but once the niceties were out of the way, St. Just was not in the mood for small talk anyway. He was grateful for the chance to simply gaze out of the window, taking in the scenery as it flew past on the short drive, his mind churning through the evidence given by the witnesses he'd met so far in the case. He was aware there were many more witnesses with potentially useful information, and every officer at Ampleforth's disposal had been sent to question them, but the situation was unsatisfactory: St. Just preferred in all cases to be hands-on and to interview witnesses and suspects in person, trusting his own judgement as to their veracity. There was no substitute for a live reading of body language – the 'tell' as subtle as a too-rapid blinking of the eyes, a tenseness in the posture, an unconscious flexing of the hands. He was aware that in this instance, as there was only one of him, he was going to have to rely on the judgement of others – others whom, in almost every case, he had never even met.

He was sure Ampleforth had assembled a good team, but on every team there would be a parent concerned for a child, a young sergeant looking for love in all the wrong places, an adult with an ageing parent feeling her best could never be enough. The sort of police officer who could set these human emotions and concerns completely aside was not desirable to have on an investigation team, either.

The Verdoodts lived in Old Headington, near to the hospital where their son's body was being subjected to the mortifications of a full post-mortem examination. Presumably they had consented to the procedure. Since the death had yet to be proven to be a murder, the approval of a family member likely had been asked as a matter of form. St. Just thought that must be the most difficult thing in the world for a parent. But any parent worth the name would want to learn the truth of their child's fate, at whatever cost to themselves.

The graceful Georgian home of Gregory and Amber Verdoodt – a brick square punctuated with perfectly proportioned windows, shutters and columns, was sited in a well-tended garden clinging to the last of the summer blooms. Parked at the kerb was a van advertising 'Ralph's Landscaping', and a worker, presumably Ralph or someone in his employ, was busy turning out a flower bed in preparation for cooler weather.

St. Just lifted the brass lion's-head knocker and gave it a few soft taps. A handsome, tanned man who could only be Jason's father greeted them at the carved wooden door. He led them into a sitting room hung with colourful still-life paintings, all looking like originals from the last century and before. On the floor was a threadbare rug of great beauty, the sort of antique only the well-to-do would feel free to tread on and risk spilling food and drinks over.

Jason's biography of a life of poverty and want on the mean city streets, as had been told to the media, was not holding up. From the moment Ampleforth told him the address, and St. Just looked up the quaint village of Headington on his mobile, he'd wondered. Even without knowing the Oxford area well at first hand, it didn't seem to him to be the address of a home on a council estate. Unless Jason's parents had quite recently come into a great deal of money, the house embodied a solid middle-class prosperity.

As they were all getting settled in the large seating area, St. Just – having murmured the expected condolences, and

Constable Lambert having commented on their lovely home – asked how long they had lived there.

'Twenty-five years.' The reply came from the woman who was presumably Jason's mother, although she appeared to be a few decades younger than the father. She'd been introduced as, 'My wife, Amber.' The age difference was so vast and so apparent, St. Just thought she had to be Jason's stepmother.

Still, to judge by the swollen red eyes in her pale, handsome face, she had not had an easy time of it since learning of Jason's fate. Her hair, while expertly cut and coloured, hung lankly, held back by a plastic clip, and her face showed only smudged traces of makeup. As she sat next to her husband on the plush camelback sofa, she clung tightly to his arm, as if his strength were the only thing holding her up. The man himself was more stoic, nearly placid, but it was clear from his own wizened, moist eyes he was taking the news like a heavy blow to the heart.

'What can you tell us, Inspector? And I hope you don't think me rude, but why is the man in charge not coming to speak with us?'

'Inspector Ampleforth realized this case called for every resource at his command, as there are so many witnesses to interview. I may be a poor substitute, and I do apologize, but finding a suspect is a priority for the Oxford police, and DCI Ampleforth is needed to keep things moving forward. I hope you will understand, not a moment can be wasted, and no lead can be left unfollowed.'

'Of course, of course. I do appreciate your coming out to speak with us. What do you know?'

His wife had taken another tack, asking, 'Please may I offer you some coffee?'

St. Just had the sense she needed something to do, something practical to keep her glued together for the next few minutes, so he accepted the offer of coffee he didn't really want or need, on behalf of himself and Constable Lambert.

Once Amber had left the room, St. Just said to Gregory Verdoodt, 'I hope you don't mind, but Constable Lambert will be taking notes while we speak. Just for later clarity and verification.'

Taking her cue, Lambert fumbled around in her uniform pocket, producing a small notebook and pen. The bright yellow pen had a stylized pattern of white daisies, the sort of thing found in gift shops. It had probably been a birthday gift from a friend or relative.

If it seemed marginally inappropriate, he didn't feel he could complain. For all he knew, a suspect being interviewed would be lulled into complacency by such a cheery reminder of the constable's name.

As soon as he had the thought, he wondered – *was* he speaking with a suspect? Surely not. The man's grief looked raw, very real, and it was a complete aberration for him to think anyone would kill their own child. St. Just knew that it happened but it was still inconceivable to him. Even as a mercy killing. He wasn't yet a parent, but he knew the instinct would be to cling to hope for a miracle, beyond any reason.

Before Amber returned from her coffee mission, St. Just wanted to ask a few questions that might distress her unnecessarily.

'I'm sorry to have to ask, and please don't take offence, but I'm sure you will appreciate that time is of the essence,' he said. 'And time doesn't allow us to observe all the niceties if we are to get to the bottom of this.'

'Ask away,' said Gregory. 'Whatever it is you need.'

'Amber is not Jason's mother, am I right?'

Gregory Verdoodt met the question with a harsh, mirthless laugh. 'Amber and I have been married for ten years. My first wife died when Jason was ten years old.'

'So your marriage to Amber – your remarriage – took place when Jason was a grown man.'

'He was twenty-two.'

'I'm sure you've seen the various interviews in the print and online media. There's a discrepancy in what has become his official biography.'

'You mean the cliché of the impoverished struggling youth, spending all his time in libraries to escape the nightmare that was his home life.' This was said with irony but not a trace of bitterness, which St. Just found remarkable.

'This' – what was the word, if not 'lie'? – 'this deception didn't bother you?'

'Not too much, if I'm honest. If anything, I had to applaud Jason's marketing savvy. I suppose he learned that from me. That was my field: advertising and marketing. There was nothing remarkable about Jason's upbringing. He didn't go to private schools, and that was a deliberate choice on my part when the time came. I could have afforded Eton and all the rest. But I wanted him to be more a man of the people than a privileged white child. To know how the other half lived. The funny thing is no one has come forward to correct this image, no friend from his background, no friends from school. There is one girl – woman now – he kept in touch with, but that's all.'

That would likely be Minette, thought St. Just, but he wasn't ready to take that detour just yet.

'And why do you think that is?' St. Just suspected he knew the answer but wanted his guess confirmed.

'He didn't have any friends. It sounds terrible, put bluntly like that, but it's true. At least, not for long. Everyone was a stepping stone to the next level. People don't like being used like that. I have no illusions about my son. Does that shock you?'

'I find it refreshing, if you want to know the truth,' said St. Just. 'We will get to the bottom of this matter much more quickly if we do away with sanitized hagiographies and platitudes. You strike me as the kind of man who has limited stomach for that sort of thing.'

'You are quite right,' said Gregory. 'My son was very good looking, very attractive to women, but he didn't specialize, if you follow. I mean to say that everyone loved him, or at least, wanted to *be* him, wanted to be near him.'

'Wouldn't we all like to be that person?'

Gregory nodded absently. He seemed to have steeled himself to say what he needed to say, even though it was distasteful on every level. He wanted to be done with it.

'He also had a gift for ingratiating himself with older people – men and women. No doubt it was of tremendous value in securing him a lectureship at Oxford. I have no idea where that particular ability came from, and it's not like he had the chance to develop it much as he grew up. Both of my parents were long dead before Jason came along, and he barely knew his mother's parents before they passed, both of dementia, one quickly following the other. But he seemed to know what was *expected* of him when dealing with an older person, if I can put it that way. He would approach them with the exact level of respect and attentiveness and politeness required. They never suspected they were being condescended to. In fact, so far as I could ever tell, it was not condescension. In his own mind he had moved into a space where he understood them perfectly. I always thought it was rather a shame he didn't go into psychology – or marketing, for that matter. But his chosen field allowed him great insight into all manner of people from all cultures and I suppose you could say he found his precise niche.'

'You found all this concerning, though, didn't you?' St. Just hazarded. Because it was a strange thing – rare that a parent would be so knowing and aware, so free of blinkers when it came to his own offspring. But something in that thought and Gregory's answers led to a sudden understanding.

'Jason was perhaps . . . adopted?' He asked the question tentatively, because if he had this wrong it would be incredibly off-putting and likely to spoil the interview. But Jason's father, it seemed, had no problem with it.

'Yes. I assumed you already knew that through your investigation,' said Gregory. 'We adopted Jason from an orphanage in Ireland. As soon as he was old enough to understand, we told him he was adopted. That he'd been put up for adoption by a mother who had no money, and no way to support him, and who wanted him to have a better life. It was the truth, of course. Well, close enough. From what little we knew of the mother, Jason would have had a very limited exposure to the finer things, shall we say.'

'And Jason was fine with this news?'

'He seemed to take it very well, at least at first. But as time went on it created a distance between us, a sort of deep-seated distrust, and I often wondered if we shouldn't have waited to tell him. If we shouldn't have dressed it up a bit better than we did. His biological mother was an addict, you see. Heroin, cocaine, and whatever else was going. I think now . . . I think that part of the story we should have kept to ourselves. Perhaps we should have, you know. Prettied up the story for him, given him a better idea of himself to cling to. Not given him any ideas he may have inherited some innate tendencies or weaknesses.'

St. Just nodded, not so much to show agreement with the decision to tell all as to show his understanding of the dilemma. The story of a biological mother torn by an impossible choice had some element of Dickensian romance, he supposed, that a child would find appealing, soothing. Was it better to fill a child's head with this comforting image of her brave sacrifice, or was it better to fill his head with the sordid facts of her existence – to implant scenarios that would only grow more grotesque once they took root in a child's mind?

'But it would have meant lying,' Gregory Verdoodt was saying. 'However, we probably should have waited until he was a bit older. The truth may have been more than a six-year-old boy could absorb. I don't suppose we'll ever know now.' He paused, 'We will never know.'

'Did his mother also come to regret telling him?'

Gregory shook his head. 'She came to regret the whole thing. She loved Jason, but she had no illusions, either.'

Constable Lambert put in: 'But, in fairness, you almost had to let him know, didn't you? At least, about the adoption. It's so easy for anyone to find out these days.'

St. Just was thinking along the same lines. That in these days of DNA testing by return mail – spit in a tube and Bob's literally your uncle – it would be only a matter of time before the boy stumbled across the truth. There was also the question of any inheritable diseases that Jason would by right need or want to know about. There might be some comfort as well as fear in knowing what might lay ahead. Especially in this day and age, with so many scientific advances, it was always possible that forewarned would be forearmed.

'As you say, it's impossible to know,' said St. Just. 'But you do feel that Jason came to dwell on the possibilities, shall we say?'

'I can only tell you he went from being a normal little boy with friends to a little boy who held people at arm's length, employing various strategies to do so. It was fascinating to watch in its way. No one could get close to him after a while.'

'And you include yourself in that, do you?'

'Let's just say I was amazed when I saw how thoroughly I had been written out of his biography. He preferred the mean streets version of what he might have been, you see. I suppose that was the novelist in him, dying to get out. I didn't approve, but I understood.'

'And then I suppose when his mother died, it rather compounded things for him.'

'You mean, of course, his adoptive mother.' Amber Verdoodt had re-entered the room, carrying a tray filled with all the makings of a coffee service, complete with biscuits. Her husband rose to take the tray from her.

'I see you've told them,' she said, without rancour, resuming her seat next to her husband and preparing to pour the coffee into cups with saucers. Looking at St. Just, she said, 'Although I'm sure you've guessed that I came late to this situation.'

'It would be helpful to us to know what your relationship was with your stepson,' said St. Just.

She stole a glance at her husband before answering. 'On the surface, he was completely accepting that his father had a right to happiness. That living alone, without companionship, does no one any good.'

'On the surface?'

'Yes. It's a bit hard to describe this but I don't think he was bothered either way. It wasn't like Jason to spend a lot of time wondering how other people were doing, whether they were happy or not. I'm sorry to say this in front of you, Gregory, but I think you know what I mean.'

'I do. Perfectly. I understand perfectly,' he said.

St. Just wondered if with Jason there hadn't been a sense of a foreign element living among them. If a biological child might not have faced the barriers Jason felt were in *his* way to full acceptance. For a beloved biological child, every transgression might be forgiven, every flaw downplayed. Did he feel the rules were different for him?

While St. Just wasn't looking for ways to blame the parents for the person Jason had become – by all accounts a selfish and self-centred man – he did wonder if his home life had contributed to fashioning his personality. His father seemed a reasonable, intelligent man, but to know him thoroughly one would have to live in the same house with him.

And of course, with his first wife long dead, little could be retrieved of the person she once had been. He knew too well himself that memories faded and shape-shifted over time.

They talked a few minutes longer but there didn't seem to be much more to learn from the clearly struggling parents. St. Just asked if Jason had any hobbies and was told he didn't have much time for that sort of thing.

'He did like visiting antique shops,' Amber contributed. 'He was buying furniture for the new house, you see.'

'Did he happen to mention someone named Minette? Perhaps in connection with the new house? Was he perhaps thinking of settling down, I mean?'

'That's the friend,' said Gregory. 'Minette Miniver, from university. But my impression was that Jason's interest in Minette wasn't romantic. At least, not any longer.'

'Ah,' said St. Just.

'They dated at one time, but I never gathered it was serious. Not with Jason the way he was. I know she moved to London. I have no idea how often Jason saw her, if at all. He always had, you know, other fish to fry.'

'I think they went to the races together, once,' said Amber. 'At Newmarket.'

'Really,' said St. Just. 'He liked the occasional flutter on the horses, did he?'

She shook her head. 'He told me he didn't bet. He said betting was for losers. He just liked watching the beautiful animals, seeing their excitement just before the race. He said they were the only pure and perfect things he'd seen in his life. Much better than people, he said.'

This memory seemed finally to do in Jason's stepmother. She burst into tears and bolted from the room.

DCI St. Just and Constable Lambert, trailing apologies to Jason's father, left soon after.

Back in the car, Constable Lambert told him, 'I'm adopted, but I didn't think it was my place to offer that up just now. The thing is I've never had the least bit of interest in my biological parents.'

St. Just waited, thinking there'd be more. There was.

'I was grateful. I had the best parents in the world and needed no others. I was afraid of surprises, to be honest. What if it turned out she was a prozzie, my father unknown? But my parents never stood in the way of my learning more if I wanted.'

'I wonder,' said St. Just, 'if you'll feel the same when you have children. Do you think that will change your feeling?'

'I'll let them decide. But I won't hide my adoption from them. They've a right to know.'

St. Just, properly abashed, maintained his silence as she executed a U-turn to take them back to central Oxford.

'Where to next, sir?' she asked.

'You can drop me as close as you can to the Turf Tavern. I'll walk from there to my next interview. I'm sure you have better things to do than chauffeur me around.'

She tossed a look over her shoulder that may have been meant to convey, *I'm sure I don't*, but did not comment.

The beauty of Oxford was that everything that could be considered central Oxford was entirely walkable, so long as one kept an eye out for traffic. The layout of the city streets hadn't changed with the centuries, although a few had likely been in the path of progress and been built over. He thought he'd see if Portia might join him, as the Turf was one of the tourist spots they'd promised each other they'd visit that weekend. With their holiday plans now overturned, perhaps no one would mind his taking a break for a quick meal. He texted her and she answered straightaway.

Love to. I'm starting to hate Reginald.

SEVENTEEN
The Turf

The Turf, inevitably referred to in guidebooks as 'one of Oxford's hidden gems', was everything a children's author like Tricia Magnum might hope for in writing about a treasure hunt. Leaving breadcrumbs to find the way back out was almost a necessity.

There was little to alert the casual passer-by to the place's existence, but an historian's knowledge that the pub was bounded on one side by the original city wall offered one clue. It had started life as a gamblers' den, built just outside the city's jurisdiction, so any illicit activity could continue unregulated. A roster of the famous who had visited included Stephen Hawking and movie stars like Richard Burton and Elizabeth Taylor and, as with the Randolph, nearly everyone connected with the *Inspector Morse* shows.

St. Just found the 'secret opening' to the maze of St Helen's Passage and, at about the halfway mark, made a sharp left turn towards the pub. He looked for Portia in the several courtyards surrounding the building, each shielded with outdoor umbrellas and provided with heaters to chase away any autumn or spring chill. She wasn't outside, so he headed into the interior, which consisted of two rather cramped rooms – especially cramped for someone of St. Just's height – joined by a central bar. She was sitting in a far corner, her handbag placed opposite to save him a seat.

'Did you have any trouble finding the place?' he asked.

'I've been here before. When I was a speaker at the St Hilda's conference, several of us met here for dinner one night.'

'Right, I remember. A book critic and some authors were with you.'

'It was a fun night. They were swamped by autograph seekers.'

'I'm sure you were as well,' St. Just said loyally. Indeed, he'd been with Portia on more than one occasion when a fan approached to thank her for writing her books. Portia was always gracious and genuinely flattered, but he could also tell she was flustered. 'If I wanted attention I'd go on the stage,' she always said. 'Or become a TikTok influencer.'

'I'm nowhere near as recognizable as some crime fiction authors and I don't care to be,' she said now. 'Truly. It would be like the Princess of Wales trying to shop for tomatoes in Waitrose. I couldn't stand to be hounded all the time, with flash cameras going off in my face and people going through my rubbish bin. I want to be able to go to the shops and eat my restaurant meals in peace, ta very much.'

'When would you find time to write?'

'Precisely. Plus, I'd be too busy trying to get my videocam to work so I could post selfies to Instagram. Anyway, this place is wonderfully spooky and atmospheric at night, with an old-timey medieval vibe. Ghosts in every corner, headless women, men dragging chains. And that jagged lane you must take to get here – at night it gives you the shivers, even in a group, especially in the part that dog-legs around, where anyone could be lying in wait. Some places just carry an aura. This one certainly does.'

'I'll bet. Perhaps a setting for a book?'

'Already on it. As soon as I put Reginald in his place and keep him there. I already regret having him as a recurring character. Perhaps I should kill him off. Push him over a waterfall.'

'Good idea, except your fans would never forgive you. Besides, he's starting to grow on me.'

'And to think you didn't even know who he was when we first met.'

He smiled. 'I am abashed by my former ignorance. So, what's good on the menu?'

'A glass of chardonnay and the woodland mushroom and ale pie, for me. If you won't join me on my vegetarian journey, I think you'll like the steak and ale pie. And the choice of beer is said to be first class. You order at the bar. When you come back, I want to hear as much as you can tell me about what's going on.'

He went to place their order for food and drinks. It was early enough in the day that the pub wasn't crowded. Returning to their table and settling across from her, he said, 'I'm not sure what I'm accomplishing here. I've spoken with the master, the wine steward of the college, the housekeeper, the scout, and Tricia Magnum, mostly because she was staying at the Randolph and within easy reach.'

'I don't suppose Tricia had much to contribute?'

'Not a lot,' answered St. Just vaguely. He always had to walk a fine line between openly discussing a case with Portia and trying to be discreet until he had a better sense of where the police investigation was headed. Now he simply said, 'There seems to have been some connection there with Jason, at least on her part.'

'I'm sure you're being diplomatic,' Portia said. 'Tricia made no secret of how she felt about Jason. I often wondered how much of what she was saying was fantasy and how much fact. She claimed to have been instrumental in bringing him to the attention of Castle Publishing.'

'Really? She didn't mention that to me. Anyway, just now I was with Jason's parents – his father and stepmother. I can't say they enlightened me in terms of who might want to kill Jason. I only came away with a sense of a rather disturbed young man, blinded by ambition.'

'You mean blind to others' needs,' she said.

'Precisely.'

'The type to collect enemies in the way others might collect antiques.'

'Strange you should say that. I asked them about his hobbies and was told that in addition to horse racing he liked to visit antique shops. I didn't really notice any antiques in his rooms when I was there, apart from an old desk that probably came with the place centuries ago. Perhaps any purchases are already at the new house he bought.'

'I believe his interest in antiquities went back even further,' said Portia. 'He was an expert on Stonehenge, did you realize? It's how he made his name, being part of the team that determined Stonehenge was probably a site of burial ceremonies at one time. Stonehenge gets a brief mention in *The*

White Owl, but no more than a mention. I suppose he didn't want a lot of overlap.'

'I suppose I really must read the thing.'

'After you *download* it, certainly. But I can save you some time. There's nothing in there that strikes me as being a tell-all tale that people would want to see suppressed. It's simply fantasy and mystery wrapped in escapism. There might be a character that borrows from someone in real life. Authors do that all the time, using hair colour and so on. Nothing to pinpoint a particular person, though.'

As they were lingering over coffee, Portia said, 'Where are you off to now?'

'To Jericho, to speak with Sir Boniface Castle and whoever else in the office might be able to shed light on Jason Verdoodt and any enemies he collected. It will likely be a long conversation. I'll walk with you as far as the Randolph and drop you off there. The publishing house isn't far from the hotel.'

'Sounds good.' She began collecting her things.

'Thanks for being such a sport about this,' said St. Just. 'I realize this isn't the break you were hoping for.'

'It's working out very well. I'm getting ahead on the next novel which is always a psychological boost for me. Please don't worry. I'm quite content. Will I see you for dinner?'

'You will indeed see me for dinner at any place you name. But at some point, it'll be back across town for me to Cowley, where I hope to find Minette Miniver.'

'The girlfriend.'

'The woman who seemed to believe she was Jason's girlfriend.'

'Or wife-to-be, if rumours are true? Which they so often are. Anyway, she and Jason are said to have known each other for ages, since university.'

'So his father told me, and yes – sadly it's true that rumours can carry a germ of truth. God only knows what Jason told her. I wonder if she'll admit to whatever it was. Or even know her true status with him.'

'What makes you think she'll be in Cowley? I thought she lived in London.'

'According to the Oxford police, who've had a word with her already, she'd come up a day or two before the party. And now she's staying on a while, presumably to learn more about the case. Or to be available for questioning. It's a rare person who is that cooperative with police.'

'And Jason had no idea? That she was in town?'

'I guess not. She meant it to be a bit of a surprise – possibly that's all she meant. Her actions speak of an ambush, to my mind. She crashed the party, after all. That's what I want to question her about.

'As to what Jason knew, well. We can hardly ask him now.'

EIGHTEEN
Battle of Jericho

The building housing Castle Publishing was Victorian lady on the outside, Starship Enterprise on the inside. St. Just knew that – in any historic town – changes to the exterior of an old building would seldom be allowed, even though in Oxbridge years a Victorian building was not old.

Still, the city of Oxford would require permits and inspections and no end of interference on an exterior remodel. It was their job, and nearly everyone was grateful they took their responsibility to preserve the past seriously.

But interiors were a different thing. Castle Publishing had taken advantage of this situation by modernizing every inch of the interior, starting with the very swooshy elevator that carried St. Just to the third floor, to the plush carpets in a modern zigzag design of black and white, to the open-plan workspace intersected by cubicles.

To his mind, there was something inhumane about this stabling of workers in stalls. In his own case, he'd been lucky: He had been promoted out of cubicle status as a very young man into a corner office, from there inching his way up the detective ranks to detective chief inspector in charge of murder investigations in Cambridge. He had not had long to suffer trying to have a personal conversation or make an appointment with his doctor with the very good chance of a room full of people overhearing.

The staff of Castle Publishing, by and large, was not what he'd expected, which was a roomful of twenty-somethings displaying their mastery of hair gel products and all shouting into their phones at once. But he supposed he had in mind a noisier business like stockbrokering or journalism.

The stereotype in publishing was that very young people

from wealthy families were hired for entry-level positions and paid a pittance for their labour in exchange for being able to boast to their contemporaries that they worked in publishing. The people in the cubicles here were all in their late forties or even fifties, so far as he could see. It was certainly not germane to the case, at least he couldn't see a way that it would be, but it was remarkable. He knew he could learn from Portia if there was a philosophy behind what amounted to some bizarre form of reverse age discrimination.

He asked at the front desk for Sir Boniface, and in due course the publisher arrived to guide him into the lift and carry him to the top floor. There they threaded their way through more cubicles, every worker suddenly springing into action to show how busy they were. Once they reached the corner suite with its views over the city, Boniface closed the interior shades of his fishbowl to afford them some privacy.

Boniface offered St. Just a chair and sat down slowly behind his desk, looking as if he had lost a great deal of sleep and as if sitting and standing were painful. St. Just's own mother had tried to hide the fact that every movement was agony for her until finally she agreed to hip surgery, after which she could barely be coaxed to leave the dance floor.

Boniface looked as if ten years had been added to his handsome face. There were bags beneath his eyes that St. Just was certain had not been there at the party. In fact, at the party for his star writer, Boniface was like a man drinking from the fountain of youth – until Jason's tardiness became too noticeable to ignore and his guests showed every sign of hunger and restlessness. The hors d'oeuvres on offer had been of the unpopular if healthy vegetarian variety, like carrot fingers, but even those had quickly disappeared, and people became decidedly edgy as the clock ticked closer to the promised time for dinner. Of course, Jason had the best excuse in the world: St. Just thought it likely he would have climbed every mountain to have been there and only death itself would stop him.

'What did you think when Jason failed to appear at the party you'd organized for him?'

'I didn't know what to think, and neither did my wife.'

'And your children?'

'David and Imogen were as baffled as I was. As we were.'

'This was not typical behaviour for Jason?'

'Not at all.' Boniface shook his head decisively. 'That is not to say that Jason was meek and mild and always toed the line, but this party – even though there had been bigger parties for him in London – this party meant recognition by his college, and I gathered he was enormously proud of that.'

'Did he feel in some way that the college didn't appreciate him?'

'No, I don't mean to imply that. So far as I know, he was perfectly respected in his field; well established at a very young age, in fact. But he was probably close to the pinnacle of success in that regard. He was a lecturer, and he could look ahead to a satisfactory trajectory, a professorship and all the rest. A retirement with a decent pension, his name in the lists of the hallowed and respected, a proper tolling of the college bells when the time came. But there are a million such people in Oxford. Well, perhaps not a million, but many hundreds who pass through, who make a mark, and who are quickly forgotten by the next century. Jason's book, his novel, lifted him to a higher level, a level that the people in his department and his college could not ignore. Perhaps they had no aspirations themselves to write a novel but the fact that someone, one of their own, had done so and succeeded so completely – well, I'm sure there was some feeling attached to that.'

'Jealousy,' supplied St. Just.

'Absolutely. No question. He had his critics but the position the snipers found themselves in was to sound petty and disgruntled, and to make people even more curious to learn for themselves what all the fuss was about. In other words, he was in the enviable position where the negative reviews sold as many books as the positive ones.'

'A wonderful spot for a publisher to be in, too, I'm sure.'

He acknowledged this by smiling for the first time during the interview.

'The party for Jason was what my children would call a big effing deal for him, and nothing would have stopped him from being there.'

'That is why you were so worried,' said St. Just. It was a statement of fact. He had overheard parts of the conversation with the butler when Boniface sent the man to find out what was the matter. Aloud, St. Just said, 'I heard you talking with the butler.'

'Yes, of course I was worried. Jason was to do a reading that night and there wouldn't be time for that as things stood.'

'A reading from *The White Owl*?'

'Yes, of course.'

'Why not from his work in progress? His second book? Surely the world and his wife has read the first book by now, thanks to your discovery of Jason and his immense talent.' This was not strictly true, as St. Just himself had not read the book, but hoped flattery might go down well with Boniface.

'Authors hate that, is why. I've never known one who would agree to reading a work in progress. They say it scares off the muse or puts a curse on the process or some rot like that. Handling authors is rather like dealing with toddlers. To an extent you must play along. Imogen can tell you more about that.'

'I look forward to talking with her. Also, I will need to speak to your son if he's here.'

This request clearly made Boniface uncomfortable. He took a sudden interest in straightening the pen on his desk, but finally he said, 'Yes, he's here. I'll see if he's available.'

'Oh, good. Please do. I'd much rather have a word with him here than down at the station.'

This had the hoped-for effect.

'I'll make sure he's available,' said Boniface.

'Anyway, what did Jason say when you asked him about it?'

'About what?'

Had St. Just been married to Boniface, he might have recognized the stalling technique so familiar to Lady Ursula.

'About the reading.' St. Just decided to play along, finding it interesting that Boniface would stall on such an innocuous topic. 'When you asked Jason to read from his work in progress.'

'I didn't ask him,' came the reply. 'I knew better. The answer would be no. Anyway, Jason had a set piece that he read on these occasions, from the beginning of the third chapter. He nearly had it off by heart, and people always enjoy watching an author reading the actual words they have written. Don't ask me why. Personally, I find it stunningly boring listening to writers reading their works aloud. Most of them are rubbish at it, as well as bad at public speaking.' He laughed briefly. 'Please don't tell that to any of my authors.'

'No worries,' said St. Just. 'I suppose they became writers so they wouldn't have to speak in public.'

'Yes, and the joke's on them. It's a standard part of promoting books these days and none of them can get out of it, although they do try.'

'Was Jason good at public speaking? At reading aloud from his works?'

'He was quite good at it. Of course, he was a lecturer at Oxford. He had years of experience behind him in this sort of thing. It was no great leap for him to go from talking about non-fiction in front of a crowd at an academic conference, say, to talking about fiction at a book fair.'

'I'll need to speak to your wife and daughter.'

'I'm afraid that won't be possible right now. Lady Ursula is indisposed, and my daughter won't leave her side.'

How very melodramatic. Victorian, even. He pictured Lady Ursula having to be revived with smelling salts. But St. Just was losing patience with the slow progress he was making. They'd never solve the case if the police had to inch along, interviewing over fifty suspects, some of whom seemed to be going out of their way to make themselves unavailable. Thames Valley Police had brought in uniforms from St Aldgate's station to help interview the witnesses, but even so, someone had to compile those statements and look for inconsistencies in time-lines and alibis. It was a massive undertaking and as usual the police were understaffed.

'Very well,' said St. Just. 'I will appear at your home this evening. This is not a suggestion, sir. If I must, I will compel you. I will be there at seven o'clock. I'm afraid there is no other time and the police need to speak with all the persons of interest concerned in this case.'

'My wife is hardly a person of interest. She was a guest at the party herself and knows no more than any other guest.'

'I understood the guest list was entirely in her charge. She was in fact the hostess for the event. The master of the college might know academic publishing, but Jason had moved into an entirely different field. Your wife's role is crucial in this and I need to speak to her without further delay. Tonight.'

Boniface was clearly not the type of man to follow orders. He was the man who *gave* orders. But in the face of St. Just's insistence, he nodded curtly and said, 'Very well. If there's nothing else, I must ask you to leave now.'

St. Just nearly laughed. He must be joking. Either he'd had dealings with the police that made him believe they could be manipulated, or he'd had no dealings at all and was naïve in the extreme. Either way, his view of the situation was cock-eyed.

St. Just said, 'We are just getting started, Sir Boniface. I need to know everything you know about this party. About Jason Verdoodt. About those most likely to want to harm him. Those least likely to want to harm him, for that matter. About this book of his and how much input you had into it. I need to know basically the entire contents of your brain, sir, when it comes to your star author – oh, and that includes your own personal relationship with him. We are nowhere near finished today and we won't be finished until this case is resolved. I'm more than happy to turn up here again tomorrow and the next day if—'

Perhaps Boniface's imagination began running wild, and the idea of his place of business being stormed by police, the doors battered down as in some television drama, was enough to bring him into line.

'All right, all right. I hardly know where to start. As to personal relationship? Let's start there. Jason and I met over drinks a few times at local pubs and restaurants, but it was never an editorial discussion. I don't have that sort of discussion with authors, anyway – we have a team of experts to deal with the misplaced commas, with poor grammar, and with the plot holes that need backfilling. The book he turned in was letter perfect. I asked him if he'd hired a freelance editor to go over it and he became annoyed by the implication he needed help. There was no need for me to comment other than to praise – for me to try to influence or change it or him in any way.'

'So, what did you talk about?' St. Just settled back in his chair, as if to say they had all the time in the world, and he was simply there to listen closely and to guide. It was the only way to get Boniface to see this conversation as less an onerous public duty than a means to help Castle Publishing weather this storm. The cost of Jason's loss would be immense, and many of the questions St. Just held in store had to do with that loss. With how Castle Publishing would cope financially with no new book from their star author on the horizon.

But for now, St. Just was content to hear more about 'social Jason'. What was the man like, away from college, away from his students and colleagues? What was he like manoeuvring through this blossoming new world of his – this world of fame and fortune?

'To be honest I found him to be an enigma,' said Boniface. 'A rather frustrating one.'

'Could you elaborate on that?'

'Not really. He was difficult to get to know, that's all. We generally met at the "Bird and Baby" – The Eagle and Child, that is. You know the place?'

'Of course. The famous pub on St Giles where the Inklings met – C.S. Lewis and J.R.R. Tolkien and that lot. I understand it's closed for renovations – hopefully that's a temporary situation.'

'Yes, indeed, I fervently hope so. There are few places that have that cachet, almost as if the universe had conspired to make it a literary shrine, to be visited by pilgrims hoping to absorb some of the genius that emanated from the spot.'

'So you chose the place of meeting?'

'As I recall, that was Jason's idea – I really don't remember as I never thought the police would be asking about it. But I'm sure he liked the thought of his own name one day being added to the list of famous names associated with the historic old pub.'

It seemed a minor enough vanity to St. Just. Certainly the man had earned the right to be proud of his fame.

'And what did you talk about?'

'Again, if I'd known this would matter, I would have noted it in my diary that evening – if I kept a diary. It was along the lines of a getting-to-know-you meeting, at first, and became more business-focused as time passed. Jason told me about his background – a background which was difficult, to say the least. He had much to overcome with parents who were not inclined to encourage literary endeavours.'

Oh really.

Boniface continued, 'He apparently had trouble at one point in his life getting together enough money to buy writing materials.'

Surely that was a tale too far, thought St. Just. What did a pad of paper cost – a pound? A pencil – fifty pence? He'd heard similar stories told by fans of other authors and decided for now to let Boniface dwell in ignorance on Jason's actual background, except to say mildly, 'That may have been a bit of an exaggeration on Jason's part.'

'Well, he was a writer, wasn't he? I suppose being a bit of a fantasist goes with the territory. Anyway, personally, I found him to be charming and engaging. He wanted me to like him, and I got the impression he was going out of his way to become a favourite of mine. We had him over for dinner one night, and I was able to observe him working the same magic on my wife.'

'You found his behaviour to be, shall we say, artificial? Like a cloak he'd put on to impress?'

'I'm not naïve, Inspector. I have been managing and supervising men and women almost since my teen years and I know that Jason was ambitious. I never saw it as a problem. Quite the opposite. He wanted very much to succeed, to cultivate the bookshops and their owners, to cultivate the reviewers, to cultivate other authors who might write him an endorsement, to make sure his book, which was already guaranteed a good response, would become something unforgettable to the reading public.'

'As you know, my fiancée is an author,' began St. Just.

'And a jolly good one, too!'

'Yes, thank you. I think so. And from her I never got the impression there was a guaranteed bestseller. That there was no such thing, in other words. That luck played a huge part in this business.'

'She's quite right about that. I may have overstated the case. But in all my years as both a reader and a publisher, I've not seen a book catch fire in the public's imagination like this one did. And it didn't happen by accident. It happened because all the stars aligned. And because Jason made sure they did.'

'How long have you been a publisher?' St. Just knew the answer from the background emailed to him by Ampleforth's people, but wanted to hear for himself how Boniface would characterize his own career. It must have been a leap from wallpaper manufacturing to book publishing. Possibly a leap too far for a man inexperienced in the ways of book sales.

'It's been just over three years.'

'And the company is in good shape financially, is it?'

'It is now. All thanks to Jason, if I'm honest. I mean, we were turning a corner but Jason put us light years ahead. It will be a very long time before we'll have to worry about keeping the lights on at Castle Publishing.'

'But what about his next book? Now that there will be no next book?'

'It hardly matters. We had taken out life insurance on him once we realized the treasure we had on our hands.'

'With his consent?'

'Of course, with his consent. It is very common practice with an extremely famous author. We can't have the whole business hinge on the survival of one man or woman. What if he were to be run over by a lorry?' Realizing what he'd said, Boniface looked abashed. 'I mean, that is to say . . .'

'Or what if he'd been murdered?' said St. Just. 'Quite the dilemma; I do see that.'

'That's certain, is it? That it was murder? But yes, if he fell ill, even if he missed a deadline due to illness, we had to be covered. Books are in the pipeline a very long time. Anything could happen to derail the process. And losing a key author – disaster. The others are all replaceable,' he added dismissively. 'Jason was different.'

This was all news to St. Just, that any author could be insured like that. He supposed it was the same as in the movie industry: a big star playing a major role could not simply be replaced without a huge loss of time and money, of film footage that was already in the can.

It certainly put a new complexion on the situation with Jason. Live or die, the publishing house would survive.

But what if he went to another publisher?

That would be a different story entirely.

NINETEEN
David

H e and Sir Boniface spoke for another few minutes but St. Just came away from the conversation little the wiser. He had entered Sir Boniface's office thinking the man might have a motive, however far-fetched, but he left thinking he had none. Finishing off his star author before he could write his next book made no sense at all for Boniface to do.

If for some reason he'd decided to kill his cash cow, the reason would have to be personal. Compellingly so. Given Jason's reputation as a Lothario, and given his daughter Imogen's reported fascination with Jason, perhaps the honour of the family had been at stake. Jason had played fast and loose with the wrong woman, a woman to whom he owned a lot, probably, insofar as Imogen had helped his book sales take off.

Boniface reluctantly called his son from his office phone to tell him the police were here and wanted a word. St. Just could hear David squawking a protest at the other end. 'I don't gather it's optional, David. Detective Chief Inspector St. Just will be there in a minute. Be ready for him.'

St. Just wondered what 'being ready for him' might consist of. Was David even now combing his hair, or closing a browser left open to some dodgy website, or shredding papers? Boniface led the way to the corner office opposite his own, showed the detective in and closed the door carefully behind. The members of the editorial staff in their cubicles had watched their passage closely, pausing in their work to see what was up. Somehow, St. Just was easily recognizable as a policeman, as if he carried a flag proclaiming his status.

Now he settled into a futuristic chair across from David Castle. It seemed David was a bit futurist in all things, to judge by the photos and action figures ranged across the credenza behind him and the movie posters hanging on every wall. Perhaps he'd been put in charge of décor for the entire office. It was the sort of display a teenage boy might have in his room, just bordering on inappropriate for a man of David's age and position. However, St. Just was willing to acknowledge that he himself was completely out of step with anything that could remotely be called current popular culture, and he suspected that David's preoccupations were very much in step with the zeitgeist.

St. Just took a moment to size up the man before him. His skin was unnaturally pale, suggesting long hours indoors in front of a computer, and he was fashionably thin, almost to the point of emaciation. As David folded his bony hands atop his desk, St. Just could not help noticing his fingers were abnormally long; his nails, which appeared to have been professionally manicured, were large and spade-shaped, covering the entire tips of the fingers.

In contrast with his father, David appeared eager to talk – eager and willing.

'This business has to be resolved,' he said. 'No matter where the clues may lead.'

'We are still determining whether this was foul play but increasingly there seems little question it was. Where do you think the clues may lead? Or, to whom?'

Clearly David had not been expecting this kind of open-ended, collaborative sort of question, let alone this level of interest in anything he might have to say. It was a fleeting impression but St. Just gathered very few people paid David any mind. Having just spoken with his father, St. Just could imagine David as a young boy being consumed by that over-whelming personality, that rather toxic masculinity that was not about feeling but about fear. The fear being that the son might turn out to be something different from the father.

It made one wonder exactly what the ideal child was meant to look like to an ambitious father like Sir Boniface. Perhaps someone tall and brave and strong, but also someone who would never leave the father's side.

Was David's choice to join his father's business voluntary? Or had David had other dreams? St. Just supposed it had nothing to do with the investigation, but it was the sort of question that plagued him in recent days. As he and Portia edged ever closer to being parents one day soon, St. Just was predictably dogged by questions of what kind of father he would be and what kind of father he wanted to be. His own father had been of the 'leave him to get on with it' school of child-rearing, and St. Just felt that – as a result – he had grown into a completely self-reliant adult.

The only thing that had ever thrown him for a loop had been his time of being a widower. He had got through it somehow, simply by believing he must. That there was no other choice. Most of all he got through it by burying himself in work. In retrospect, Portia's arrival in his life had been like walking into a lighted room after an eternity in darkness.

David had been speaking as this was going through his mind – he'd been listening but only with one ear. St. Just gave himself a mental shake, returning his attention to the moment.

'Do they really think it could be anything but murder?' David asked.

'What an interesting comment,' said St. Just. 'You almost make it sound as if Jason had a price on his head.'

'Only in a manner of speaking. I suppose my father has told you about the insurance policy? That's quite rare, you know. But there are insurers like Lloyds who will insure absolutely anything and we found a group that drew up a plan that was a masterpiece of a safety net for the company. We never did anything like that for any other author, and I'm sure we never will again.'

'How much money are we talking about?'

'Twenty million pounds of insurance payout.'

'How extraordinary. I would have thought the premiums would be so astronomic as to make it not worth the while.'

David shrugged. 'What can I tell you? My mother is very wealthy. I should say her family is very wealthy. Once having put her shoulder behind the business, so to speak, it simply could not be allowed to fail. Too much was riding on the success of Jason's book. The fact was while we get manuscripts in every day, almost none of them are publishable, let alone guaranteed bestsellers like *The White Owl*.'

'I was just speaking with your father about these guarantees. He said something to the effect that no matter how much a book might tick all the boxes, whether it coincided with what the public happened to want at that moment was anyone's guess.'

'Well, yes, that is true, also.'

'But are you saying you feel the motive for doing away with Jason was financial?'

'Definitely,' said David. 'To be perfectly frank, he was difficult and demanding, and I think I can speak for everyone when I say it will be a relief not to have to deal with him further.'

St. Just was astonished by this proclamation, leading as it did straight to the door of Castle Publishing. On further reflection he realized it was perhaps not so astonishing if the son were trying to overthrow the father in some elaborate takeover plot. Get rid of Jason, get the insurance money, perhaps cash out with whatever parachute deal he might be eligible for. It was all a bit in the realm of conspiracy theory, but one never knew.

There was however another possibility, and he led the conversation round to that.

'I understand your sister was quite taken with Jason.'

'Who told you that?' David went immediately to the defensive, unable to hide his alarm at the turn the conversation was taking. While St. Just could only applaud his loyalty to his sister, it was necessary to explore all avenues before resorting to far-fetched theories around life insurance policies.

'I don't suppose Jason was anyone's idea of an ideal future brother-in-law,' he said mildly.

'It had never reached the stage of brother-in-law status. And I'll be honest with you, I don't think it ever would have reached that stage, had he lived. Jason's interest in my sister was merely practical and I am sure would have been short-lived. Had he lived.'

They were once again in the territory of family honour. The prospect of his own sister being dumped by the man on whom so much hope and money had been lavished had to rankle.

But was it enough to provoke David into murder? Or her? Still, St. Just decided to ask the standard questions as to alibi and whereabouts.

'At what time did you arrive at the party?'

'I told this to some bloke from the police already.'

'Now tell me.'

'I arrived with my sister and my parents. We were all together. We got there just as the party was starting – was due to start, I mean. Which would be seven, nearly on the dot. We were all together rather constantly that night, I would say.'

'I see. So you can alibi each other.'

'If you must use that word but it is not appropriate. It would be as true to say everyone in that room provided an alibi for the next person. It was a small room. There were people everywhere.'

Which was part of the trouble the police were having, as St. Just was aware. The room was small, slightly *too* small to accommodate such a crowd. It would never have passed pandemic standards. But that meant anyone trapped behind a tall person or a large person or a bookcase could not really say who was standing across the room from them. To the police's frustration, this had already proved to be the case more than once in the investigation.

'Again, you are saying each member of your family can provide an alibi for the other.'

'I wish you would stop using that word but yes, we were all together – not really mingling because mingling wasn't easy in that crowd. A few people came up to us and spoke. That children's author – I suppose I shouldn't say this, but I find her rather alarming. She stood for a long time talking to my father and mother, trying to ingratiate herself. Her sales are really not what they used to be, you see. The only thing keeping her afloat is her first book, which spawned an industry, but frankly she's just phoning in rubbish at this point. Maybe small children don't notice – who can say? Anyway, people like that came up to talk – a couple of other authors, the master of the college, various support-reading people like Lord Whatshisname and his lady wife. The event was couched as a fundraiser, you see. At one point my father went to speak with the butler, I do remember that. He was getting agitated over the delay.'

'It does sound as if you can be accounted for, for the most part, since you observed so much. But I'm sure you can appreciate, sir, that a family providing alibis for other family members . . . this is not too compelling.'

'I'm terribly sorry about that but that's what we've got. Now, if there's nothing else?'

'Just one more question,' St. Just said smoothly. 'I know you're busy. I wonder what your personal relationship with Jason Verdoodt was like? I understand you discovered him. That must have created a tight bond.'

His eyes shifted away, landing on a *Star Wars* poster decorating a corner of the office nearest the door. At last, David said, 'You would think so, wouldn't you?'

'Would you care to elaborate?'

'I may as well. The man saw himself as God's gift to women and to literature. Gratitude was not really in his vocabulary. I have absolutely no doubt he would go elsewhere for an advance of even five shillings more. There was no loyalty in that man. Castle is a small publisher but we threw everything we had into his book, into making it the rousing success it became, but he had his eyes on a big American publisher, you can count on it. Because their distribution and resources, to be honest, still exceed our reach.'

'Did his treatment of your sister make you angry?'

'That is two questions. But yes, it made me angry. Imogen can fight her own battles, and sometimes she gets on my last nerve, but seeing Jason play with her made me dislike him a great deal more than I already did. Before you ask, however, I never considered harming him. I was betting he'd be gone soon enough.'

They chatted a while longer about the perfidy of ungrateful authors, but David seemed to have little more to add, and St. Just didn't have enough information yet to ask him questions that might get him further in the investigation. Finally he looked at his watch – it was getting on to late afternoon, and he was hoping to catch Portia and arrange dinner with her.

'I'll find my own way out,' he said. 'Thank you for your time.'

He closed the door behind him, leaving David shuffling papers in what looked like a frantic attempt to distract himself. His mind clearly was elsewhere, and St. Just would bet it was on Imogen. Was David trying to protect his sister? He didn't seem to realize he himself was at risk, for Jason's leaving, despite what David had said, would be a disaster. How far would David go to save the company he surely was set to inherit one day?

As St. Just was leaving, he was met by a young woman who – first looking over her shoulder to make sure she was unobserved – sidled up to him and handed him a business card.

On the back were the words, *Meet me at Freud's, 119 Walton Street. I have something to tell you.*

TWENTY

Gita

S t. Just gathered from the young woman's furtive manner this was meant to be a private meeting. He quietly slipped away from the crenellated premises of Castle Publishing and made his way, with the help of a map app, to the nearby café-bar in Jericho.

Once outside the building, he looked more closely at the card the young woman had thrust into his hand, never meeting his eyes before returning to her cubicle just outside David's office. The card identified her as Gita Patel, assistant to the editorial director at Castle Publishing, which would be David Castle.

The café-bar turned out to be housed in a deconsecrated church, St Paul's, opposite Oxford University Press. They had just opened the doors for the late afternoon crowd and the place was filling up quickly. The bartender was busy setting up, creating a clatter of glasses and silverware.

As St. Just waited for Gita, he browsed the history of the place on the back of the menu, where he learned the Greek Revival building, labelled 'FREVD' in Roman-style lettering above the portico entrance, had been erected in response to a cholera epidemic in 1831.

St. Just had asked for the table against the wall and furthest from the door, a spot that seemed to offer the best privacy. As he sat beneath intersecting strings of fairy lights, he wished fleetingly for a potted palm to hide behind. It was evident that whatever Gita had to say to the police might be putting her job at risk. He wondered that she hadn't chosen a place further from the offices of Castle Publishing, but he supposed she couldn't vanish from her job for any length of time without drawing attention to her absence.

Within ten minutes she appeared at the main entrance, still

looking over her shoulder for anyone on her trail. St. Just was beginning to believe the culture of the publishing house must be rather toxic if its workers could not simply announce they were taking a coffee or tea break.

She spotted him immediately – with his height and broad shoulders he was always easy to find in a crowd. He stood to greet her, holding out his hand, but her anxiety level seemed to rise as she allowed her small hand to be enveloped in his. It was clear she didn't want to be seen fraternizing too openly with the enemy.

Resuming his seat, he pointed her to a chair opposite, asking if she wanted coffee or tea. She accepted the offer of coffee gratefully and St. Just signalled one of the waiters.

As they waited, she introduced herself. 'As you can see from my card, my name is Gita Patel and I work directly for David Castle as his assistant.'

'I would imagine you have quite a bit of responsibility,' he said conversationally.

'You have no idea,' she said. She wore her hair combed back from a heart-shaped face and woven into a glossy bun at the nape of her neck; she now smoothed back the sides in case any strands had escaped in her rush to meet him. She had enormous brown eyes fringed with long black lashes, and everything about her manner exuded a grave intelligence. St. Just would not be surprised to hear that, despite her age, she was a key player in the firm.

Now she added 'I've been there from the beginning. My family is exceedingly proud of my job, knowing how big the competition was when Castle Publishing first began announcing openings.'

'What are your qualifications?'

'A double first in English lit and languages. And I was willing to work for very little money. But they surprised me in that. Editorial jobs are notoriously low paid. Castle was determined to break that mould and get the best. I wasn't about to tell them I would have worked for a fraction of the salary they offered, and it's not as if I don't earn every penny twice over, but I could never find a job to match what they've given me over the years. It makes it difficult, you see.'

St. Just waited. She was getting to it at last and wouldn't need much nudging.

'But there have been things that made me wonder . . .'

She seemed prepared to stop at that and bolt for the door. St. Just thought a bit of gentle prodding might be in order.

'Did these things have anything to do with David Castle?'

'In a way, yes. He's my boss, but I am in fact more and more responsible for his position, especially when he's on holiday. Which he is, more and more. The entire thing falls to me. You see what I mean. I am paid well but I also earn the salary.'

'Yes, and?'

'It was when Sir Boniface was on holiday that the manuscript of *The White Owl* came in. David takes credit now, but I was the one who spotted it. David threw it in his rubbish bin. Can you imagine? I don't think he did more than glance at it. Honestly, if something isn't a *Game of Thrones* rip-off, David simply isn't interested.'

Clearly David having seized credit still rankled, and who could blame her?

'Anyway. You understand, we have many thousands of manuscripts come in each year and a small staff. We also have a policy, instituted by Sir Boniface himself, that submissions must be typescripts – meaning no computer files. Everything must be printed out on paper and mailed in, rather than submitted by email or using an online submission form like anyone else in the twenty-first century would insist on doing. It's a wonder Sir Boniface didn't demand everyone use a quill and parchment – he is sort of stuck into this idea that the *real* heyday of the novel was in the time of the Brontës and Dickens and everything since then has gone downhill. So anyway, one day Jason Verdoodt's manuscript arrives in the mail and later I found it in David's rubbish bin.'

'You found it? How very lucky.'

She looked abashed, but said, 'I do it all the time. David really has the worst taste in the world and should never have been trusted with these decisions while the cat – Sir Boniface – was away. If it wasn't science fiction or fantasy, David wasn't interested. I read the first ten pages, thinking yes, this is good.

This is very good indeed. I read ten more then I put it aside to take home. I was so taken with the story I immediately wanted to clear my calendar of anything that might interfere with my reading. So – and I'm sorry to admit this – every other manuscript that came in that day got very short shrift. Even more so than normal. Everyone that day got the standard rejection slip. "Not for us", kind of thing.'

Momentarily she hung her head, then looking up at him, said, 'I still feel bad about that. It's a brutal business for writers struggling to get a toehold. But I called in sick the next day so I could finish reading Jason's submission – it was that good.'

St. Just could see why she felt that way, but he was wondering what this had to do with the death of Jason. He could only see that David might have found his position in jeopardy should Sir Boniface come to hear of this manuscript retrieved from the trash, thrown there by his own son. And he didn't think Gita would have told him.

'Was this the first time you had to resort to this subterfuge? In other words, were there other manuscripts David didn't bother to read but that you rescued?'

'There were one or two. But nothing that was going to make or break the company. Of course, with the right marketing one can make a silk purse out of a sow's ear. But with Jason the potential was immediate and obvious. Oh, I forgot to mention he enclosed an author photo with the manuscript.' At that she smiled. A tentative but charming smile that let him know how ridiculous this was.

'I gather that's not usual?'

'It rather depends on what the author looks like, but it was somewhat unusual. What they tend to do is send their manuscripts in with a box of gourmet biscuits, or hard-to-get tickets to a show, or a stuffed animal, or some other kind of bribe – anything to make their submission stand out. One time the author left the manuscript down in the lobby with balloons attached to it. Sometimes the bribery is tempting; more often it's absurd.'

'And it doesn't help?'

'Honestly, it sends up alarms. Balloons one day, an

incendiary device the next if the manuscript is declined? But even in dealing with slightly unprofessional behaviour, one must be professional and weigh each manuscript on its own merits.'

'And David tossed Jason's manuscript in the rubbish, photograph included.'

'Yes. Considering what Jason looked like – and he was drop-dead gorgeous; sorry, bad taste, I mean he was gorgeous – one would think David would have given the manuscript a quick read, a quick once-over.' She lowered her eyes.

But St. Just was wondering if that was exactly the problem. David was expensively dressed in the way most wealthy men are well dressed, and he had the sleek, polished look of a well-fed politician, but he was never going to stop traffic with his good looks. Jason was the opposite.

Could there have been a soupçon of jealousy behind David's action? Was it the photo that turned David off, some sort of instinctive revulsion – perhaps a need to even the score against a good-looking playground bully of the past?

She continued, 'I stay out of the marketing side of things; it doesn't interest me and it's Imogen's area, besides. And one does not want to cross Imogen. But it became more apparent to me, the more I read the manuscript, that the movie tie-in was there, possibly a long-running series with that whole lucrative sideline of merchandising, too.'

'I don't follow,' said St. Just. 'Merchandising?'

'That's where the real money is made now. When you look at the Harry Potter franchise, that's the business model all publishers want to follow. All the costumes and wizards' hats and video games and puzzles – all the spin-off merchandise. I don't get it myself; I just know if the author can tell a "ripping yarn", as they say. But certainly, I grew up with Harry Potter and I understand the appeal. I have younger brothers who are complete nutters on the subject, and quarrel over whatever Hermione does as if she's real.'

'And *The White Owl* had all of this spinoff potential?' St. Just was beginning to understand why the insurance policy on Jason had been so large.

'Oh, certainly. Yes, indeed, in my opinion. Again, I leave

that to Imogen, but it required no great imagination to see the possibilities.'

'And from descriptions I've read, it had elements of *The Da Vinci Code* and *Raiders of the Lost Ark* and "quest" stories like that. It was rather a treasure hunt of a book.' How odd that David didn't see the potential – assuming he read any of it. Then again, his interests were clearly more towards science fiction.

Could David's envy of the author have goaded him to try to stall his career before it got started? Did he simply not see what others could plainly see? Did he, for whatever obscure motive, want to make sure the company failed?

Or had being in charge in his father's stead simply gone to his head?

He tried out these theories on Gita, but she simply shook her head at all but his last suggestion.

'If you're asking me, I would say that yes, being in charge went to his head. David is rather a sad creature, I've always thought, hidden in his father's shadow most of the time. My own father is much the same – he rules the roost, or at least we let him think so most of the time – so there are times I can sympathize. I don't think David could think much beyond the excitement of running the company in Sir Boniface's absence.'

'That does not bode well for the company if Sir Boniface ever stood down or was forced to resign due to ill-health. He's not a young man anymore.'

Again, she shrugged: *Not my problem.* 'I will be long gone by then. I've applied for an editorial position in London. And if they accept me, I will certainly be on the first train out – I can never advance far at Castle Publishing, not with the family in charge. The glass ceiling at Castle is that I'm not a blood relation. The pay at what I hope will be my new job doesn't match what Castle pays me, and the cost of living in London is almost as obscenely high as it is here in Oxford, but with Jason gone . . . The company was exciting to prospective employees, you know. Now it's a dead end.' Realizing what she had just said, she hastily added, 'Sorry. You do know what I mean. There's just no way I can advance there and I need the challenge.'

'Completely understandable,' said St. Just. 'But was this what you wanted to talk to me about so urgently?'

'Um. Not entirely.'

What she told him next turned the case in an entirely new direction.

TWENTY-ONE
Gita Tells All

Having said so much to indicate she knew where the Castle Publishing bodies were buried, Gita now hesitated, taking a sudden interest in the restaurant's stained-glass windows. They were interrupted at that moment by a waiter arriving with their order and St. Just was afraid he'd lose her. She was so clearly regretting the impulse that had made her put the note in his hand, suggesting she had valuable information to share with the police. St. Just hoped this wouldn't prove to be a waste of his time by an impressionable young woman with a wild imagination.

'You see, it's just that, Jason invited me into his rooms at the college.'

St. Just braced himself for a story as old as time. Knowing Gita was in a position to help him succeed with his manuscript, Jason had set out to seduce her or at least win her to his side.

He hazarded a guess. 'This was before he submitted his manuscript?'

'No, no.' She shook her head firmly. 'Sir Boniface had bought the manuscript. The contract was signed. Editing suggestions had been submitted to Jason, but he'd rejected most of them, if not all. He knew what he had, you see; he knew his worth. Most authors at bedrock have no belief in themselves, a tendency publishers try to exploit, but Jason's confidence was *total*. The cover had been chosen – you've seen it? Really a gorgeous job; we paid a lot for the original artwork, and normally we cut corners there. The printing plates were set up, the presses were running, and copies were flowing off the conveyor on their way to the shops. It was "a done deal".'

'I see.'

He waited as she took a deep breath. When it didn't seem she would continue, he said, 'I hope you'll forgive my saying so, but you're an attractive young woman and Jason was known for taking an interest in attractive young women. If the book was as far out of the pipeline as you indicate, what was his interest, do you think?'

She laughed, for the first time relaxing into the interview. 'No, no,' she said again. 'It was nothing like that. He had Imogen for that. She oversaw the marketing for the book, besides. I had done my small part and there was nothing further to be got out of me on that score. The endorsements were flying in, so I didn't even have to go cap in hand to other authors and their editors to ask them for a marketing blurb.'

'Jason didn't show a, shall we say, a personal interest in you?'

'No. In some ways, you have it the wrong way round, Inspector. I have a suitable boyfriend, a husband-to-be, in fact, and my father would have wrung the neck of anyone he thought might interfere with my plans to marry. And my mother would help him to do it.'

'I see. So . . .'

'The visit to see Jason was my idea. I invited myself. That is to say, I was there to drop off a carton of author copies in person. I was on my way home, so it was no big deal to carry the box from my car into the college. And Jason was a perfect gentleman. Offered me coffee, offered me wine. I never felt compromised or that I might be. He was a perfect gentleman.'

'All right. So then . . .' So St. Just's working theory, that Jason had assaulted her in some way and that like most victims of assault she was embarrassed to talk about it, as if she were somehow to blame, flew out of the window.

'Besides, Jason Verdoodt simply was not my type. Too old for me, for one thing.'

'And for another?'

She lifted her head and looked directly at him for the first time. 'It was clear to me early on what kind of man he was. Dishonest to his core. And I don't just say that now that I know so much more about him. He just gave me a bad feeling. Just a feeling, you know, and I acted on it by making it clear to him – without really having to say anything; body language can work wonders – that if he should try anything he would be wasting his time. Or worse. That I might scream bloody murder. Sorry! The English language is full of mine-fields like that. That I might scream the place down. But I suppose thinking of him having been murdered, it weighs heavily on me.'

This was refreshing to hear, thought St. Just. Finally, a woman who had not almost immediately succumbed to Jason's famous charms. He didn't think it was because the women who had been pulled into Jason's orbit were unintelligent, but human beings were a needy lot, some more so than others, and like any good predator, Jason seemed to have known how to spot the needy ones. St. Just could only applaud Gita's savvy in clocking him and being able to resist the temptation to align herself with a rising star like Jason. This young woman impressed him as someone who had been born with a solid bedrock of common sense reinforced by her upbringing.

He had dealt with many victims in his day. The true victim, abducted or attacked out of the blue, perhaps in their own home, was of course blameless. But there was another sort of victim who ignored all the warning signs and blamed them-selves when they really should not. Either lack of money, or fear, or concern for others in their care would too often keep women, especially, trapped in situations that turned out to be deadly.

It was easy for people looking in from the outside to wonder why these victims had either missed the warning signs or, having seen them, thought they could cope, adapt and over-come. But sometimes leaving everything behind was the only answer.

'That story about his tragic upbringing was nonsense, for a start,' she said, 'but overseeing his biography wasn't my job. I left all that to Imogen, as I've said. And besides, by the time I realized, there was no putting the toothpaste back in the tube, as the Americans say.'

'How did you find out about that?'

'Ah. So the police figured it out. I thought you might.'

'But how did you?'

'I was curious,' she said. 'Something happened that made me curious. I once needed to reach him and I called St Rumwold's and asked to be connected to his rooms. They have a very old-fashioned set-up there. Normally I spoke with him on his mobile but I wasn't able to reach him that way on this occasion – he may have had his mobile turned off. So they plugged me through from the porter's lodge or whatever it is they do, there's some kind of old-fashioned switchboard – can you believe it? Anyway, when there was no answer, the porter came on the line and said he thought Dr Verdoodt was out visiting his parents and would I like the address.'

'I'm surprised he would give you that information.'

'Are you? I suppose it wasn't strictly in line with procedure, but when I told him I was from Jason's publisher he seemed to have no problem with it. I forget the man's name now but he was very helpful. Anyway, he gave me the address and I was amazed. Because I was expecting him to give me some south-of-the-Thames dodgy address. Something in a postal code that would indicate people with few resources or, at best, a neighbourhood on the cusp. I know London well; my family lived there for years. But he gave me an address in Headington. Now I happen to know that area quite well. When my mother was in hospital, I visited her nearly every day. And sometimes I couldn't park where I wanted to so I got to know the area, finding spots I could leave the car for several hours if I needed to. Anyway, I knew exactly where Jason lived and, unless his father had got very lucky betting on horses, there was no way Jason came from the kind of background he had claimed.'

'So what did you do with this information – I mean, what did you do with your suspicions he might not be telling the truth? Did you tell Imogen or anyone else at Castle Publishing?'

She shook her head. 'I couldn't see the point, and when you think about it there was little point in my blowing his cover story. Probably he was not the first author to embellish his background into something more interesting than a dull life in a two-up two-down with a father who drove a lorry and a mother who took in laundry. Although I think that's an interesting background for a writer, myself. That sort of native-genius tale. But did I blow Jason's cover? No, I did not, and that may have been the moment, I realize now, that I was setting myself up to keep even more of his secrets.'

Oh, really? 'And what secrets would those be?'

Again, she dropped her eyes. He had time to admire the expert application of coal-black eyeliner, which to him seemed coals to Newcastle – her eyes, like Portia's, were mesmerizing without any cosmetic enhancement. 'I need to tell this story in my way, because it is difficult. All right? It is so very difficult for me. I am in a terrible position, but it is a position of my own making. It is my fault. But a man has been killed. I feel I must speak up. You do see? I have no choice.'

'I'm very glad you feel that way. I wish more people did.'

'You may change your mind when you've heard what I have to say. I would rather you think well of me. But I must not let that stop me.'

He waited as their coffee grew cold. Having come near the point, she was clearly under duress, and he did not want to push. She might shut down, change her mind at any moment. Whatever was on her mind, he suspected it might put her or someone she cared about in a bad light.

'I went into his rooms, as I say, where he offered me coffee or a glass of wine. When I declined the coffee and reminded him I didn't drink, he said something like, "That's a shame", and went into the next room to retrieve a bottle and a glass for himself.'

St. Just nodded. *So far, so good.*

'Have you been in his rooms?' she asked. 'Yes, I suppose you would have by now. Then you know there's a main area that's sort of a sitting room-slash-office, and a separate bedroom. I assume, because he offered coffee, there is also a small kitchenette, or at least a place to make tea or coffee as well as a bathroom. It was quite a nice space as these things go. When I was in college myself, the accommodation was variable, let's say, but of course I didn't stick around to become a lecturer. And I believe Jason was a special case. I mean, he was always treated as a special case by the college. They gave every indication of wanting to hang on to him and a good set of rooms with a great view over the quad would help.'

She clearly was detouring into trivia, but he let her go on, waiting patiently.

'Anyway,' she said finally. 'Well, since Jason was gone, having stepped into the next room for his wine, I began browsing the bookshelves in his room. In his living area. It's an occupational hazard for someone who works with the written word all day, you understand. It's such a window into someone's brain to see the kind of books they read. Jason's shelves were filled with the expected anthropology and archaeology books, things of an academic nature, and there were no signs of popular literature. No Booker Award winners, no *New York Times* bestsellers. It was all pretty much what you would expect of a lecturer at Oxford but, given who Jason was, on his way to becoming a hugely successful commercial author, I must say I was a bit surprised not to find his tastes to be more . . . wide-ranging.'

A logical observation, thought St. Just. 'Perhaps he kept his more mainstream reading in his bedroom. Wanting to keep the two halves of his work separate.' He was thinking of Portia as he spoke, whose books on criminology occupied her office space at home but were stored on shelves in a separate area from her crime novels. During the pandemic, she'd had extra shelves built to allow her to work from home. Her own published crime novels now had a shelf to themselves. The areas of her expertise often overlapped, but the manifestations of these areas never shared the same space.

'I thought so too. But then I noticed the books on a bottom shelf in the corner, nearest the door. These books were all written in foreign languages, and neatly sorted by language. There weren't many of them, as most of his books were in English, so it was easy to peruse this one shelf. I had completely forgotten that Jason was fluent in more than one language: French and Spanish, to name two, but the books in Dutch seemed to predominate.'

'And what did you make of this discovery?' asked St. Just, who was increasingly baffled by this recitation.

'I speak Dutch, you see. I'm quite fluent, as my father was a diplomat and we lived some years in the Netherlands where I completed some of my schooling. So of course, those were the books that attracted me. It had been some years, but I was able to read the titles without any problem.'

St. Just had a feeling he knew what was coming, but he let her continue without interruption.

'There was one book that was older than the others. Most of them had clean, modern jackets. Only a few were antiques or used books, probably from second-hand shops. They were by and large classic tales, translations of Jane Austen or Herman Melville, all that sort of thing. A few Simenon detective novels translated from the French into Dutch.'

His impatience got the better of him. 'Were any of these books by any chance entitled *The White Owl*?'

She nodded, pointing to him as if to say, 'Got it in one.'

TWENTY-TWO
Gita Tells More

'Of course, it wasn't *The White Owl* in English,' Gita Patel continued. 'The title on the spine was *De Witte Uil*.'

'The original novel, one supposes.'

'Yes,' she said. 'Of course, I was intrigued. What a coincidence! I thought. It seems incredible now, but that was my initial thought, that Jason had got his title idea from this book. Just as I was reaching for it to take a closer look, I could hear Jason returning. I could only catch a glimpse of the author's last name on the spine, and since it was a dark corner and it was an old book besides, it wasn't easy to read the letters through the cracked binding. But I thought it was either Boogaard or maybe Boogman.'

'But you didn't ask Jason about it when he came back into the room?'

'It's funny you should say that. Because I've often thought back to that moment and wondered why I didn't simply make a joke of it or draw his attention to the book in any way. Instead, when I heard him coming back, I moved over to the window and stood there as if transfixed by the view. You see, I must have known in my gut even then something was up. And I didn't want to discuss it with him – or with anyone – until I knew more, until I had had time to investigate it more, until I was sure. Even though I told myself it was just a book title, and that a title didn't matter, it upset me. And I wanted time to decide what to do if what my gut was telling me was a bigger problem than it appeared to be on the surface. There's no copyright on titles, you see. Titles get reused all the time.'

'Listening to your instincts,' said St. Just. 'Very wise. Go on.'

'So once I left his place that day, my problem was how to

somehow gain access to the book again. And my mind went down all sorts of avenues there. Perhaps I could sneak back into his room when he wasn't there. But that was breaking and entering – I mean, you would know. Maybe that's the American term for it – I watch a lot of their shows on the telly. But I was sure that it wasn't exactly *ethical*.

'Still, I had to know. And I thought there might be more . . . legal ways to go about it. The first thing I did when I got back to my office was to search the Internet for a book with the same title – first in Dutch, then in any language I could think of. In English, of course, all the references were to Jason's new book. There was nothing – I could find nothing about this old book in Dutch. I came to the conclusion that the book had been self-published, and many years before by the look of it. So getting hold of a copy was becoming more and more problematic, you understand. I decided – well, I decided I had to try to get into his room and get my hands on that book. At least long enough to take photographs with my mobile phone of a few pages and confirm it was a completely different story with, only coincidentally, the same title as Jason's book.'

'Or perhaps, rather than breaking into his room, get someone else to have a look around,' hazarded St. Just.

'Ah, yes. I thought of that.' Again, she looked completely abashed for a moment, but recovering quickly, she added, 'I realized that would require some form of bribery of someone – perhaps the housekeeper, or perhaps the scout who did his room for him. Maybe one of his students who took tutorials in his rooms? And once again I was into an area where I simply was out of my depth. I mean, what do I know about bribing people? And besides, having been in the college atmosphere myself, I know how completely trustworthy the staff are. Once in a great while, I'm sure, there's a problem with someone pilfering or whatever, but for the most part you can guarantee those people are not the sort to succumb to a bribe. At least not the low-level bribe I would be able to offer. That seemed like a dead end. I had no idea who his students were and, as to trusting one of them, I dismissed the idea almost immediately.'

'I do understand. So what did you decide to do?'

'I decided on the lesser evil,' she said. 'I hope I don't get in any trouble for this, but I was frantic and I had to make sure my suspicions were wrong. I wasn't looking for evidence that I was right, you see, I needed—'

'Never mind all that. What did you do?'

'I knew something of Jason's schedule. I knew he held his tutorials in his rooms Tuesdays and Thursdays, and the rest of the time he was either at the Institute of Archaeology in Beaumont Street, or in the lab, or at the Pitt Rivers Museum. I could always ask him, of course, but I thought my sudden interest in his whereabouts would be suspicious. I was getting deeply paranoid over the whole subject very quickly, I realized that, but so much was at stake. My own reputation, the reputation of the publishing house. We would be a laughing stock in the industry if what I suspected to be true turned out to be true. And every book we had published in the past, every book in the pipeline – they would likely be held up to special scrutiny by some diligent reporter.'

'Yes, of course. I quite see the problem.'

'I wouldn't have been so suspicious if I didn't already know Jason's biography was a tissue of lies. I should have realized. I really feel I should have realized and I should have told someone early on, at least about his biography. Like I said, you can't put toothpaste back in the tube or the genie back in the bottle, or so I thought. Well, I believe now I thought wrong.'

'So what did you decide to do?'

'I pieced together as much of his schedule as I could. Here and there I made random calls to his department asking if I could speak with him. If they said he wasn't there, I might call back the next day at a different time. Finally, I struck lucky. I called the Institute of Archaeology and was told, yes, he was there and they would put me through to his office right away. I hung up, ran out of my own office, and hotfooted it over to St Rumwold's. The porter recognized me from before. I thought he might but that didn't matter; I used it to my advantage. I was now a known quantity. I told him I had left a personal article of mine in Jason's room. And would he be so kind as to help me retrieve it? Of course he couldn't leave his position at the gate, which I knew and was counting on, but he told me the scout who did for Jason could let me in. I felt bad about this as well – the man clearly trusted me. But I stood there while he got the housekeeper to locate the scout – her name was Tess – and asked her to let me into the room. Once there I went straight over to the bookshelf. My plan was to pretend that book was my own, you see, a book I had loaned to Jason. I would put it in the tote bag I had brought for that purpose. And that would be that.'

'And things went as planned.'

She gave a mirthless laugh. 'Hardly,' she said. 'Not at all. No, the book was gone. At least it was not on the shelf where I'd spotted it. The shelf was dusty and I could see an empty spot where the book had been. And with the scout standing there watching me, I didn't have time or the opportunity to do a full search of the room.

'Now I was really in a fix. Having lied my way into Jason's rooms, you see, I could only hope Tess didn't mention it to Jason and the porter wouldn't mention it, either. But if they did, my cover story to him would be that I'd lost my pen or something. It was lame, and I already suspected that he suspected.'

'I'm sorry, I don't follow.'

'I believe he'd moved the book. Possibly he had hidden it, realizing I'd seen it or at least thinking someone else could stumble across it as I had. Maybe he'd destroyed it, for all I knew. Now I was really stumped. What could I do? And it was then I remembered I still had old school friends in Amsterdam, and possibly they could help me. Help me find the title in their own National Library. It was an off chance that if the book had been self-published, the author might have submitted a copy, but I know my authors, you see. They want that little slice of immortality. I thought it highly likely Boogaard or Boogman or whatever his name was would have submitted a copy for posterity.'

'And did that work?'

She smiled, showing the same relief she must have felt at the time. 'It took a week or two but my friend came through. She was a professor at the university there, you see. It was a matter of some quick research on her part, and filing for permission to obtain a copy took a longer wait, but she was able to retrieve the book from the archives. They have a system similar to what we have here, in which a copy of every book published in Great Britain is kept at the British Library. Now, if the author had had his book privately bound, I might be out of luck, but if he submitted it himself – there was just a chance.

'The author turned out to be W.E.B. Boogman. How Jason came to own a copy I still didn't know; probably he found it in an antique or second-hand shop. But now I had access to a copy. And rather than get my friend to post the copy to me – which would have been breaking the law, by the way – I flew over there.'

'And it was the same book?'

'It was the same book. It's rather a shame. The author never knew how good his book was – I mean, how popular it would be. It never reached a big audience, since he had indeed published it himself. And this had all happened in the days before self-publishing online was a common thing. It had been published nearly a century before, you see. All of this was pure luck I was able to retrieve it. It was very lucky indeed that the book had not simply vanished without a trace.

'Anyway, I made a copy of every single page. Whether that was legal, God knows, but I had to find out. It was so obvious to me at a glance that Jason had stolen the thing and passed it along to us as his own work.'

St. Just pondered what she had told him, trying to slot the pieces of this new knowledge into the case. Jason was a liar, a fantasist and a plagiarist. It was not terribly surprising that he was killed, adding all of that up, and not forgetting that he was also a philanderer. But was this really a motive to kill him, the fact that he had stolen this book and passed it off as his own? It was certainly news that needed to be handed over to Ampleforth. Perhaps he would have some ideas.

St. Just asked her if she would provide him with an electronic copy of what she had copied from the Dutch book. She agreed readily.

'The question is what to do now? I suppose all of this will have to come out. Does it really have to come out that I talked

my way into Jason's rooms like that? Do all the details have
to come out? As I told you, I will be leaving Castle Publishing
very soon, God willing, and I don't want a story like this
following me. I don't want it foxing my chances with my new
publisher either. They hired me on the strength of being
involved in acquiring Jason Verdoodt for the Castle Publishing
catalogue. I almost don't see a way this won't ruin me. You
have no idea how much sleep I have lost over it. *Does* all of
this have to come out?' She looked at him pleadingly; he could
only tell her the truth.

'The outcome may be completely out of my hands. But I
will do my best. As far as I can tell, you saw a wrong and
you tried to right it.'

'Yes! That is what I was trying to do. But do you know,
my experience has been that doing the right thing often comes
with a special kind of punishment. I hope to escape that
punishment – even if I deserve it.'

'I will do my best,' he repeated. 'Thank you for being
honest.'

'But does this have anything to do with what happened to
Jason? His murder? I've thought and thought about it and I
can't think of any way it could be related. The Dutch author
of the original book is long dead. If anyone was seeking retri-
bution, like a descendant or heir of his, surely they wouldn't
kill Jason. They would simply come forward and stake a legal
claim. Against him *and* against Castle Publishing, alas.'

'At this point it is all still a guessing game,' St. Just told
her. 'But thank you again for letting us know.'

TWENTY-THREE
Ampleforth Wonders

St. Just walked with Gita to the door of the restaurant where they went their separate ways.

As she headed back to her office, and he in the general direction of the Randolph, he wondered if she could overcome this career obstacle, should the details come out. He could understand the choices she had made all along the line although, technically, she had left the company open to a huge lawsuit. He didn't envy her having to face the wrath of Sir Boniface Castle. But she might have little choice now. Having come clean to the police, she eventually would have to let Boniface in on every detail, as she just had done with him. What he would choose to do with the knowledge was anyone's guess.

St. Just needed to talk all this over with DCI Ampleforth. He rang him and he answered immediately. To judge by the cacophony of sounds in the background – phones ringing, people shouting – Ampleforth was again in the incident room at Kidlington.

'While it is increasingly clear Jason stole the book, and that can certainly be documented,' St. Just said, concluding his summary of Gita's information, 'what is not clear to me is why it would end in Jason's death. Do you have any thoughts on that?'

'I'll confess I am baffled,' said Ampleforth. 'Since the real author must be long dead – and we will be learning all we can about him – the question becomes, was Jason killed by some relative? A sort of punishment? Revenge? I suppose it's possible that, seeing the kind of money Jason was raking in, a descendant of the true author might become totally unhinged. Especially if that person was just scraping by financially. But more likely they would sue Jason and the publishers.'

'That's what I thought, too. Also, it seems to me the whole thing is the wrong way round.' St. Just stepped back on the pavement to allow a young woman to pass with her child in its pushchair. 'Isn't it more likely that Jason would kill to silence someone giving away his lucrative game? But that's not what happened. Besides . . .'

St. Just was thinking perhaps no one knew the truth about Jason's plagiarism of the Dutch author's tale – no one but Gita. But that put the police even further away from tying Jason's plagiarism to his murder.

'Besides what?' said Ampleforth.

'I suppose we'll first have to establish whether someone knew about Jason's plagiarism and acted upon it. And it will be very hard to establish that, don't you think? Perhaps we could run the passports of Dutch nationals and see if someone has made a sudden visit to England that ended in Oxford. And then extrapolate from that to someone who is a blood relative of the true author. It will require establishing the family tree for the man's descendants and then tracking their whereabouts and their movements. Especially on the night Jason died. It's a nightmare of a problem, don't you think?'

'I do indeed. Let me think about that. We have a genealogy expert we call in on occasion. As you know, genetics are more and more often helping us solve cold cases, and there is a growing field of experts who can decipher and trace family trees. Even in this case, where DNA is not a factor, Sarah can at least put us on the right track to getting birth and death certificates and so on and so forth. If the man never married or had descendants, though, we may hit a dead end very quickly. Especially if there's no marriage record – no legitimate line of descent. Oh well, I'll see what we can do at this end.'

'Any news on the rest of the investigation?' asked St. Just. He'd found a quiet alleyway just off the pavement to keep him from blocking foot traffic.

'My team have managed to track down everyone at the party that night, and they claim, if they left early, it was merely to go over to the dining hall. In other words, all are accounted for, no one ran off to South America or anything, but there are so many of them to talk to. Some of them were in town only for the event itself and have since returned to London or wherever – in one case to New York. For obvious reasons of budget, we're having to deal with those people by telephone. I'm not sure it gets us much further forward. Everyone claims not to have seen anything before or during the party. I suppose it was foolish of me to hope to find a witness who had watched Jason falling down the stairs.'

St. Just said, 'The only person who saw him fall was almost without question his killer. Possibly there was an innocent witness now too frightened to speak but, given the layout of that stairwell, I would say it's unlikely. They'd have been spotted by the killer.'

'I would agree. So, where are you off to now?'

'I thought I would go and speak to Jason's girlfriend myself,' replied St. Just.

'Which one?'

'Ha. I mean, Minette Miniver.'

'Yes, one of the team, I believe it was Constable Lambert, spoke to her just after helping in the search of Jason's rooms. Ms Miniver was distraught, according to Lambert, and could contribute nothing. Perhaps the woman has had a chance to collect herself and can be of more use to us now. But she's in Oxford only temporarily, as I think you know, so yes, it would be helpful if you would speak to her right away. She will be leaving, as I recall, the day after tomorrow. She wanted to visit Jason's parents before she left. Pay her condolences, that sort of thing.'

'I barely touched on the topic of Minette's place in Jason's life when I spoke to them. I didn't gather she played a big part now, if ever. They seemed to imply that with Minette in London, the two had drifted further apart.'

'Her inserting herself into the party is certainly suspicious. At the least, it was a daft thing to do.'

'Indeed, it was. But since she left the party early – was told to leave early – it may put her out of the running as a suspect. I suppose she could have sneaked back in, but surely the college's security cameras would have spotted her.'

'I still have people going through every frame of footage

– the early evening footage as well, in case she or someone else came in earlier. So far, though, there's nothing.'

'Anyway, I will let you know what I learn from her. Then I hope to grab a bite to eat with Portia, after which I've arranged to go over to the Castles' home to talk to the wife and daughter.'

'Blood from a stone those two, Ursula and her daughter, Imogen. They're not giving anything away and it's obvious they're hiding something – something in terms of their relationship with Jason. Or maybe they're naturally cagey – I've noticed people with money only want to be in the spotlight on their terms, if at all. And both the father and the brother are trying to block our access at every move now, threatening lawyers and so on if we keep turning up. Very good luck there.'

'Good,' said St. Just. 'It sounds as if I touched a nerve.'

TWENTY-FOUR
Whoever Loved?

'All right, yes, I crashed the party,' said Minette Miniver, sitting bolt upright on the tatty sofa in her cramped rental flat. The room had about it an aura of desperation, of failed attempts to make ends meet. She pulled her brown cardigan tightly against her body. 'It's not a crime.'

'Technically, it *is* a crime. It's trespassing.'

St. Just had found Minette in a narrow Victorian terrace in Cowley, a far cry from the gracefully restored Victorian building housing Castle Publishing. This building had been carelessly divided into rabbit warrens, some of which seemed to be occupied by students while others appeared to be available for short lease by a motley assortment of drifters. The entire space could have done with a coat of paint and perhaps an unannounced visit from the council. He wondered why Minette had chosen to stay here when, as a doctor, she almost certainly could afford better. Oxford boasted several high-end hotels apart from the Randolph.

But apart from her odd choice of accommodation, which might simply reflect a personal desire to be in Cowley for unknown reasons, he wondered how much she could contribute to their knowledge of Jason – not so much as a doctor but as someone who apparently had known him longer than anyone but his parents.

Making his neglect of her, leaving her off the guest list, even more puzzling.

'They found high levels of a commonly prescribed anti-anxiety medication in Jason's system,' he told her. 'Do you have any idea if that is something that would have been self-administered?'

She shook her head at the question. 'Jason was the least

anxious person you'll ever meet. Well, obviously you'll never meet him now in person, but take it from me. He'd never be using drugs, especially that type of drug. Not recreationally, not to treat a condition. He just would not be using that type of drug.'

'Is there a type of drug you believe he would favour?'

This question with its tinge of sarcasm was a mistake, and St. Just wished he could call back his words. Her back immediately went up. St. Just thought she must have loved Jason very much to be this offended by any suggestion that he might have had feet of clay. The interview was going to be uphill-going, in which case, if she was that deluded.

'No, and I didn't mean to imply anything,' she said hotly. 'He didn't use *any* type of drug. He was always too . . . too careful of himself. You people really do know how to twist things, don't you?'

The transformation was amazing. Anger almost instantaneously dried the tears with which she had begun the interview, dabbing occasionally at her eyes as she verified witness accounts of her short time at Jason's celebration party. St. Just wondered if she might have had a run-in with the law in her past. With some people, even a parking ticket could fester in their minds forever. But Ampleforth's team had given her clearance in that regard. She was a respected doctor with impeccable credentials working at a well-known London hospital, which made her uninvited appearance at the party seem completely out of character.

If anything, there was a suggestion from the team that she was obsessed with her job, working all hours with little time for a personal life. St. Just supposed dedication could tip over into a sort of mania, a quest for perfection in a profession where death – the ultimate failure – was inevitable. He'd often seen the pressure of responsibility bring down the highest flyers in the police force.

'He jogged,' she was saying now. 'He ran marathons. He ate mangoes and organic cereal and oat milk for breakfast, for God's sake. His favourite vegetable – he was a vegetarian – his favourite vegetable was bean sprouts. I hate bean sprouts, don't you? It's like eating worms. Anyway. He never touched coffee and he'd only drink a certain hard-to-find tea from some speciality shop in Oxford.'

'But he drank? I mean, evidently, he drank on occasion. The college madeira.' All the wine on offer at the party had come from bottles stamped with the college crest. This didn't make it ineligible to contain poison, of course. The question might even be how *long* ago it had been poisoned. The corked bottle that became in effect a murder weapon could've lain about for decades, tampered with, long ago, by a vintner or someone else holding a grudge against the college.

Except no one at the party had reported feeling any ill-effects. Only Jason's system had held substances seemingly chosen to impair his ability to function.

And there was a single glass containing traces of the drink that had been used in his murder.

'He barely drank,' she said, her voice even sharper than before. 'Now you're making him out to be a drunkard. I'm telling you, whatever happened to him it was not, how do I put this . . . it was not self-administered. Someone *did* this to him. Someone . . . someone *murdered* him and here you are talking to me, asking me about his bad habits, when you should be looking for his killer. I'm telling you he had none. No bad habits.'

Of course, St. Just now knew better. There seemed little point in pressing her further on it for the moment, however. It would only reinforce her position that Jason had been Godlike in every way, right down to his bean sprouts, which St. Just happened to like but now doubted he could feel the same way about again.

Instead, he said, 'No bad habits. How about enemies?' Holding up a forestalling hand in case she once again leapt to Jason's defence, he added, 'Most successful people have them. And he was highly successful.'

'Hugely. *Hugely* successful.'

'So he had enemies?'

She seemed torn between admitting her lover had not been universally loved and a need to insist on his importance, for fear the police might not make too much effort on behalf of a lesser man. Fortunately for the investigation, she decided on reflection to come down on the side of law and order.

He just hoped she wouldn't lead the police down a few garden paths in her eagerness to make sure someone – anyone – paid the price.

After a brief hesitation, she came out with, 'He had a problem with his scout.'

'His scout?'

'Yes, you know, the person who cleaned his rooms. The person who did for him.'

'Yes, I know what an Oxford scout is, but I meant, tell me more about what happened.'

'I'm not sure,' she admitted reluctantly. Clearly the scout would be her first choice of murderer and she wanted to help the police see that in any way she could. 'He only mentioned in passing that he thought she'd been going through his papers in his rooms and he was livid. His papers – I mean, can you imagine?'

St. Just nodded. Much like messing about with the Dead Sea scrolls, given the author's fame and sense of self-importance. Now he came to think of it, Jason's rooms had been a model of order with few papers to be seen, and none of them looking scattered. He assumed Jason's work would be on his laptop, now safely in the hands of Ampleforth's forensic technicians. Anything of interest on the hard drive would yield itself to their probes, however encrypted or hidden behind a password.

'What a complete violation of his privacy!' she went on.

'There was an open quarrel with her then?' he prompted. 'They exchanged heated words?'

'No, nothing like that. But I think he tried to get her fired. Typical Jason. I mean, it was a bit of an overreaction, and in this case – perhaps it was a bit mean-spirited. The woman wouldn't have many employment opportunities, looking like she did, and scouts aren't paid much to begin with.'

'You knew about her, then? He spoke of her?'

'Just in passing. I saw her a couple of times in the collage. He called her Scarface.'

'That was unkind.'

'Yes, I suppose it was. She'd been in some sort of accident, I guess. Jason had a tiny bit of a cruel streak.' *Now* we were getting to it. So much for Jason the perfect paragon.

St. Just sensed a relief on Minette's part that the scout would not have been a temptation for Jason. She must have lived her life on tenterhooks, waiting to see who Jason was attracted to next, and wondering when he would leave her behind forever. With the stunning success of his book, that day could not have been far in the future. And could only have been prevented by his death.

But all this assumed she had some awareness of his true, unfaithful nature. Did she?

'You don't know any more details of the incident with the scout? Her name is Tess, by the way.'

'I wish I could remember. I just know he was livid, and he went to the head of scouts or whatever you call them now at Oxford – at Cambridge, they're called bedders – and insisted the woman be replaced.'

'He tried to get her fired? You're sure of that?' This sounded like a motive if St. Just had ever heard one. Was it an over-reaction on Jason's part or was it somehow justified? Had she stolen money or something else of value?

'I'm not sure. Just . . . replaced. Maybe just not allowed to clean his rooms anymore. He wanted a new scout.'

'When did all this happen?' he asked.

'I don't know. A few weeks ago is when he told me about it.'

Perhaps a few weeks was a long time for Tess to hold a grudge, he thought, but it wasn't without precedent. Sometimes the longer a grudge was nursed, the more malignant the desire for revenge grew.

Still, jealousy seemed to be the theme as much as revenge, wherever St. Just turned: editors and publicists, fellow authors, people Verdoodt had jettisoned on his way to fame – all with some axe to grind; all nursing some slight, real or imagined; all wanting what Jason had. There were issues of personal jealousy, as well as professional: the handsome academic seemed to have developed a bit of a groupie following, surely much to the dismay of Minette, a friend from his younger years whom he might have been trying to discard since his first brush with success. She was probably not alone in being someone he had simply outgrown the need for. The numbers of the outgrown might be legion.

St. Just wondered about his apparent wish to leave Minette, in particular, behind. Was it his *privileged* background he was ashamed of? Often people will shed themselves of people from the past not because they're suddenly boring but because they know too much about the real man being hailed as a genius.

St. Just suggested this theory, but Minette dispelled it quickly.

'Yes, his impoverished background was a fairy tale. But so what? That was for the official biography.'

'You knew, of course.'

'Certainly, I knew. Far from being impoverished, he never had a moment's want growing up. I'm sure he thought it would help sell books to portray himself as a struggling genius who came out of nowhere, who practically taught himself how to read and write. The fact was, as you now know, he was solidly middle class. His father was a marketing guru and did very well. His mother was a housewife. They were people who stayed at home in the evening and went to church on Sunday and watched the telly and voted for the Conservatives no matter what, at least to hear Jason tell it. Probably that's why he thought they should be kept in the background. People want their authors to be exceptional in some way, unusual, and they'll buy any story about them so long as it's entertaining and, best of all, redemptive. Hopeful. Drug or alcohol problem? Great. A stint in rehab? Even better. Abusive parents? Tick that box, for sure.

'To be fair and give him credit, it's not as if his parents set him up to be a famous author. There were no books in the house that I ever saw. Apart from his books from college. I suppose he got the tools for being a writer from some of the lecturers at Cambridge, who were very good and took an interest in him. Most people did – take an interest in him, I mean.'

'Women in particular?' St. Just asked mildly.

'Yes, but he and I were an item,' she said fiercely. 'You can ignore anyone who says otherwise.'

'What time did you arrive at the party?'

'I can't say for certain.'

'Try.'

'A little after seven.'

'Let me ask you this,' he said. 'Did you ever doubt Jason wrote *The White Owl*, the book that made him so famous?'

This brought her up short. 'Why, no. What an astonishing idea,' she said. Then she seemed to hesitate. 'Well, I did write a few essays for him when we were in college together. But that's only because he was so busy with extracurricular activities, not because he wasn't capable of writing them himself. No. You're barking up the wrong tree there. He wrote scads of academic papers. It's a different sort of writing, yes, but . . .'

But the thought of Jason's plagiarizing seemed to have struck a chord within her, stirring up some memory or other. He could almost see the wheels turning as she replayed the times he had cajoled her into doing his work for him. Or the times she had willingly done everything she could to help him. Someone like Minette, who had known Jason a long time, who well knew Jason's inclination to take shortcuts, would not be too amazed to hear of his audacious deception.

Still, Minette was so loyal it might take her more than a few minutes to come to terms with the idea.

It might take her a lifetime.

TWENTY-FIVE
Portia

One of the Randolph Hotel's charms was its central location, making it ideal for a murder investigation, as the fictional Inspector Morse could have testified.

However, the decision had been made to establish police headquarters in Kidlington, nowhere near as convenient as what was depicted in the *Morse* series, but no doubt chosen because the price of property in central Oxford was sky high.

Dominating the corner of Beaumont and Magdalen Streets, the Randolph was another creation in the Victorian style, but with a Gothic façade done in brick rather than stone. It was a place where the wealthy and the famous came to stay. St. Just realized the fact Sir Boniface was paying for their room presented an ethical question from the moment Jason was killed and the situation ticked over into a police investigation. It would taint the appearance of an impartial investigation, an investigation in which St. Just was by now thoroughly embedded.

St. Just supposed he and Portia should have switched hotels – preferably to something less expensive. As it was, St. Just had already decided that – for convenience's sake; the convenience of not having to move and try to find accommodation elsewhere – he would be picking up the tab, outrageous as it was on a policeman's salary. But nothing could be made to appear as if the police were beholden to Boniface. Just thinking what the media would make of the situation made St. Just cringe, since technically Boniface and his family were as much suspects as anyone else at that party for Jason.

St. Just had a word with the uniformed receptionist at the front desk, providing his credit card information, and making sure the room and incidentals would not be charged to Castle

Publishing. As he waited for the reservation to be updated, he admired the décor, a carefully planned jumble of arched Gothic windows and doorways and opulent wallpaper, the plush carpet leading up to the desk and to the left, the broad staircase leading to the guest bedrooms. He recalled that the famous hotel had survived a kitchen fire not too many years before, but no trace of damage remained.

Having concluded his business with the receptionist, he went to meet Portia in The Snug, the hotel's library-style cocktail lounge attached to The Alice restaurant. She was already waiting, resplendent in a blue-black dress, taking in the Bohemian splendour of the room and completely at ease, reminding him of the first time he had ever set eyes on her. Whether alone or in a group, Portia always seemed comfortable in the world, content within herself, and with a striking ability to treat every challenge life threw at her as an adventure. It was a welcome quality for a woman who would soon be a policeman's wife. He had tried to warn her, but didn't believe anything could really prepare her for the reality of the cancelled plans at the weekends, and the three a.m. phone calls. It was like being on call as an A&E doctor.

On call much like Minette Miniver, now he came to think of it. Possibly Jason had been her only escape from a gruelling job of daunting, life-or-death responsibilities.

Briefly he wondered what she would do now. Return to London, after having seen Jason's parents, and then what? Bury herself even more in work? He found himself hoping one day she might find happiness.

He greeted Portia with a kiss and she handed him a menu, saying, 'You must be famished.' He realized that he was, but tonight would not be the night for a long, leisurely meal, as he had to meet with the Castles later. Still, he was determined to make the meal an experience for Portia, to try to make up for his having to keep running off to interrogate witnesses. She never complained, but he never wanted to take advantage of her good nature.

'So, what can you tell me?' she prompted, once the waiter had taken their order for cocktails. 'What's going on?'

He knew Portia could be trusted not to repeat what she

knew to the wrong people, although at times she had trouble staying out of an investigation – with the best of intentions. But in the case of Jason Verdoodt's murder, tied as it seemed to be to Castle Publishing, he thought she might be able to offer special insight.

He told her then, in confidence, much of what Gita Patel had told him. About the true provenance of Jason's famous book.

The stunned reaction she gave him was all he could have hoped.

'You must be joking,' she said at last. 'Of all the audacious, dishonest, crooked, crazy things to do. Just insane. I mean, he was almost certain to be caught out, wasn't he?'

'I don't see why. The book could not have been more obscure, its author long gone. Ampleforth is looking into it, but I am going to guess the author had no close relatives so, when he died, his book died with him. Probably Jason did his own research along the same lines to make sure the scam would work, that he would not be detected. I'm going to guess that as time passed, he gave himself full credit for the translation of the work and decided that it was therefore his – a bit of mental backflipping that I wouldn't put past the man now that I know more about him.'

The waiter interrupted them just then to take their order. They briefly returned their attention to the menu, St. Just aware of how little time they had. He picked almost at random the wild sea bass and Portia chose the mushroom risotto with a side of broccoli to share. Both chose the scallops to start.

'How tragic,' Portia said, once the waiter had retreated with their order. 'You are describing every author's worst nightmare. Not only the plagiarism, which at least indicates some success for the author – stealing being the highest form of flattery these days with the Internet. I wonder sometimes why I bother when my eBooks show up for sale at a steep discount on the dark web where *I* certainly didn't put them. But the thought that when you die your books die with you . . . well. I can hardly bear to say it aloud, it's such a chilling thought.'

'I agree. It's pure theft of intellectual property. And I can only hope that what Jason tried won't catch on. As you say, the web is like the Wild West. It's too easy to steal, too easy to pretend something that is not yours is yours. Something that perhaps took the true author decades to create. Jason's fraud was only possible because the book he stole only existed in physical form. Had it been out there as an eBook, someone likely would have stumbled upon the truth long before now. Anyway, it's a fine kettle of fish for the people at Castle Publishing.'

'But what does it have to do with Jason's murder?'

St. Just sighed his frustration. 'You have arrived at the very heart of the matter. If the author whose work Jason stole had any surviving relatives, would they really have killed Jason out of revenge? Of course not. The very idea is preposterous. Unless they're quite insane, they would have recourse to the court system. They might have the true author's notes, or his diary, but even without that sort of evidence, the existence of the physical book, the old book in Dutch, is proof enough. It would be a nice tidy windfall for them. But with the author dead . . . It would be rather like killing the golden goose.'

'I suppose,' she said, 'they could sue Castle Publishing, even with Jason dead, or come to an agreement with the firm. Some kind of financial agreement, I mean. A payoff.'

'But talk about tipping your hand,' said St. Just. 'No, that makes no sense. They kill Jason and then show up demanding money from his publisher?'

'Right. You may as well take out an ad announcing that you're the murderer.'

'My reasoning exactly, and Ampleforth's.'

'Do you really think the Castle family have no idea what Jason pulled on them?'

'I don't know.' St. Just shook his head in frustration. 'It's one of the things I hope to ferret out tonight. I suppose it's just possible they were in on the scam, that they used Jason as a sort of front man. Good looking, intelligent, Oxford background, well spoken . . . It's just possible, and I will certainly be looking for anything that indicates they had knowledge of what was going on, or were in fact the master-minds themselves.

'But in the case of Sir Boniface, I would guess he believed

what he wanted to believe, which was that by lucky chance he'd stumbled upon a gold mine that could save the company from ruin. Nothing in their accounts indicates they were doing well until Jason came along.'

'What about David? As the acquiring editor—'

'I must correct you there. David really had nothing to do with the acquisition. His assistant discovered the manuscript. Gita Patel.'

'Well, there you have it.' Portia put down her drink decisively.

'There you have what?'

'I would look very closely at Gita Patel,' said Portia. 'What would be more logical than Jason luring a young, vulnerable woman into his net – rumour has it he was very good at that – and convincing her to take on the book.'

'Even knowing it was a fraud? That Jason hadn't written it – had in fact stolen it?'

'It would be very hard to prove, but it all fits together.'

St. Just was thinking it would all fit together very beauti-fully in a crime novel written by Portia, who was famed for her twisted and unguessable denouements. But having met Gita for himself, he was reluctant to think her capable of such a scam. She had struck him as honest and above board, wanting to do the right thing and genuinely distraught at the situation created for her by Jason's deception. Why would she tell the police the truth if she was in on the scheme, after all? When chances were very good that she would completely get away with it so long as she kept quiet about what she'd learned? There was no reason for anyone to ever find out the book had been stolen from a long-dead author.

He said as much to Portia, who shrugged and said, 'It's a possibility. She wouldn't be the first woman to lie to the police. But perhaps she just found the whole thing to be too much of a strain once Jason was found dead. Lying is exhausting, even for the most dishonest. If she is basically an honest person, as you seem to think, the lying would quickly get to be too much.'

'Still, all the more reason to keep quiet about his fraud. Jason's death put the whole thing into new and dangerous

territory for everyone – suddenly everyone was a suspect. But
you're right. Sometimes people with a conscience will break
wide open over the smallest thing and will want to get it off
their chest – if without admitting their total complicity in the
scheme.'

'Is she trying to place the blame anywhere else – on
someone else?'

'She's not. In fact, she's very torn, not wanting it to come
out, but knowing it might have something to do with Jason's
death, thinking it *must* have something to do with it.'

St. Just sighed.

'If only,' he said. 'If only I could see exactly what.'

The waiter had arrived with their starters. Between bites,
Portia asked, 'What about the woman at the party in the red
dress. Doesn't she rather stand out as a suspect? I mean,
crashing the party like that. It doesn't look good for her. Even
though I'm sure Jason was deserving of a good fright.'

'You think that's why she did it? To frighten him?'

'It is hard to say,' she said. Portia sat back, having finished
her scallops. 'My guess is she had some hare-brained idea of
letting him know how much she cared rather than having a
well-thought-out plan for murder. It was the kind of scheme
that was sure to backfire. Are you thinking she met him just
before the party started but he rejected her, so she decided to
make him pay? Once she was ejected from the party, she may
not simply have left quietly. She could have sneaked back into
the college somehow – have the police looked into that?'

'Without a doubt,' he said, putting down his fork and taking
a sip of wine. 'The security cameras should tell us, if so. The
problem is the college is hardly airtight. She could have walked
in behind a group of raucous students entering through the side
gates who weren't paying attention and wouldn't care even if
they had spotted her. But no one has come forward to say so.'

'How about the porter?'

'There's really very little chance of his noticing anyone
entering or leaving from the side gates. But if he had turned
away, or gone to answer a call of nature, something like that,
the video cameras would have captured Minette on the grounds,
especially in that dress.'

'Were they able to pinpoint Jason's time of death?'

'Pinpoint is seldom a word used by pathologists,' St. Just replied. 'As you know.'

They were veering away from the topic of Portia's publishing expertise, but she was an expert criminologist as well. He'd found her insights in that regard useful more than once.

'But they estimate Jason was killed around the time the party started. The video would record any interlopers that night at whatever time, so we'll know if she did return. Or if someone who shouldn't have been there was there.

'Ampleforth of course has someone going inch by inch over the video. But this is showing every sign of being a closed circle murder. Your favourite kind.'

She laughed. 'My favourite in fiction, you mean. In real life, it's a different story, and rather chilling. When you think about it, we were in the same room as a killer and didn't know it.'

TWENTY-SIX
Castling

Constable Daisy Lambert had again been dispatched to pick up St. Just at the Randolph and drive him in an unmarked sedan the short way to North Oxford and the home of the Castle family. He apologized for keeping her so late at the end of what had certainly been a long day for her, as well as for himself. She probably had children, a husband, a family – all having to adapt to the reality of being related to a policewoman.

'I don't mind, sir,' she said. 'To tell you the truth, this is the closest I've ever been allowed near a murder investigation like this – I mean a high-profile case like this. Usually it's domestics. Not that those aren't tragedies, but when the bloke is found standing over his wife with a knife dripping blood and shouting, "I'm glad she's dead", it's not hard to figure out who is the guilty party. This is more like those golden age crime stories. Have you read those books? Agatha Christie and that lot?'

'When I have time. I seldom do – have time, that is.'

'I read them to unwind. Also, to pick up clues as to what to watch out for as I'm on a case. So whatever it takes. I'll drive you wherever you need to be.'

'You've been in the force long, have you?'

'Just three years, sir. Only in homicide for the past year.'

'That's a fast rise up the ranks,' he said.

'They are having trouble recruiting people to the police,' she said modestly. 'Women especially. My timing has been lucky, and I've worked very hard. I want to lead my own team one day.'

St. Just was both surprised and pleased to hear of her ambition. He still wondered at her being relegated to chauffeuring him about, but he would make her part of the interview with the Castles – mother and daughter and whoever else was about – as she'd been part of his interview with Jason's parents. In that case she had acquitted herself nicely in not inserting herself into the conversation. However much she might have wanted to bring up her own adoption, she seemed to know her own happy experience was not going to be useful to the grieving parents.

His Sergeant Fear back in Cambridge was likewise a model of discretion, and skilled at picking up the clues people dropped under the pressure of an interview.

Besides, Ampleforth had told him she'd been sent on her own to talk with Minette Miniver, so perhaps being his driver wasn't the demotion that St. Just had thought at first.

The Castles' house, standing at the end of a short drive, proved to be gargantuan. St. Just thought it was a good thing it was isolated on a large tract of land from its neighbours, who otherwise could not have avoided using the term 'eyesore'. It was more a villa than a typical manor house, and more akin to something the Borgias might have had built. Someone had added turrets and stuck unnecessary things on to it like carbuncles. It scarcely blended in with its more sedate neighbours, despite its evident cost. St. Just supposed it wasn't meant to blend.

They were met at the front door by Lady Ursula herself, who managed to look both annoyed by what she clearly saw as an intrusion, and terrified. St. Just imagined the terror was for her daughter, Jason's plus one on the fateful night.

Lady Ursula stood back sullenly from the door and motioned them into the sitting room off a marble hallway. The front door shut with a clang behind them.

No expense had been spared on the plaster ceilings and mouldings of the hall; the sitting room was crisscrossed by wooden beams rather at odds with the style of the entryway. Stuccoed recesses had been created throughout the room to hold reproduction busts of Roman emperors; hanging from the walls was a Mona Lisa – a reproduction, of course, as was da Vinci's drawing of Vitruvian Man. The whole overlooked a terraced garden any pope would have been proud to call his own.

St. Just was no expert but surely the décor lacked imagination. Someone of Sir Boniface's wealth could have afforded things that weren't such obvious fakes.

Perhaps the decoration was Lady Ursula's choice. In any event, the thought of fakes brought him back to the point of their visit. How much had she known, if anything, of Jason's treachery? What might the rest of her family – particularly her children – have known?

At first, St. Just didn't notice Imogen was in the room, sitting bolt upright against a mound of pillows. Her brocaded dress tended to make her blend into her surroundings. She began to stand, perhaps to offer a greeting, but St. Just waved her and her mother into their seats. He and Constable Lambert took two chairs opposite, across an ornate coffee table. The surface of the table was probably a reproduction, but he had seen something like it in a catalogue of an exhibition at the Ashmolean Museum. It was a floor mosaic from Pompeii of a grinning skeleton holding two wine jugs, a morbid reminder to seize the day – the sort of thing wealthy Romans had used to decorate the floors of their dining rooms.

St. Just trained his eyes to ignore the disturbing image as he began the interview with Ursula and Imogen Castle. He introduced Constable Lambert, adding, 'I do apologize for disturbing your evening, but I'm sure you realize time is of the essence in an investigation such as this. And any help you can provide—'

'An investigation such as this?' asked Ursula. 'Are you saying you are certain now this was not simply an accident? That Jason Verdoodt did not perhaps just have one cocktail too many, trying to quiet his nerves before his big night?'

'Mother,' said Imogen in a warning voice. St. Just imagined the two of them had had this discussion already in anticipation of his arrival.

At Imogen's sharp tone her mother turned towards her on the sofa quite suddenly, saying, 'I need to know. I need to know *everything* and without delay. And I need to make sure the police understand *clearly* that whatever happened to Jason, it had nothing to do with any member of this family.' To St. Just, she said, 'We, as a family, are devastated by this loss.'

She didn't look devastated. Upset, wary – yes. But not devastated. It sounded to St. Just like the opening lines of a media statement such as might already be being readied for distribution. In other words, damage control had begun. Lady Ursula had a reputation to protect.

St. Just, who had done his homework, said, 'I believe you are descended from the Blackenthorpe family.'

This turn of the conversation surprised her, and he could see her mind teetering between pleasure that he had spoken the name so reverently and suspicion. Because it was the name Blackenthorpe, he was certain, that she was desperate to protect, even more so than her husband's name.

'I wasn't aware that you knew,' she said. She sat up straighter, her posture becoming regal. Next to her, Imogen – sensing what was coming – rolled her eyes. She had heard all this before, *so* many times. 'But yes, the Blackenthorpes have been part of the warp and woof of this nation for many hundreds of years.' At 'warp and woof' Imogen toggled her head slightly back and forth, mocking her mother's pretensions. 'There has never been a hint of murder in all that time. Perhaps a judicial murder here and there, but that was how they did things back in the day. In recent times, as well you know, we have been pillars of the community. Absolute pillars.'

Nonsense and balderdash, thought St. Just. Not that it mattered, but a cursory search of the Internet had revealed the Blackenthorpes had dirtied their hands in more than one scandal, mostly financial. None of them had shown an over-riding regard for their marriage vows, either. Their house parties in the 1930s had been notorious as set-ups for weekend trysting amongst members of the nobility and the occasional royal, as well. The murder of Jason Verdoodt was just one in a long line of scandals to be hushed up, never discussed, shoved into a trunk in the attic.

He could sense that Constable Lambert beside him was tense and still, no doubt picking up on the older woman's fear and anxiety beneath the bluster, waiting with him to see how Lady Ursula would play her cards.

It seemed to Daisy, as she confided to him later, that attempting to boss St. Just about would not have a good outcome. The lady herself must have arrived at the same conclusion, for her next words were in a lower register of voice. She reverted to the 'we are devasted by this loss' theme of a few moments before.

'We will of course do anything to help the police in their inquiries. Of course,' she said.

St. Just said, 'Good,' and otherwise ignored her. He turned his attention to her daughter, Imogen.

'I am very sorry for your loss, Imogen – if I may call you Imogen?'

'Of course, call me Imogen.'

'Please tell me all you can recall of the preparations for Jason's celebration party.'

It was Lady Ursula who said, 'I was in charge of the guest list, which I have of course provided to the police in the full spirit of co—'

'Yes, thank you. Now, Imogen, I understand you were Jason's date for the evening. His "plus one". How long had you two been dating?'

This was clearly one of her favourite topics. Managing a smile, she leaned forward and said, 'I met him last year when he came to the office to discuss marketing plans for his book. He had some wonderful ideas. So intelligent, so handsome, so . . . well, everything. It really was love at first sight.'

'For both of you?'

'Yes, of course for both of us,' she said. 'Why do you ask?'

This was a poser because St. Just didn't see it would help the interview to lay bare for her the facts of Jason's inconstant nature. If she were unaware of it, what good would it do to disillusion her? And if she were aware, she would struggle to maintain at all costs the fantasy world she had built up about her deep and abiding mutual relationship with Jason.

Looking at her now, it was impossible to judge. She didn't appear to be devastated, either. It was more as if she was struggling to decide how to market Jason's loss for a wider audience. The insistence on their love to last the ages might be her first foray into how to present herself, and her role in Jason's life, to the media.

Which suggested she may have known or suspected what

a rotter he'd been. Now he was gone, she was free to tell whatever story she chose about the nature of her relationship with the famous author.

He simply didn't have time to wander through the garden of love with her, so he said, 'That's good news. Because what the police need is someone close to Jason, someone in whom he would confide, someone who knew his day-to day-activities, someone who knew most of all anyone who may have wanted to harm him. You can be invaluable to helping us apprehend whoever did this to him.'

Unless, of course, you're the person who murdered him, he thought. But they would get to that eventually.

Thrilled at being cast as Jason's confidant in this drama, Imogen said, 'Of course. Jason did tell me on many occasions that I was the only person he trusted – the only woman he had ever been able to trust in the world. It was such a special moment, I—'

'Yes, and where did you meet? In private, I mean?'

'Well, it was difficult meeting at the college, of course. Tongues do wag and we weren't ready to openly declare our love. Jason had bought a new house and it was being renovated, so we would meet there whenever we could break away. I was helping him pick out the furnishings and the decorations. He said I had marvellous taste.'

St. Just tried to keep his eyes from straying to the décor around him. Perhaps it had taught her what to avoid in decorating schemes.

'We would sit on a blanket in front of the fireplace and we would, you know . . . we would talk and, you know . . .'

'Yes, I see,' he said, to spare her and himself the details. And to spare her mother, to whom this was clearly news. Beside him, Constable Lambert had begun to scribble madly in her notebook, first flicking to a new page. What on earth could she be writing?

'We'll need the address of this house of his, even though I'm sure the police have that information on file somewhere.'

She rattled off an address in North Oxford, not far from where they sat. Surely the police would have searched the place, but St. Just made a mental note to ask DCI Ampleforth about it. What were the chances that Jason might stash any secret projects he'd been working on at his new house? Particularly any handwritten notes for his translation from the Dutch book from which he had lifted his bestselling story?

It was probably where he had hidden the book itself, since Gita Patel had said it went missing from the shelf where she had first seen it in his college room.

Or would he have destroyed it? Burned it in that fireplace? Surely the time of its usefulness to him had passed, but he might have attached sentimental meaning to it.

'Have you spoken to the media about this?' he asked Imogen.

'Yes, I'm hoping to be interviewed by Sky News, the BBC and Channel 4. There may be radio interviews and print journalists, as well.' Seeing his expression, she added, 'I'm doing all I can, you see, to bring Jason's killer to justice.'

And bring yourself centre stage as the bereaved girlfriend, thought St. Just.

His heart sank at the news, but he had rather been expecting this. Imogen clearly had a flair for the melodramatic, and she would take every opportunity to put out a call to the public, probably in the process muddying the waters of the investigation, bringing out every nutcase in England and beyond. They would get the usual false confessions, and every tip, however insane, would have to be followed up. He imagined her motives for this included some complicated combination of grief and a desire to keep Jason's book in the public eye, circulating widely and driving up profits for Castle Publishing.

He was strongly reminded of his recent conversation with Minette Miniver. Imogen Castle had been besotted with Jason at some point, as well, but had he died before she'd had the wool pulled from her eyes?

Or had she come to realize his true nature? Had she already sensed that Jason's roving eye could quickly become a problem?

Imogen struck him as a woman used to having her own way, a woman who had grown up in the lap of luxury, a woman who had walked into a ready-made family dynasty, created for her by Sir Boniface. She might have been born lacking the humanitarian gene Minette seemed to possess, the gene which had inclined her towards a life of service to others.

What might the more self-centred Imogen have done if Jason moved on to greener pastures, having wrung from her all he wanted?

As they drove away from the Castles' house, St. Just reflected on the interview. The term 'castling' came into his mind, a play on the Castle family name. Castling – a manoeuvre in chess to protect the king and to deploy the rook to the centre of the field. He had the feeling that's exactly what mother and daughter had been doing, either consciously or unconsciously. Protecting the king – in this case, Sir Boniface – and moving the rook into a position of greater power. The rook being Imogen or her brother David.

Despite the obvious friction between the two women, he felt certain they would come together in the face of a common enemy. The common enemy being himself and Constable Lambert.

Daisy Lambert's mind seemed to be running along similar tracks.

'They didn't like having us there.'

'Most people don't like having the police in their sitting rooms. We always bring either bad or terrible news – there is no in-between.'

She manoeuvred the car back on to the main road, slipping in behind an oversized Mercedes. 'I wonder why David and his father didn't make an appearance?'

'I wondered the same,' said St. Just. 'It was almost as if the women had been sent on a scouting mission to find out what we knew.'

'Do you know, I almost wonder . . .' she began.

'Go on, Constable.'

'As you say, no one wants the police in their sitting room. But they especially feel that way if they've had prior dealings with the police. Dealings that went against them, or almost did.'

'I'm sure you've been looking into their backgrounds. Have you turned up something interesting that makes you say that?'

'Not so far,' she acknowledged, slowing the car at a roundabout. The traffic was increasingly heavy as they drew nearer to the centre of town, and it was more difficult to talk over the cacophony of noise.

Oxford had changed so much over the years from a sleepy academic town – like his Cambridge still was, in many respects – to something approaching the noise and chaos of London. St. Just hoped the city planners would be able to hold progress at bay before the entire medieval ambience disappeared behind sheets of glass and intolerable, soul-destroying decibel levels.

He asked Daisy to repeat what she had just said.

'I said it's early days yet, and we should remember that the Castles haven't lived in Oxford all their lives. They're from London – "The Smoke".'

'Of course, you're right. We haven't begun to scratch the surface, but certainly the Met will give us anything they have. I think we've done as much as possible for one day. Once you drop me off at the hotel, I hope you'll have a good meal and perhaps a drink. And get some rest.'

'I think I'll drop back into HQ and have a look around the computer files, see if anything new has come in. I'll let you know tomorrow if anything turns up.'

He had seen this kind of dedication before. He had himself put in those kinds of long hours, especially after his wife died, before Portia came along to give him a reason to go home at night.

He knew this dedication would catch up with Daisy, that she would one day reach a point where she'd worked herself to the point of exhaustion. He knew from experience how sharp that point could be.

He also knew that nothing he said would stop her.

She executed a U-turn to drop him at the front door of the Randolph. A livery-clad doorman hurried down the steps to open the car door.

St. Just, who always over-tipped for good luck, slipped a five-pound note into his hand.

Constable Lambert sped off as he went to meet Portia for a nightcap in the Morse Bar.

TWENTY-SEVEN
Coffee Klatch

Later that night, St. Just found a text from DCI Ampleforth asking him to meet at a nearby coffee shop for breakfast.

He left Portia having a lie-in in their room and, as he made his quiet way out through the door, put the 'Do Not Disturb' sign on the handle.

It had been nearly midnight before they got to sleep, and he didn't see why the investigation should ruin her for the next day's work. She'd told him over brandies in the Morse Bar that – between the excellent hotel room service and sound-proofing – she was making great headway, and hoped to have most of a rough draft finished before they left Oxford for home.

She tactfully did not ask when he planned to leave. But they both had somewhere else to be on Monday morning in Cambridge. They both knew he might have to stay behind while she took the train home. Sergeant Fear could handle the office for him for a day or two more, but no more than that. The clock was ticking.

Walking into The Black Sheep coffee shop, he was not surprised to see Constable Lambert sitting at the table. Judging by the bags under her eyes, she might not have slept at all.

'Does this mean you have news?' he asked her, pulling a chair back from the wooden table.

'I'm not certain,' she said. 'It's all a bit tentative.'

'I'm telling you, it's too vague,' said Ampleforth. 'I'm not dismissing it,' he added, seeing her reaction. 'But we'll go into all that after we've talked over a few other points.'

'Yes, sir,' she replied, with no evident rancour but with an alert posture that suggested she would be looking for the first opening to discuss her findings.

St. Just asked Ampleforth, 'Has anything else come to light? Anything from your interviews with people from the guest list for Jason's party?'

'Not really. Almost universally their information is unhelpful. They all say much the same thing: they showed up for the party, the guest of honour was very late, some began drifting towards the back exit in search of nourishment, slipping away quietly, unnoticed. Then, of course, the rest were instructed by the master to leave out the back, through the garden, and they complied. Some simply left the college altogether, however. Those who were only there to see the famous author decided to call it an early night.'

'They're all cooperating?'

'Yes, but there's little to cooperate with, if you follow my meaning. No one claims to have seen anything unusual. No one admits to seeing anyone leave the party via the normal exit – the door leading to the main stairs at the bottom of which we found our victim. They all tell a version of much the same story. They hung about the library drinking and laughing but growing incrementally more restless as their dinnertime approached and then passed.'

'It was Lady Ursula who drew up the guest list,' said St. Just. 'As I'm sure you know. And I find that odd in one respect. She really had nothing to do with the day-to-day running of the firm, so it's likely she didn't know the people who would need to be invited or who would expect to be invited. I suppose she might have consulted Imogen, but no one's saying so.'

'I'm not sure that's unusual or unexpected,' said Ampleforth. 'I gather the whole idea of the thing was to impress – to invite those with deep pockets who could help the college, having been suitably impressed by its ability to draw a major, popular figure such as Jason. It's the kind of thing people probably won't admit to, but when they're looking at paying exorbitant fees for tuition, they're going to want bragging rights for their offspring. They want to be able to say "my youngest, Primrose, went to St Rumwold's College, Oxford, you know. The place where Jason Verdoodt was a lecturer".'

'You're right,' said St. Just. 'Lady Ursula would know who those deep-pocketed people were. The publicity from hosting the party at a renowned college would burnish the sheen of the publishing house. And if Jason was a draw in life, he certainly will be in death. Unless people are put off by having their lecturers drugged and pushed down stairwells.'

Ampleforth shook his head. 'In my experience, and I'm sure in yours, once the initial fear wears off, people are fascinated by that kind of thing. By murder. The college will feature in one of those true-crime shows before too long, you mark my words. I don't know why, but being part of a crime seems to make people feel important and interesting, if at one remove.

'Anyway, the size of that guest list resulted in a multitude of suspects, including the lady's own daughter and the lady herself, of course. But the sheer number of suspects, or witnesses, wasn't too large a problem for us in the end, thanks to their herd-like behaviour in dashing off – almost as one – to the trough for dinner. There don't appear to have been many strays.'

St. Just said, 'Maybe we should be asking who was left *off* the guest list and might be angered by the omission, if there are any who fit that category. Perhaps someone who would be expected to cause a ruckus if they *were* invited.'

'Minette wasn't invited,' Constable Lambert reminded them. 'And she was knives-out with Imogen.'

'That's right, she wasn't,' said Ampleforth. 'Still, I don't see . . .'

'And that begs the question,' Lambert continued, 'why was she there?'

'I don't follow,' said Ampleforth. 'She just pushed her way in. Angry she'd not been invited. Woman scorned, and all that.'

'Perhaps Jason made sure she was there, just to stir the pot,' said Constable Lambert. 'I think he knew she was desperate, at her wits' end, so he made sure she knew there was a party she wasn't invited to. Just to egg her on, see what she'd do. He may even have mentioned his official date was Imogen.'

'That seems a stretch,' said Ampleforth.

'Do you think so, sir?' she asked politely. 'I think Jason was a master manipulator. A perfect monster. I think he knew her very well after so many years. He knew she loved him to the point of obsession, and to make her feel this one night was her last chance to persuade him to stay with her – I think that sort of game fits with what we know of him. For all we know, he let her in early himself, through the college's side door.'

'To make sure she was there with Imogen,' said St. Just slowly. 'Just to see what would happen. To light the blue touch paper and step back. I suppose that fits with what we know of his nature. And the more we know, the more we know the man was pure poison.'

Lambert said with growing confidence, 'And the way she was dressed that night, overdressed in that flash frock – more than one witness mentioned it as all wrong for the occasion. I put it down to snobbery until I saw it for myself. She showed it to me as she was packing to leave; she had decided to leave it behind for someone to donate to charity. She said she hated it, and it would only carry bad memories for her now. I do think that dress gave away her mental state, like. Because she struck me as someone so conservative, she'd never in her right mind have worn it.'

'Hmm,' said Ampleforth. 'Perhaps we should try her again. But unless she tells us, we can't know for sure that Jason goaded her into attending. Anyway, so many people were at the party who might have feared or disliked Jason and had a grudge or grievance against him. What sort of guest list is that? And what are the chances now that they'll own up to it?'

It was a very good question. The investigation had thus far taken St. Just, Ampleforth and Lambert down the winding streets and alleyways of Oxford, with its long history of town-versus-gown feuds, its venomous skirmishes for academic prizes, and its scandals too numerous to count. The inquiry had been hampered by uncooperative witnesses – the Castles, most notably – and by people with something to hide, like Gita Patel, until she had decided to come clean. Even the college master had seemed less interested in who had killed Jason than in wanting it all cleared up quickly.

St. Just wondered if they might be looking at the case the wrong way round. Had Jason been a threat to someone not just for his selfish behaviour, and his basic dishonesty, but for what he knew about someone? And what he might do with that knowledge?

Could he have been killed by someone with secrets he had threatened to expose?

Or had already exposed?

Could it be a case of murder committed not out of jealousy, but out of fear and revenge – equally strong motives?

He noticed a signal passing between Ampleforth and Lambert.

'Go ahead and show him,' Ampleforth said to her with a sigh. 'May as well, for what it's worth. Maybe St. Just will see something I don't. That's why he's here, after all.'

'Thank you, sir. I'd like to start by asking if either of you have read Jason's book?'

They both shook their heads rather sheepishly.

'There's scarcely been time to sit about reading books, has there?' said Ampleforth.

'Too right you are, sir,' she said. 'It so happens, I had read the book already. How could I not, when it was in the front window of every bookshop I passed in Oxford? And something I read in it stayed with me – rather, one of our suspects made me think of something in the book. So much so that last night I went back, downloaded an e-version, and did a search of the pages, looking for the words that had caught in my mind.'

St. Just was kicking himself, and he was certain Ampleforth was kicking himself as well. Someone should have been assigned to read the book written by their victim, the book which had propelled him to fame, as being potentially useful to the investigation. It was on St. Just's to-do list, he told himself. There simply hadn't been time, as Ampleforth had said.

Constable Lambert, warming to her topic, said, 'I wondered if the true-to-life descriptions in Jason's masterpiece that reviewers raved about were exactly that: drawn closely from the author's actual adventures in the hallowed halls of learning. We now know that the book wasn't his to begin with, but that wouldn't prevent him from changing a sentence here and there, adding a character or description, perhaps, to someone else's work. Since he was translating it into English, he was free to do what he wanted, correct?'

'Correct,' said Ampleforth, in a 'will you get on with it' way.

Turning to St. Just, she said, 'There's something I want to show you, sir.' She flipped through the pages of a manila folder she'd brought with her and took out a pencil drawing. It was of a young man, his thin face all sharp angles and edges.

'Is that David?' asked St. Just.

'We don't know who it is. But it certainly looks like David to me.'

'To me, too,' admitted Ampleforth. 'But it's only a sketch. A resemblance, at best.'

She said, 'In *The White Owl*, there is a character who . . . especially now I see this sketch of a much younger man . . . a character who has all the basic characteristics of David. Tall, thin as a skeleton, with pale skin and a snake's head and heavy eyebrows and so on. It was the description in Jason's book of the long, thin hands and the spade-like nails that drew my attention. Very specific, it was. The rest of the characters are lightly drawn, but this character got an entire paragraph of description to himself.'

'So you're telling us this because . . .' prompted Ampleforth.

'It came up in a search of the suspects in the case using a photo of David and facial recognition software I've installed on my computer. It's a composite drawn by a victim who claims David attacked him.'

'Attacked? Just randomly walked up and attacked him?'

'Solicited him first, sir. And something then led to an altercation between the two men. There was an element to the story of money owed for services rendered, if you follow. The officer taking the report claimed he couldn't really make any sense of it and – I'm reading between the lines now – he didn't much care. He thought the victim got what he deserved.'

'How long ago was this?' asked St. Just.

'Ten years ago, in London. Not that anything's much changed in ten years. That sort of prejudice hangs around.'

'Yes, it does. Any charges brought?'

'No. It's a dead end. The attacker fled, so the composite

sketch – which the victim drew himself – ended up in the file on the case. But I thought it was interesting.'

'I think it's a stretch,' insisted Ampleforth.

'I would think the same, except for the clear visual resemblance to David. And in the text of the book there's a claim made that the character, somewhat unimaginatively named Davide, is a predator. That is the word used: predator. David's resemblance to a key character in *The White Owl* – well, we can't dismiss it out of hand. Sir.'

'But how would Jason have found out about this attack?'

'That I don't know, sir, but perhaps there'd been gossip in publishing circles? Or Jason's use of the word predator wasn't based on the legal sense of the term, if you follow. He just generally had a sense of the man as predatory.'

'It's probably time to have another word with David,' St. Just agreed. 'We don't know what we have here, if anything – perhaps a subtle form of blackmail on Jason's part? Was he simply playing with David, for laughs? Or perhaps he thought it didn't matter – that David wouldn't read the book closely or recognize himself in it if he did? People do have rather a blind spot in that way. But there's also every chance David only pretended to have read *The White Owl*. We know it wasn't really his cup of tea at all; Gita was the one who discovered it.'

'I had much the same thoughts myself,' said Lambert.

'I'll go and have a word with him,' said St. Just. 'I want to show him this sketch and see his reaction for myself.'

Did her face show a flicker of disappointment? St. Just imagined she had been picturing a similar scene, perhaps with her in a starring role as the constable who unlocked the famous case. Watching for David's reaction, knowing he was guilty, and badgering away as long as it took to get the truth out of him.

'You can come with me if you'd like,' said St. Just, looking to Ampleforth. She was his team member, after all. St. Just was the interloper.

But to his surprise, she shook her head. 'I have other fish to fry today, sir. Just let me know what happens, will you?'

TWENTY-EIGHT
Sketchy

St. Just put in a call from the coffee shop to Castle Publishing. Gita answered on the first ring.

'Castle Publishing. David Castle's office.'

'Hello, Gita.'

'Inspector, hello,' she said. 'Was there something more you wanted to ask me? If so, I can't—'

'Possibly later. First, would you tell me if there's a scene in *The White Owl* where a character goes over a cliff?'

'Where a character . . . what? Why, no. Nothing like that happens.'

'Thank you. Please keep my query to yourself. Now, will you see if David Castle is available to see me this morning? Right away, as soon as possible.'

'I'll check.'

While he waited, St. Just glanced though the folder Constable Lambert had given him before she left with Ampleforth. He'd refused her offer of a lift to Castle Publishing as it was a short walk from The Black Sheep and, besides, he wanted to work off the pastry he'd consumed for breakfast.

The file was thin, containing little more than the sketch of the David Castle lookalike and a copy of the brief police report taken one day in June, ten years previously. The report noted that the sketch had been provided by the accuser in the case, and after reading the police officer's notes, St. Just felt it was something of a miracle the sketch had survived – that the officer had not simply binned it as extraneous. The report stated briefly that a young man named Jonathan Asquith had turned up at the station in London's Notting Hill to report he'd been attacked by a man, whose sketch he duly provided. Jonathan reported that the man told him his name was Stephen, but that he, Jonathan, recognized him from the neighbourhood where his nickname was Castleman. Asked by the policeman how he knew these names, Jonathan replied, 'He's a regular. We all know him. And he's a real [expletive deleted].'

The officer noted that Jonathan 'presented with a slight bruising on his face under his left eye'. Unfortunately – and St. Just, thought, suspiciously – no photo had been taken of the bruise, or at least none that appeared in the file. Asked whether Mr Castleman had sustained any injuries, Jonathan said no, that he himself had walked away when the man had threatened him with a penknife, even though 'he owed me money'.

There was a brief notation suggesting the officer thought the altercation was the result of a rent-boy situation gone wrong, and it was clear the officer had sat back and waited to see if anyone from the other side filed a report. Or perhaps whether Jonathan might return with a solicitor to press his claim. Neither event having transpired, the file had disappeared into the pile of daily happenings in a busy London precinct. With no subsequent follow-up, the complaint had remained in the computer system until Constable Lambert had come along to piece the various parts of the story together via facial recognition software, possibly combined with a search on the name Castle and variations thereof.

Ten years later, St. Just sat back in his own chair in a trendy Oxford coffee shop, staring at the massive wall mural of a boy and a girl kissing, and wondered if the officer knew exactly who 'Stephen Castleman' was – the son of a local, monied man and his noble wife – and thought it best to bury the whole thing.

Gita came back on the line.

'Mr Castle says he's busy but perhaps he could see you tomorrow.' He could hear the smile in her voice, though he was certain she had the sense to keep a poker face.

'Tell Mr Castle he will see me today. Whether our interview takes place in the privacy of his office or in an interrogation room at the police station is strictly up to him.'

'I'll tell him,' she said.

A minute later she was back. 'What luck,' she reported,

deadpan. 'He's just had a cancellation and can see you in his office in half an hour.'

'Tell him I said thank you.'

The office of David Castle, editor-in-chief of the company that bore his name, looked largely unchanged, although St. Just thought the space felt a bit more cluttered, and that there were a few new outer space gewgaws scattered on the shelves behind David's desk. For all St. Just knew, these were collectible items worth a small fortune – he could just recognize a Luke Skywalker action figure and a Princess Leia doll, her hair coiled in buns around her ears. Remembering David was a man approaching middle age, it seemed a harmless but slightly preposterous pastime. The background run on him at the start of the case, besides failing to turn up that long-ago report which would never have been found without the diligence of Constable Lambert, had revealed nothing of interest. He lived in a separate cottage on his parents' estate, rent-free, as did his sister. St. Just thought that was nice work if you could get it. It was rather like being related to royalty without the onerous duties of ribbon-cutting and ship-launching.

But there was no hint of a personal life in the background, no known associates of a doubtful or commendatory nature. David lived a solitary life, on the surface. The London police report was the only hint of a secret life, albeit a life lived years ago.

Even if the old report was to do with David 'Castleman' Castle, St. Just was willing to withhold judgement, knowing how easy it was to accuse someone falsely. Too often a so-called victim was lying, making lies believable through practised guile and the sheer force of charm.

Apart from all that, for all he knew the run-in with Jonathan Asquith had frightened David into mending his ways, and he had retreated into a harmless fantasy world, the evidence of which now surrounded him.

Gita had greeted St. Just's entrance with a wide smile, announced his arrival over the intercom, and walked him over to David's office. After that she tactfully disappeared. He wondered if there had been progress with her new job application. Certainly she would be well advised to leave the inhabitants of Castle Publishing to their own devices and carve out a fresh new space for herself with her fiancé in London.

St. Just again sat in the chair across from David and opened the conversation with a compliment. It seemed much the best way to set a calming tone for the interview, and David looked to be near his wits' end. St. Just suspected he was on edge much of the time, but the investigation seemed to have worn him even thinner than before, sharpening his already sharp features. St. Just wondered if he had given up eating altogether.

'Having read Jason's book, I feel I must commend you on discovering him and bringing along his career. Engaged as I am to an author, I know how much chance is involved in these discoveries – but more than chance is involved at your end, I'm certain.' He smiled guilelessly.

'Of course, it's more than that. It takes, if I may say so, a certain genius just to spot another genius.'

'It takes one to know one. Absolutely,' St. Just agreed.

'You could put it that way.'

'The scene in the book that stays with me,' said St. Just, 'is where that minor character is pushed off a cliff. What is her name? Jane? Of course, that's it – one character calls her "Plain Jane" at some point. That is such a powerful scene.'

'Yes,' said David, thereby confirming for St. Just that David had no more read *The White Owl* than he had. 'That is indeed a powerful scene. Quite . . . symbolic. Jason was good with symbolism. Is that why you're here, to talk about the book?'

'In a way,' said St. Just. 'What I've been turning over in my mind is, despite insurance and any other safety nets you might have in place, I simply can't help thinking how Jason's death will impact the company, perhaps catastrophically. Surely he was irreplaceable.'

David laughed, showing a set of very white, very expensive, and very sharp teeth. It gave his entire look a vulturine aspect. 'They all like to think they're irreplaceable, writers. But the fact is not one of them is that important.' He shrugged, holding out his long, bony hands. 'Writers are like buses; there's another one along every few minutes.'

'Yes,' said St. Just, thinking he wouldn't be repeating David's comments to Portia anytime soon. 'I suppose that's true.'

David was just warming to this theme. St. Just imagined he found it safer territory than any others St. Just might have in mind. 'I've dealt with hundreds of writers at conferences and book fairs. And I can tell you this: the smaller they are, the harder they fall. They all start out with these big dreams, believing they're something special. Well, they get the stuffing knocked out of them very quickly.'

'But surely you don't see it as part of your job to do that? To wash the starch out of them?'

'No, as a matter of fact, I don't. It is just a by-product of the process. The confident ones can deal with it. The others . . .' David shrugged. *Who cares?*

'I understand you lived in London before coming to work here at your father's firm in Oxford.'

If David noted the change of subject, it didn't seem to cause him much alarm. Rather, he took it as an opportunity to brag about his family's wealth.

'Yes, we have a house in London, like most people.'

'Really?' said St. Just. 'Most people of my acquaintance are happy with the one house they have, sir. But during your time in London, did you come across a young man named Jonathan Asquith, by any chance?'

St. Just, who had been watching David's face closely, saw the small tell – the sudden shrinking of the skin against the facial features, the giveaway that the name had indeed registered. That, in fact, it was a name he had for some time dreaded hearing again.

'The name doesn't sound familiar,' he said.

'That's very strange. He seemed to have known you – how shall I put this? – intimately.'

'I'm telling you the name means nothing to me.' He didn't dare try to bring the interview to an end. Instead, he sat waiting quietly as if for the next blow, calculating how much the police would know about an incident from so long ago.

'Perhaps this will refresh your memory,' said St. Just, pulling the file jacket containing the police report out of his portfolio.

He opened the file, gratified to see that he had David's full attention. Extracting the sketch, he shoved it across the desk blotter so it was right under David's nose.

David glanced down at it briefly and said, 'What is this?'

'That, I am told, is a sketch of you. Has anyone ever mentioned how memorable your features are?'

'No. It looks nothing like me,' said David. 'Anyway, where did you get it?'

'Oh, the police have their methods,' said St. Just. 'We all talk to one another. So you deny this is you?'

'Deny? The word "deny" implies there's been some sort of accusation. I don't care for that word. I will only state – again – that this completely amateurish sketch doesn't look anything like me. Should I have a lawyer present?'

'Absolutely, you would be within your rights to have your lawyer present. Now, I'm one of those people who may not know much about art, but I know what I like. What if I told you Jonathan Asquith is adamant that this is indeed you, that this sketch – quite an accomplished one, in my unsophisticated opinion – is of a man who assaulted him years ago after refusing to pay him for his time and effort? What if I told you this was drawn practically from the life, and that Jonathan presented it as evidence to the police in filing a complaint in your London jurisdiction? What if I told you further that, even after all these years, Jonathan has perfect recall of the trauma he endured that night?' That last was nearly the truth. Even now, he was sure, Constable Lambert was busy trying to locate Jonathan Asquith to get an update to his statement, and to show him a recent photo of David Castle for confirmation.

'Why on earth would he do that? Create this drawing, I mean?'

St. Just was reminded of the oldest legal advice in the world. Never ask a question when you don't know what the answer will be. However, in this case he felt certain David knew the answer. He did seem surprised, however, that this image existed, and wanted to work out what the police knew.

He attempted to return the drawing to St. Just, pushing it back across his desk, but St. Just said, 'That is simply a photocopy. We have many copies, plus the original. Feel free to keep it. Personally, I would say it's suitable for framing.'

'What an interesting choice of words,' said David. 'Framing.'

'It is, isn't it? Is that what Jason tried to do to you – put you in the frame for a past misdeed? Was he trying to blackmail you, sir?'

'I have no idea what you're talking about.'

'I'm talking about the fact that there is a character in his world-famous book describing a figure he calls Davide. This description matches you in every way, and this description also includes the word predator. The character is described as a predator.'

'Really? I don't remember that being in the book.'

'I'm not surprised to hear that,' said St. Just.

David, missing the life raft St. Just had just floated out to him, reached behind him for what was undoubtedly a first edition copy of *The White Owl*.

'Show me the description you're talking about,' said David.

'I think you'll find it's in chapter twenty-seven. But are you denying you had any conversation with Jason about this passage in his book, a passage describing you, a passage accusing you of being a predator?'

David hesitated for the first time. 'Now you mention it, Jason did try to draw my attention to chapter twenty-seven. I didn't understand what he was talking about, and I sort of never got round to it.'

St. Just found this believable only because it was apparent to him that David had never read the book or done much more than skim the jacket copy.

David might very well be guilty of accosting and injuring Jonathan Asquith in London just over ten years ago, but any attempted blackmail by Jason seemed doomed to failure, for the simple reason that his own editor had never read his book. How that must have irritated the author, known for his very large ego.

'If that's all,' said David, 'I really don't see how I can help the police further. I do wish you well in your inquiries, however.'

'That's very kind of you, sir. Our inquiries are going quite well but we're always grateful for the well wishes. I'm going to ask that you not leave Oxford until this investigation is concluded or until you are given permission by the police to leave. I hope I make myself clear.'

'You must be joking. I'm to be in London tomorrow for a publishing awards dinner. Castle Publishing is a nominee.'

'That's too bad. If I were you, sir, I would send someone else in my stead.' He was thinking Gita might enjoy a night out in London. 'Either DCI Ampleforth or someone from his office will be in touch.'

TWENTY-NINE
The Chase

St. Just left the futuristic offices of Castle Publishing feeling rather dispirited. The interview with David Castle had cleared up a few things while clouding others. As he emerged out through the front door into the chill of the autumn day, his mobile buzzed. It was DCI Ampleforth.

'There's been an attempted murder. Lambert just called it in, asking for backup.'

'Where?' demanded St. Just. 'Who?'

'In Cowley. In a bedsit in Cowley.'

'What in hell was Lambert doing in Cowley?' Then he recalled Ampleforth's saying something over coffee about pressing Minette again.

Please, not Minette, he thought.

'It's Minette Miniver.'

'Will she be all right?'

'Early days, but she's unconscious. I'll swing by Jericho to pick you up and we can talk on the way, but I'm worried. Lambert's not answering our calls.'

DCI Ampleforth collected St. Just in his own car, a sedan with a flashing police light temporarily attached to the top, as all other units had been sent to search for the murder suspect.

'It's all hands on deck at the moment,' he explained. 'Just keep a lookout for anyone acting suspiciously. It's all we can do for now.'

St. Just found it an alarming ride, for Ampleforth turned out to be quite near-sighted and many a pedestrian from that day owed his or her life to St. Just's shouted warnings as the car careened down the streets of Jericho. He finally prevailed on Ampleforth to pull over and let him take the wheel.

The police eventually caught up with the suspect in Port

Meadow outside Jericho, near the canal bridge. It took two men and a man-trailing dog to subdue the killer.

'It was a dog-walker who spotted her,' DCI Ampleforth told St. Just. 'One of the wild ponies got involved, as well as some geese. I gather she tried to escape on one – one of the ponies, that is – but it threw her off. She's at the station if you'd like to listen in on the interview.'

'I would indeed.'

Many hours later they sat in the police canteen. They'd been running on coffee from the vending machine for hours, only to find the canteen version was worse.

St. Just now said apologetically to his colleagues, 'It had to have been her.'

'You might have let me in on your thinking,' said Ampleforth.

'I would have said something if I'd been more certain. But I couldn't figure out the *why*, so I rejected the idea out of hand. It seemed like time-wasting, leading us all down a dead-end path. For the longest time I couldn't see the motive. But of course, once I realized she was terrible at her job, it all made sense.'

'I don't follow, sir,' said Constable Lambert. She looked down at her phone, which had been a casualty of the day, only just retrieved from the canal and still waterlogged. She'd joined in the chase for the culprit once the emergency services had arrived to take care of Minette.

She'd have to see if that new guy in IT, reputed to be a genius, could save it. Weren't you supposed to dry it out in a bag of uncooked rice or something? She'd have to remember to keep some uncooked rice in her desk, or learn not to wade into canals after criminals.

'Jason's rooms were dusty in places – dust that had accumulated for a while,' St. Just explained. 'Dust that the scout should have been seeing to. The college doesn't retain people who are lazy or who don't know what they're doing. From the scouts to the master, these are professionals. Proud of their jobs.

'It wasn't that the scout didn't try; it was that she had to try so *hard* and work so many hours just to keep up. She seemed to do her job well in other areas – the habitués of the Senior Common Room especially would have complained if she hadn't. So what was she doing in Jason's rooms *instead* of cleaning? Was she using the time for a good look through his things? It did make me wonder – if only briefly – if she was what she claimed to be. Or if she'd talked her way into the job even though she was underqualified – if so, she wouldn't be the first person to do that. But we had stronger suspects, so I ignored my instincts. You know, that nagging sense you get that something's wrong but you don't know what.'

Ampleforth seemed determined to ignore this reasoning with its touchy-feely, New Age vibe. The inspector still couldn't believe it. He had had a favourite suspect all fitted out for this crime.

'It *can't* have been the scout,' he protested. 'Surely it was David, enraged that Jason had exploited him for his book, exposing his secrets in the process. "Davide Chateau", indeed. Wouldn't fool a child.'

Let it go, thought St. Just. 'I have no doubt David – if he ever noticed Jason's portrayal of him – would be annoyed. The potential for embarrassment was real, but he might well count on no one recognizing him. And no one did. How many aristocratic sons are there in the UK who fit the general description of being a "long, lean, louche layabout", in Jason's words? But it's clear David had no idea what was in Jason's book. Why would he murder somebody over something he didn't know about?'

'Very well then.' Ampleforth took a sip of his coffee, made a face, and set the cup back down. 'The children's book author. Alarming individual, isn't she? And childish, like her books. No doubt given to tantrums. Absolutely the type who would want to eliminate anyone she viewed as competition. Certainly Jason had surpassed her in sales, practically overnight, with just the one book. Plus, he'd moved on to greener pastures, hadn't he? She was just another of his tossed-aside conquests. If it can't be the son, it must be the children's author.'

As if the whole thing were a guessing game, a game of Cluedo. St. Just chalked the inspector's attitude up to

disappointment. Ampleforth was used to guessing right and
this time he'd been dead wrong.

'If we can ignore the fact that the scout attempted to murder
Minette, I'd agree with you.'

'Right,' said Ampleforth, stirring more sugar into his coffee.
'Can't get round that. She was as good as caught red-handed
by Constable Lambert here at the bedsit, and then she tried to
flee. Might have made it, too, if the pony had cooperated. All
right, tell me your reasoning.'

'It had to be someone with access to the wine glass Jason
drank from that evening,' said St. Just.

'So the bottles of wine really had nothing to do with it.
Nobody gained access to the college cellars and tampered
with the bottles.'

'That's right.'

'I thought so.'

You did not. St. Just, exhausted, was getting tetchy. He
wanted to get back to the hotel, back to Portia, and back to
Cambridge. He said, 'Had solving the case hinged on knowing
who had access to the cellars, we could immediately have
eliminated all the invited guests. Well, perhaps one of them
could have had a connection to a member of staff who helped
them out, much in the way a prison escapee might seduce or
trick a guard into providing a key and other means of escape.'

'Or access to the cellar.'

'Correct. But the college is like a fortress – far from being
lax in their security, they've had centuries to establish their
rituals. Especially when it comes to something as important
as the wine cellar.'

'I should think so.'

'So the first order of suspects was the college master, the
college butler, and Professor Monet, who had been put in
charge of the keys by members of the Senior Common Room.
One of those three could easily have gained access to the cellar
and tampered with an additional bottle of wine in advance of
the party. Even if they were seen doing so, they would have
a ready excuse. The master not so much, but the butler and
Professor Monet? Absolutely. The problem was the bottles
were all accounted for. So said Monet, and I believed him.

'Then, as it turned out, the lab tests showed only a single glass had been tampered with.'

Ampleforth insisted, 'Anyone arriving at the party early could have got hold of one of the bottles in the library, opened it, contaminated a glass, and made sure Jason drank from it. And that tells us it was someone making sure no one else was affected. No innocent bystander. Otherwise, they'd have poisoned the entire bottle – much simpler. That suggests someone with a finer sensibility than most killers, don't we agree?'

'By that logic we were looking for a depraved killer with an honour code. I saw no need to eliminate the scout on that basis – nor the master, the butler, Professor Monet, or anyone else. Like you, I've met with perfectly civil criminals whose only fault was a penchant for violent crime. Many of them love having the power of life or death over people. *They* decide who dies and who is spared. They are often perfectly polite, even loving, to the ones they choose to spare.'

Ampleforth sighed, his shoulders drooping in surrender. 'Out with it then, man. What else made you suspect her?'

'Apart from the state of Jason's rooms? Her access, for a start. She knows this college because her job is to clean so many of its nooks and crannies.'

'Except she couldn't get into the wine cellar.'

'Couldn't she? But you're right – at least not without involving someone else by bribery or other means. She probably thought first of sneaking her way into the wine cellar with a copy of the key, then realized those ancient keys can't be copied. She could steal the keys but there was a risk of the staff being suspected, of her being caught out. It was all too risky.

'She did know all the secret passages and byways of the college, however; she learned St Rumwold's ways from the undergrads who routinely climb the walls after the main door to the college is closed and locked. That could come in handy for pointing the finger of blame at an outsider. More to the point, she knew about the book lift and saw the potential for putting it to use to hide the body until she was ready for it to be found. It was important to her to blur the time of death as much as possible.

'Anyway, she finally realized it was best to wait to tamper with the wine once the butler had set the bottles and glasses out for the party in the library. She made sure she was there early, volunteering to help set up, making herself indispensable; it was all part of her act. The role she'd been playing since she first got the job.'

'It's too ruddy convenient,' insisted Ampleforth. 'She wants a job at the college, a job opens up, and she gets the job.'

'Precisely. You have put your finger on the very crux of the matter.'

Ampleforth beamed, wondering what on earth St. Just meant, but unwilling to admit he had no idea.

St. Just added, 'It would help the prosecution mightily, I suspect, to find out whom she replaced and why. Which scout, I mean.'

The penny dropped at last. 'You suspect foul play?'

'I do. And it will be one more confirmation of her cold-bloodedness. Her psychopathy, and the premeditated nature of this crime. I suspect that she removed the former scout because she wanted her spot. Full stop. She eliminated her in the same way someone might steal a parking space.'

'I'll get someone on it right away,' Ampleforth said, reaching for his phone.

St. Just stilled his hand. 'I've taken the liberty of having Constable Lambert search the relevant dates for potentially suspicious incidents involving scouts employed by the college.' Daisy Lambert steadfastly kept her eyes on the table as he spoke, not daring to meet her superior's eyes.

'I hope you don't mind,' St. Just rushed on. 'The head housekeeper says the former scout, one Mrs Bottle, was killed during a robbery as she was leaving a nearby pub one evening. I'd like to hear more about that. Was she poisoned first with sedatives, like Jason was, to make attacking her easier, to keep her from crying out?'

'I'll be damned,' began Ampleforth. 'So she . . . so we've been dealing with a monster. An even bigger monster than we realized.'

'To return to the scene of Jason's murder,' St. Just continued, 'the wine bottles and glasses at the party were not left unattended, according to several observers. Some are adamant about this, others didn't notice. But the overall impression was that none of the guests could approach the table and interfere with one of the glasses. From start to finish, drinks were handled by members of college staff only, who were basically barricaded behind a table. The question was: why would any of them risk everything to tamper with one of the glasses? Was the scout doing it for someone else, perhaps under pressure? Doing it for herself? Those are the questions that follow but the initial question of who had the opportunity to tamper with the wine became clearer.'

'It still could've been someone who interfered with the glass before the servers came on the scene that night. It could have been one of the guests, during the party, just slipping poison into Jason's glass, with no one noticing.'

'You're forgetting that Jason was killed around the time the guests started arriving. It must have been before their arrival, perhaps just before, or else someone would have witnessed what was happening.'

'Oh.'

'The butler is certain no guest arrived early to tamper with Jason's glass, poison him, kill him, and hide the body before the others got there. The butler took possession of the unopened bottles, oversaw them being lifted upstairs to the library. He oversaw their removal from the book lift – the dumb waiter. And he left the servers, including the scout, whom he trusted absolutely, in charge. She had ample time to open one bottle, poison one glass, and make sure Jason drank enough from the glass to make him pliable. All she had to do was arrive early.'

'That was the other question. Why did *he* come to the library so far ahead of the rest of the party? What drew him there?'

'She did, of course. So we have to ask, what would be the draw that got him there early? What could she have said that would have lured him to his death?'

'If you're ready, let's go and find out,' said Ampleforth, heaving himself to his feet. 'She's had enough of a break from questioning. Come with us, Lambert.'

THIRTY

In the Wind

B y the end of that day, she answered most of their questions under caution, although she quickly threw caution to the wind. Ignoring her solicitor's advice, Tess began to speak freely.

The woman who sat before them in the drab Kidlington HQ interview room was unrecognizable from the disfigured, put-upon scout St. Just had met in Jason's rooms. Even now, windblown and under pressure, her hair loose and her makeup fading, she was stunningly attractive. She sat straight up in her chair, a picture of perfect posture, and St. Just was struck again by how appearance was at least fifty per cent attitude. No wonder Jason hadn't recognized her.

'I didn't kill him,' she said stoutly. 'You have no idea what you're talking about. It was self-defence.'

No, it wasn't. 'Tell us what happened.'

Tess's appointed solicitor, one Mr Monroe, Esq., gave her one last pleading look. Clearly he'd given up, his client having refused his very good advice to stay quiet.

'I got him there early by telling him I knew his secret about the book he stole, and for a certain price I would keep quiet,' she said. 'But no sooner did he get there than he attacked me. I acted in self-defence.'

This was the story she would stick to for hours until, finally, Constable Lambert playing good cop to Ampleforth's bad, she broke.

As St. Just said to Portia later that night, 'We're going to let the lawyers sort that one out. It could even be true. But it doesn't explain her cold-blooded way of attacking Minette, and if she's tied to the death of the former scout . . . well. That was planned, even if the attempt to kill Minette was all instinct and reflex – improvisation, which is second nature to her. I truly believe that she fits the definition of a sociopath who sees people as obstacles. It wasn't Jason's money she wanted. He probably refused to pay her anyway, to succumb to blackmail. What she wanted was revenge.'

'Revenge for his having left her? As simple as that? She was just another of his conquests?'

'He dumped her as he had so many others. He had a gift for targeting, shall we say, unstable women, but this time he had the misfortune of choosing to dump a sociopath. Jason had got away with bad behaviour all his adult life. She decided he'd got away with it for the last time.'

'I'd say they both met their match,' said Portia. 'I'll say something else. It wouldn't surprise me to learn that his PhD thesis turns out to be based on research that can't be verified.'

'Funny you should mention that. Constable Lambert will be having a word with the head of his department. It's up to them to sort that one out, and it may take years to verify all the cited sources.'

'Lambert deserves a promotion.'

'Ampleforth will be putting in a word. I'll see to it.'

'Tell me what happened – and what you think happened,' said Portia, pouring them both another glass of wine. It was their last night at the Randolph, their last night in Oxford, and because he'd got back at such a late hour, they had ordered room service. Tomorrow, duty would call them both back to Cambridge, and before long St. Just would be involved in solving yet another mystery.

St. Just said, 'Having ditched her scout's apron, Tess dressed as one of the servers that night – black slacks, white shirt, bow tie, dark hair pulled back in a short ponytail. They are all trained to blend into the shadows, after all.'

'She'd also look not much different from the men wearing formal black tie for the occasion.'

'Right,' said St. Just. 'In case she was seen getting there early, that would come in handy. As it turned out, she was not seen.

'Here is what I think happened. I'm piecing this together from what Tess said in the interview, and what she didn't say.

She veered away from certain topics, much to the relief of her counsel. But I have no doubt they'll get the full story. When I left, Ampleforth and Lambert were still hard at it. Without Jason around to hate and plot against, I think life has lost meaning for her.

'Anyway, Tess, as we came to know her, or Theresa – is an actress who met Jason in the Netherlands when he returned there on a visit. We know he lived for years in Belgium and the Netherlands and matriculated at Leiden and Cambridge before coming to Oxford. That part of his biography, at least, was true.

'They had an affair. What I'm sure he thought of as a fling, and she saw as something more, as I'm sure he led her to believe. That was his pattern. She follows him to England, where she's landed an understudy role on the London stage – fittingly, a modern remake of *Witness for the Prosecution*.'

'The woman with the scar. Of course!' said Portia.

'Applying the makeup for that part of the story, making it look realistic, would have become second nature to her. But once in London, almost immediately she catches Jason with another woman. They fight. He tells her effectively to get lost. And she realizes how gullible she's been. She vows to get even and conceives this elaborate plot. Once the run of *Witness* ends, she has nothing but time on her hands until her next role begins at the Royal Shakespeare Theatre – she was keen to tell us tonight how in-demand she was as an actress. Pure ego.'

'Jason really did meet his match.'

'A match made in hell, one could say. Anyway, she takes a job as a waitress in Oxford, rents a bedsit – all to establish a home base, a reason for being in Oxford in case the police ever want to talk to her, which they do. She arranges to be interviewed at St Rumwold's for the scout position – an opening we believe she created by killing the poor woman in that position. With her background in service as a waitress at the Turf Tavern, she's easily taken on in a probationary position at the college.

'Now she has full access to Jason's rooms, where she finds an old book and realizes it's the same book – but in Dutch

– that Jason is representing as his own. It is clear to her that all Jason has done for the most part is translate the manuscript into English. Her Dutch happens to be as fluent as her English, the only giveaway being her trouble pronouncing the word idea, which she pronounced without the "a" at the end: "eye dee". I noticed this when I spoke with her initially. It was a small thing, unimportant at the time, easily explained as a regional British accent, and mostly buried beneath the thick cockney accent she'd adopted.

'Tess also happens to be the Dutch nickname for Theresa.'

'Was Tess even her real name?'

'More or less. To everyone at St Rumwold's she is Miss Tess Babbage as she goes about her cleaning duties – Babbage being the name of an ex-husband, long gone. Most people at the college know her as simply Tess. On the stage, she has appeared in supporting roles as Theresa Bakker, her maiden name.

'At the college, she makes herself unattractive, lumpy and plain – she put on some weight and muscle deliberately – with a horribly scarred face, a terrible burn mark that no one can bear to look at. Certainly Jason doesn't care what her name is. For him, beauty is a requirement before he'll even acknowledge a woman.'

'He doesn't recognize her. How remarkable.'

'Not for a minute; he doesn't really *see* her. She counts on that. He doesn't recognize her when she gains access to his room wearing a headscarf and makeup and speaking as little as possible but using a heavy cockney accent when it's unavoidable. Her makeup includes a fake latex burn scar to disguise her identity further. As she herself told us today, "Why should he notice me? I was just his effing servant".'

'She admits to the ruse.'

'Oh, completely. She's rather proud of it, you see. Her finest role! It's the murder she denies – murders, I should say.'

'What a remarkable woman. I mean, horrible, but remarkable. Such a nerve it took.'

'Is remarkable the word? I suppose so. Anyway, another small thing that bothered me was that she'd taken a cut in pay compared with her job at the pub. Why? I wondered. The housekeeper mentioned the snob appeal of the job and I supposed that was so. But really: why trade a well-paying service job at a popular restaurant for a job as a housekeeper, cleaning and hoovering and scrubbing toilets? The answer was plain, if only I'd seen it: because she wanted to be near Jason, inserting herself into his life. And as a scout she would be granted unlimited access. Not just to his rooms but to most of the college. There was no end to the mischief she could have got up to, theft and desecration and the like, but her target was and remained Jason.

'It was the master who suggested we speak with the scouts, who know everything. If we'd followed that good advice sooner, we might have solved the crime in time to save Minette from being attacked.'

'Hindsight,' said Portia.

'What I wouldn't give for a crystal ball in this business.'

'Minette will be all right, though, won't she?'

'She has concussion, and that can be tricky. But the doctors at the hospital are confident that, with bedrest, she'll recover fully. Let's hope that as a doctor herself she respects the advice.'

Portia sat back in the upholstered chair, cradling her glass of wine. An hour ago, she'd declared she was sleepy. Now St. Just could see she'd not sleep until she knew everything he knew.

'So Tess set all this up, actually killed someone, just to get into his room?' she asked. 'That's insane.'

'That's exactly what it is – insane. Her plan might not have been well formed at first, mind. It might have taken her a while to screw up her courage. Besides, she was enjoying herself, playing with him, with everyone. She's an actress, after all, and what a role! It was the role of a lifetime. Initially she might have had in mind a spot of mischief, perhaps a bit of fun with things gone missing from his room, or things moved about, or things left in his room that would make him think he was losing his mind. A gaslighting game, in effect. A subtle revenge.

'So her motivation was murky at first – although she was determined and would let nothing get in her way if the opportunity arose to really harm him. She had time on her hands between jobs – "resting", as they call it in the theatre – and wanted to cause a little trouble. Or so she tells herself and wants us to believe. But when she realizes there is serious money to be had through blackmail, her plans change.

'She knows she has stumbled on to something big when she finds that book in his room. This was something that could really bring Jason to his knees. She decided to play with her fish in a bigger way, for higher stakes.'

'But when she confronted him? At the party?'

'It all turned bad when she confronted him *before* the party at the top of the stairs, demanding money, taunting him, waving a copy of his bestselling book in his face. She says he lunged for her, she hit him with the book in self-defence, and he went down the stairs, landing hard at the bottom. She could see he was dead and – not knowing quite what to do – in a panic she stuffed him in the book lift. I think it more likely that's when she delivered the *coup de grâce* – hit him with the hardback copy of his own book.'

'And none of it explains the fact he'd been drugged beforehand – to make him more pliable.'

'Precisely. As a scout she had access to many people's rooms and medicine cabinets, which would have made it easy for her to collect drugs, probably a bit at a time. As a server at the party, she simply added the drugs to the glass of wine she planned to give him. Then the guests started arriving and she assumed her role serving drinks as though nothing had happened. Once she was sure all the guests were upstairs and she wouldn't be seen by any late arrivals, she stole a moment to go downstairs, retrieve him from the book lift, and arrange him artfully at the bottom of the stairs to make it look like an accident.'

'An accident. Do you believe her?'

'I don't, and not just because of the callous way Minette was attacked and nearly killed. I'm getting to that. Bear with me.'

'Always.'

St. Just smiled and went on. 'As I say, her initial plan in taking the job at the college was to look around his room, see what he was up to, see who his current girlfriends were, especially – because there would always be more than one.

She may have had some vague idea of warning them off as to Jason's true nature. Perhaps a poison pen letter or two, anonymously sent. Or perhaps, she just liked tormenting herself with the knowing.

'She searched his computer at leisure while she was supposed to be cleaning his rooms, of course – he kept all his passwords hidden in a notebook by his computer. A foolish practice against which we are all warned, even though I do it myself.

'Above all, I believe, she wanted to find any manuscripts currently in progress: Jason's much-anticipated second book. Inspired by the outlandish, stage-managed kerfuffle surrounding the release of every Harry Potter book, she wanted to make copies and post them online anonymously before the book went to press. Sell advance copies on eBay or something like that, see if she could damage his sales and make some money while doing it. The trick would be making sure none of it could be traced back to her, of course, but she felt safe in the knowledge no one would ever suspect a scout of having the audacity, let alone the brains, to pull off such a stunt.

'But her plan never got that far. No matter how hard she looked, she told us, she could not find any document that seemed to be the promised follow-up to Jason's hugely successful first novel. That was odd. That was very odd indeed. All that stuff in the media about him staying at the Ritz, desperate to get away from it all, wanting a bit of peace and quiet to work on the new book for which the world held its breath in anticipation. She didn't really know how these things worked, but surely he should be scribbling down at least a few ideas by now on sticky notes, and there was no trace of anything like that. He seemed to be reading a bunch of boring rubbish about ancient cultures, that was it – not surprising, as that was his chosen field.

'She did go through the papers in his rooms – he left much of his stuff out, thinking a cleaner would be too stupid to know what it was – and she learned some things he didn't want her or anyone to know. What she learned was that at some point he had been translating something out of Dutch into English. More boring stuff on ancient cultures, she thought. It wasn't until she found the original book that she realized what he was up to.

'The book was of course the basis for *The White Owl*, the novel that had brought him wealth and fame. Knowing the Dutch language, she took an even closer look at that book. *Et voilà*. She wasn't to know, as we now know, it had been written by an obscure Dutch author who had died in disgrace and poverty decades before, and she didn't need to know. She could see for herself he'd stolen the text. Jason must've come across it in one of the antiquarian bookshops in town. The book had never been published in the usual way. It had been a vanity project, pure and simple. Jason had bought what might have been the only copy outside of the Netherlands.

'When she realized what she had, she made a classic mistake: she got greedy. She had been playing a game for revenge but realized she had knowledge in her possession that could destroy him. And stringing him along, making him think if he paid her off she would go away – that was more fun than she could ever imagine. She thanked her lucky stars. Or the gods of revenge, or whoever had made this book of Jason's, his stolen book, fall into her lap.'

'She hid the book, right?'

'She's not saying . . . yet. Gita couldn't find it when she went to look for it is all we know. Anyway, Jason wouldn't want anyone to know what he did, or what he was capable of doing. Not now, not as he had just reached the pinnacle of success. He would do anything, pay anything, dance to her tune – the way she'd been forced to dance to his.

'She knew all about the planned party, of course, and she volunteered to serve – the college was always shorthanded for these occasions and often put out a call for help among the day staff. She threatened Jason that – if he didn't pay up – she would reveal the truth at his special party in front of all these people he so wanted to impress.

'She is a physically strong woman but, to play it safe, she made sure there was something a little extra in his drink. As you say, she wanted him malleable, pliable. The last thing she wanted was a scene, for she knew his temper, and in any hand-to-hand combat she'd be bound to lose. She arranged to meet him before the party; they met at the top of the stairs leading into the library. A note she left him the week before demanding money for her silence was of course unsigned. She let him believe that some clever professor of English had caught him out. And that would be the person he would be meeting just before the party to pay the money he had been instructed to bring, in cash. When he showed up to meet his blackmailer, he found his scout, dressed for the evening in her server's outfit. She offered him a glass of the wine that would be served to the guests that evening, saying she wanted to be sure it had the guest of honour's approval.

'He could have gone to his death never realizing this server was an old girlfriend, let alone that his blackmailer was his current scout.'

'His bank records would show a large withdrawal, surely.'

'But they did not. We think his plan was never to succumb to blackmail. His plan might have been to silence his black-mailer for good. We may never know, unless Tess starts telling the entire truth. Anyway, his amazement when he realized he had been caught out by a mere scout with no special academic qualifications would have been something to behold.

'The scar had done its work; it was so disfiguring people couldn't bear to look too closely at her and didn't want to be caught staring. She doubted he'd remember who she was, anyway. But perhaps it was enough for her, his knowing he had been had by what he considered to be a lesser human being. I think, just before she killed him, she'd reveal she was the woman he'd taken once advantage of.'

'And she nearly got away with it. But then, Minette somehow got in her way.'

'Yes. Minette, like the former scout, was expendable. It would have been an unnecessary death, of course, but Minette became an obstacle to be got rid of.'

'How did Tess find out about Minette?'

'The question is how did Minette find out about Tess? You see, Tess was living in the same temporary boarding house as Minette. For both women, short-stay accommodation was a matter of convenience, if for different reasons. Tess could have afforded better rooms, but she had to play the role of a scout

who could only afford such a low-rent place. Minette wanted
a place convenient to town but just outside the centre, in case
Jason spotted her in town. She was there to surprise him, if
you'll recall. Dressed in that slinky dress, making one last
desperate attempt to attract and keep him.'

'I'm just glad she got out of this alive. And hopefully, she'll
choose a better man next time.'

'Let's hope. Her obsession with Jason nearly got her killed.
Anyway, you should have heard Tess on the subject of Minette.
"I should feel sorry for her", she said, "but I have nothing but
contempt for anyone who is as stupid as I was in falling for
his line".'

'I still don't understand the attack on Minette,' said Portia.
'I mean, why?'

'Minette saw her without her scar.'

'Oh.'

'Minette had seen Tess at the college on the rare and special
occasions Jason allowed her to visit him. But, unlike most
people, she didn't turn away from the scar on Tess's face. As
an emergency room doctor, she'd seen far worse.

'But then here is Minette in her temporary bedsit with its
shared bathroom, and who does she run into but Tess in the
hallway? Unlike Jason, she recognized her immediately but
. . . where was her scar? Minette knew something was up. She
knew it was a disguise and there was no good explanation for
it. She suddenly realizes: the whole scout thing is an act.

'She couldn't hide her reaction, being basically honest. And
Tess being the opposite, she immediately picked up on
Minette's stunned expression. And she knew, without hesita-
tion, Minette had to go. Minette was a loose end.'

Portia nodded. 'Anyone would have to wonder why a scout
would be walking around the college in disguise? Tess knew
Minette was bound to tell the police.'

'Yes. To Tess, she was collateral damage. During the initial
investigation, Tess had given the police her Cowley Street
address – it wouldn't do to be caught in a lie about something
so basic. She had to; she had no choice. So Tess realizes she
must kill Minette before disappearing back into her real life
– I suppose being an actress counts as real life, as much as

being a bin man. Anyway, Tess had told me when I spoke with her in Jason's rooms that she was going to return to work as a waitress, said she was tired of picking up after the nobs or whatever, but her real plan was for Tess Babbage to disappear, once the excitement about the college murder died down, and return to her glamourous theatrical life as Theresa Bakker.'

'Then Minette forced her hand.'

'Yes. Tess attacked her without thinking it through, but once it was done, with Minette almost certainly dying at her feet, she knew it was too big a coincidence – both women living in the same place – for the police not to figure it out.'

'That two women with a connection to the murder were both staying at the same street address in Cowley was one thing,' said Portia. 'That one would end up attacked and left for dead was another.'

St. Just nodded. 'I'm sure Tess thought she had killed her when she ran for it. Constable Lambert found Minette lying in a pool of blood and called nine-nine-nine immediately, no doubt saving her life. Tess had shoved her hard and she'd hit the sharp edge of a coffee table on the way down.

'Minette was able to tell us that when Tess attacked her, Tess was wrapped in a towel and had just come from the bath. That's why she was without her scar disguise; she'd washed all that stuff off her face. She had to "borrow" something of Minette's from her room so she'd have something to wear on her way out. And she thought it might give her an alibi for the time of Minette's death.'

'How is that?'

'She was seen from the back wearing the red dress and, because of that, when police began questioning people, it was assumed Minette had still been alive and walking around at a specific time. The witness who swore he'd seen her was adamant about what he'd seen, and quite right in stating the red dress was unmissable, one of a kind.

'He told police it had been three minutes before noon (he'd set his mobile alarm) and at noon every day, the man said the prayers of holy office. He was in Oxford training for the priesthood, so as a witness, he was essentially above reproach. He just happened to be mistaken about who he saw. But no worries. Tess's bright idea of using that unforgettable dress to establish an alibi for the time of the attack on Minette turned out to be her downfall. She ended up having to rush through town in heels and a tight red dress, in broad daylight.

'Minette had sworn she'd never wear that dress again, telling Constable Lambert in an earlier interview that she wanted to be rid of it and was going leave it behind to be donated. Lambert found Minette's near-lifeless body clothed in jeans and a jumper, so whoever left the building wearing that dress, Lambert knew it was not Minette.'

'No wonder Tess had trouble riding the pony,' said Portia. 'It's lucky Constable Lambert got there when she did, but why was she there, anyway?'

'For one thing, she wanted to ask her if Jason had goaded her into showing up at the party. But she'd also left her note-book behind the day before, along with her daisy pen, and she didn't want Ampleforth to find out. She was afraid he'd hold it against her, being so careless with her witness notes. She's been angling for promotion for a long time, and she was afraid this might scupper her chances.'

'Oh, my. But I'd say she's indispensable, wouldn't you? Anyone that young is bound to make a mistake.'

'At least she won't make that mistake again.'

'Probably not. Most of us go through life making brand-new mistakes.'

'That reminds me,' he said, pouring the last of the wine into her glass and his. 'Constable Lambert's research has turned up the person who is undoubtedly the one remaining heir of the true author of *The White Owl* in its original version. If this person gives permission to Castle Publishing – gives them rights to continue publishing, in other words, and does not decide for some reason to sue them – the book will continue to be out there in the world, enjoyed by millions. But this time with the real author's name on the front, and with a small fortune going to the true owner.'

'In which case, why sue?'

'Exactly.'

'Then, all's well.'

'That ends well. Yes. Cheers.'